Amazon Harvest

Book 1 of the Harvester Trilogy

Amazon Harvest

Amazon Harvest

Book 1 of the Harvester Trilogy

By John Wilson Berry

Amazon Harvest

Special thanks to my wife Linda.

I would never have completed this book without her encouragement and support.

Amazon Harvest

Book 1 of the Harvester Trilogy

©Copyright 2016 by John Wilson Berry

Contents

Chapter 1 …………..…………..3

Chapter 2……………………....21

Chapter 3…………………….32

Chapter 4……………………..44

Chapter 5……………………..53

Chapter 6…………………….71

Chapter 7………………..……97

Chapter 8……………..……119

Chapter 9…………...………..155

Chapter 10…………...……….166

Chapter 11…………...……….186

Chapter 12…………...………202

Chapter 13……….…..………223

Chapter 14……….…...………236

Amazon Harvest

Chapter 1

The world around David Morgan seemed to tilt, sending a weird jolt through his eyes that reached all the way down to his gut. The blue walls of the tent rippled and the tablet he was playing *Zombie Apocalypse* on twitched in his hand as though given a soft tug to the right. The gut twisting tilting sensation lasted a fraction of a second and then everything snapped back to normal. Or rather, everything except his head, which felt fuzzy for a moment longer, then nothing.

"What the hell," he mumbled, blinking his eyes in confusion. The strange feeling broke his focus on the game and a swarm of zombies marched out of the dark depths of the tablet toward his guy. Before he could react, the undead horde attacked and tore his avatar to pieces with a chorus of zombie growls and a splash of gore. With a sigh, he stopped the game, although it was far too late. At least he wasn't very far along this level.

That tilting feeling had been...weird. It felt...well, sort of like everything had been tugged to the right for a moment. Did I almost fall over? That's what it felt like, but not exactly. Crap. With his luck, he had caught malaria or some other deadly tropical disease. Of course, they had been given countless injections before leaving, every one of which had hurt like hell, so they were supposed to be protected from all that stuff. Whatever it had been was gone now and he did not feel the least bit sick. Doubt crept into his mind if he had really felt anything at all, but he rejected it with a slight shake of his head. No, he had felt something, he was sure of it. Very, very strange.

Did playing his games on this stupid tablet instead of a normal, full sized screen make him dizzy? A small snort forced its way up and out his nose. *That's dumb. I'm not dizzy. Dizzy don't feel like that.* But...maybe this was a different kind of dizzy? Could it be eye strain from looking at the small screen?

Thinking of the tablet's shortcomings made him give it a scornful glare. It sucked to have to play on this little thing. But here in the middle of the damn Amazon rainforest, mile upon mile of snake infested jungle from...well, everything, there wasn't a whole lot of choice. His stupid sister had flat out refused to let him bring his VR headset, which double sucked. However, he had been playing on the tablet for almost three weeks without any dizzy feelings. Why now? Weird.

Nothing else made sense, though, unless he really was getting sick. *Well, I feel fine now. Maybe I'm just tired.* He decided to finish this level and get some sleep.

Dismissing the odd sensation, he tilted the camp chair back against the table and wiggled in a vain attempt to get comfortable. One of the legs beneath him creaked and he froze. No additional sounds of complaint came from the chair so he relaxed. His sister kept telling him he was too fat to lean back on two legs like this, but it was the only way to get comfortable in the folding piece of crap. It wasn't like he was leaning out over a concrete floor or anything. Falling onto the spongy floor of the tent wouldn't be the end of the world after all. Sally was such a worrier. Shrugging off the dizzy feeling and his sister's warning, he focused on the game once more.

The pain of The Memory and all the other stupid stuff of the world faded away as he played. The painful fingers of doubt, and fear, and shame released their hold on his brain and he slipped into the universe of the game. A universe where he could move with the grace of an athlete and the confidence of a rock star, traits he sorely lacked in the real world. Here he felt alive, more so than he ever could in real life. Real life sucked, games ruled.

Everything shuddered and twisted sideways again, making him blink in an effort to get his eyes to focus. No doubt about it this time. Either he, or the world, had experienced something. But what? Crap, maybe he was getting sick. Strange, strange, strange. A trace of fear tickled along his back. Something was not right. But he had no clue what it might be. After a few moments however, doubt once more crept into his head about actually feeling anything.

No! He had felt dizzy…or something. Though dizzy still didn't quite seem to fit. It passed too quickly. Whenever he had been dizzy in the past, like after a ride on a wild rollercoaster, the feeling stuck around in his stomach and took time to fade away. This dizziness had hit like a snake and faded away to nothing almost as fast. That didn't fit with this feeling.

The world had certainly seemed to tilt and twist in front of him. But no, dizzy wasn't the word for it. No, for sure, it wasn't dizziness, not really. But it was something like being dizzy. Twisty. That seemed to fit it better. Twisty. Whatever the hell that meant. Sometimes his mind came up with expressions he couldn't quite explain, even to himself.

Okay. I must be more tired than I realized. Or else that last shrink Sally took me to was right about having, "Events," whatever that was. Like most head doctors, the guy was a nut bag. But the idea of having what amounted to brain spasms was a sobering thought. His life sucked bad enough as it was without a whole new level of crazy to deal with.

He shook his head in denial, tinged with frustration. *No, I'm tired, that's all.* So, get through this level and then off to bed. Most likely he was worn out from lack of sleep. Having to sleep in a tent in the hot and smelly sauna of the Amazon Basin was a bunch of crap. He had never sweated so much in his whole life.

Anger still burned in his chest over being forced to come here in the first place. His older sister was his legal guardian and had made him come with her to this uncomfortable green hell. All in the name of science and personal development. Although of course, it was her science and his so-called personal development.

Personal development, especially his, was Sally's favorite thing to talk about. David's shortcomings and what he needed to improve on came up at least once a day. Something he did, or failed to do, would trigger another long winded sermon. Sermon after sermon after sermon, day after day after day. This had been his last year of high school and her efforts had reached new heights. Instead of working to become a scientist, she should have been a priest. Lord knew she had plenty of experience preaching to her a reluctant congregation of one. All the sermons really achieved was to give him maybe a smidgeon of guilt and make him cling all the harder to his games. This was no doubt the reason she had decided to drag him along with her to the jungle.

Most such speeches tended to begin with angry yells like, "What were you thinking!" or, "You've got to get your life together." Of course, she'd use a whole lot more words to get across that basic idea, all of them loud, but that was the gist of it. Over time, he'd learned to let the words flow over him. He'd nod, promise to do better, and then forget about it as soon as she was out of sight. His life was as together as he wanted it to be.

Yes, reality sucked. She didn't understand how much he needed the games. He clung to the worlds in the games to keep from going crazier. Crazy in a way much that would be much worse than a so called, "Event." They helped him from having to deal with things he was just not strong enough to handle.

Although he had not actually seen his mother's mangled and torn body after the tornado, his mind's eye could provide an image horrible enough to bring tears. That was when his life started to turn gray. But this gray was a light mist, only partially obscuring the world. The saddest thing about avoiding the memories of his mother was that it blocked access to all the wonderful things he associated with her. All the love and guidance on how to be good had to be kept walled off, lest they take his mind to other thoughts that did not bear thinking.

That memory, The Memory, was the reason he hid his thoughts away in the gray clouds of his mind. The Memory to not remember was about his father. A memory so bad, so hurtful to his soul that he fought to suppress it to this day.

Oddly enough, sometimes the effort to avoid The Memory triggered it. With dismay, he realized his thoughts were on just such a path. The strange dizziness interrupted the game and made him wish for the comfort of his mother. This led to fierce sadness over her death and then, as it inevitably did, to the total abandonment he had experienced by his father. Tears welled as that very bad day forced its way into his mind.

The Memory began to play like an old, flickering horror film through his mind. Some parts were super vivid and hurt like the cut of a knife, other parts tended to be indistinct and fuzzy, leaving behind a dull, lasting ache. All of it was bad.

It was a sunny Thursday afternoon, one year to the day after his mother's death. Over the past year, David had been in a funk but was making progress in dealing with his grief and putting it behind him. The nightmares almost never woke him up anymore. Sally had become the center of the family and a new kind of normality set in. Yet, when he got home after school that day, he had known something was wrong when only echoes answered his yells as he walked through the house. It was cleaner and neater than normal, cleaner even than mom had kept it.

Father was supposed to be home. David searched the house and then thought of the garage as being the last place he might be. Sure enough, there he was. Dead, hanging with his feet dangling above the concrete and a face as blue as could be. The body slowly revolved with a greasy yellow rope around the neck. This was the great betrayal of his father. The abandonment of a son already questioning his place in the world. A son so unworthy of love, his father had taken this terrible route to escape.

It took a lot of effort to force the gray over The Memory. But he had learned how to do it years ago and bit by bit, the gray returned. He sighed with relief as the pain faded. Yes, he much preferred gray nothingness to reality. Reality hurt like hell. The games helped, the games were best of all. They were something and helped wall off other thoughts. Plus, they were much better than nothingness while still not actually being real, which was fine with David. They had become the perfect place to escape. Wiping away the last of his tears, he refocused on the tablet.

The game level he was on had been kicking his butt all night. At least he had managed to pause it this time before his guy got killed. If he got past the last big bunch of zombies, he should reach a save point. That would help clear his mind. Once he got there, he would go to bed. That sounded like a good plan.

It took a moment to get back into the game. But soon he was blasting his way through the first easy challenges. Then he was free, a super hero in a world of adventure and free of pain. The massive wave of zombies he knew to be the last big boss of this level started to march forward with murderous intent. The heavily armed character on the screen stood poised and ready, as was David. Both the gray and last vestiges of pain were swept aside as he tensed with pleasurable anticipation of the fight.

Then the world lurched sideways harder than ever. It came with a pronounced whoosh from the surrounding trees.

The sudden motion was much stronger than before and almost knocked him over. The precariously balanced camp chair groaned and popped with protest. He flailed his arms to maintain balance and managed to keep from falling, but his tablet didn't fare as well. Slipping from his fingers, the device flipped into the air and pirouetted almost gracefully before falling. It bounced off a chair leg and hit the ground, a victim of his less-than-athletic prowess. Fortunately, the canvas floor softened the impact and the screen continued to glow up at him.

David's hazel-green eyes swept the blue walls of the tent, his round soft face a mask of bewilderment and fear. "What the hell?" That had been way worse than the dizziness he felt earlier.

On the tablet's screen, zombies once again overwhelmed his now frozen avatar.

7

"Crap." It had to be his sister screwing around with him somehow. Snatching up the tablet, he tabbed it from the game to the overdue report his sister was making him write. The abused camp chair groaned as he turned an apprehensive look at the still-closed tent flap, and then he felt silly. Unless Sally had come up with a way to tilt his tent, there was no way she could make him feel that sense of vertigo. Moreover, if it had been Sally…well, there'd be a serious ass chewing underway, not a silly mind game. That just wasn't her style.

Heck, for that matter, Sally wasn't even in camp. She'd flown off to Rio Estrada earlier in the day to spend the night in air-conditioned comfort. He'd begged to go with her. She'd replied, "You haven't done anything to deserve going. You need to grow up a little first."

There was no way she'd come back early. The helicopter would never make the trip in the dark. Even if they did, the chopper was loud as hell and he would have heard it. He let out a sigh of relief. Thank God he wouldn't have to hear yet another sermon.

The relief was short-lived, though. If it wasn't his sister, then what was going on? Nothing seemed out of place inside the tent. The soft patter of rain hitting the nylon, accompanied by the songs, chirps, growls, and groans from the surrounding jungle, seemed as annoying and normal as ever.

Rain hissed against the nylon tent and tippy-tapped on the ground as it dripped down and off the surrounding leaves. This was a disgustingly normal event despite the region being in the so-called dry season. The first month of the dry season here averaged as much rain as the wettest month in Alabama. Overall, a typical night in the rainforest for the University of North Alabama research team: wet, uncomfortable, rancid, and disgusting.

His tent was one of thirty clustered together at one end of a small clearing where they'd set up the base camp. During the day, the tents were a riot of color that stood out starkly against the green of the forest. Now it was a little past midnight and only those few glowing from within were visible, marking tents whose occupants were still awake.

All around the camp, huge trees stretched skyward. When the team first arrived, his sister had gushed, "It's a magical dell. A cathedral of life." From that point on, the sickly-sweet descriptions found their way into her rainforest sermon. Whenever she started, David would roll his eyes and try to sneak away. All that lovey-dovey forest stuff wasn't the least bit how he would describe the clearing where they set up camp. The very thought of the damp, smelly, buggy and hot clearing being a cathedral for anything made David want to puke.

So what about this dizzy stuff? The first two times were nothing compared to that last one. This had been much worse and nearly knocked him over. At least, that was what it felt like. Did I fall asleep or something? Not long before leaving for Brazil, he'd been driving on a back road late at night. One moment he was cruising along and the next he was off the road, surrounded by dust and tall grass. He had jerked awake and managed to turn just before hitting a tree, making his heart leap into his throat.

But no, this was different. That night he'd been tired and the road long, hypnotic, and boring. This time he'd been fired up, focused, and in the zone, about to take on a mass attack of zombies. The idea of simply dozing off didn't seem right.

Shadows dancing in the corner of the tent pulled his eyes to the small LED light suspended from a nylon loop above him. It swung slowly back and forth. "Humph," he grunted. Something had disturbed the tent, or the light wouldn't be moving. Was one of the older students in the camp messing with him? He kept to himself most of the time, so that was unlikely, but not impossible. Could someone slapping the tent push the tent pole into the table he was leaning against and cause him lose his balance? Anger washed over him for a moment. His opinion of the people in the camp wasn't a whole lot better than those he held for the jungle, even if he had no good reason for feeling that way. The anger faded away with the sad realization that no one in the camp cared enough about him to bother messing with him.

Fear, along with a knotted gut, sent gooseflesh across his skin as the world tilted again. Something pulled him to the left and then stopped, causing him to sway back to his right. No, no, no, this was impossible. His gaze roamed the tent, looking for a cause, but there was nothing. There was no way that twisty, rolling sensation had come from somebody simply hitting the tent.

At least this time he hadn't nearly fallen off his seat. With the chair sitting on all four legs, it was easy enough to counter the motion. The sensation reminded him of a time on his father's boat the year before his mother had died. A large wave from a passing barge had caught him by surprise, rolling the ski boat and nearly dumping him into the water. He'd only just managed to catch himself and tumbled to the bottom of the boat instead.

After making sure he was okay, his father had laughed and told him he needed to work on his sea legs. Being large, overweight, and clumsy his entire life, learning to maintain his balance on the boat wasn't a skill that came easy. After a few dozen more falls, he figured out how to roll opposite the motion of the waves. While never graceful on the water, he managed to move about the boat without bruising various body parts. It was a skill he'd never imagined needing here in the middle of the Amazon.

David shook his head in confusion. *This is just too strange. Am I getting sick?* Shadows dancing on the walls of the tent pulled his gaze back to the small light, which now swung with more vigor. The dancing shadows gave ample evidence that he wasn't suffering from some kind of hallucination or inner ear problem. Something had rocked the tent, that was for sure. An earthquake? Maybe, but he'd experienced an earthquake on a trip to Stillwater, Oklahoma with Sally, and this tilting sensation was nothing like the shaking rattles he remembered.

An excited voice called out from somewhere in the camp. Another answered, Dr. Allen by the sound of it, the expedition's leader. He couldn't make out the words, but the voices carried concern, and maybe a twinge of fear. He wasn't the only one disquieted by…whatever.

Additional sounds of people moving about the camp came as more nervous voices joined the first two. Whatever had disturbed his tent had also gotten the attention of the rest of the camp. At least he knew he wasn't going crazy. In a way, the thought wasn't very reassuring. Visits to numerous therapists during his young life had made it plain his mind wasn't normal. He had learned to deal with that. But this was different. Something very much out of the ordinary was alarming the camp's inhabitants.

The voices from outside the tent tapered off, and a strange silence settled over the area. David froze in place as well, hoping that whatever had passed through the night was over.

The normal sounds of the jungle stopped as well as if the creatures of the forest declared a sudden truce in their never-ending battle for survival. The abrupt silence left a noticeable and disturbing void. Of the usual cries from the wilderness, not an insect, frog, monkey, or bird could be heard. A tingling shiver crept across David's chest and up his back. The team had spent six weeks in the Amazon and the shrieks, screams, and growls had never gone silent before.

He hated the cacophony of life and death from the rainforest. It had made his first nights at the camp a nightmare, invading his dreams and robbing him of sleep. Even now, screams from the jungle sometimes filled his sleep with images of sharp teeth and rending claws. However, this sudden silence was worse; it was very real and very much out of place.

The soft patter of rain and the drip-dripping of water from the leaves remained, but this seemed to accentuate the quiet rather than dispel it. One particular drip that been veiled until now by the noise from the jungle was especially loud. The water ran down leaves fifty feet up and fell unimpeded onto a tarp covering some equipment with a loud metallic tink, tink, tink. The sound was like the timer on a bomb marking away the seconds. The whole world sat motionless and tense, waiting for the next impossible surge.

It struck, only much stronger this time, tilting the world and making the small light in David's tent swing so fast it thumped into the sloped nylon ceiling. The lamp began spinning and cast shadows that danced and twirled. This turned the tent into a surreal stage as light chased dark in a mad ballet. Cries of fear echoed through the camp when another, and then another invisible wave turned the world on its side. Had gravity itself gone mad? David fought to brace himself in the flimsy chair as the earth rolled beneath him. Each wave tugged him northward, ebbed briefly, and then tugged on him again.

The waves increased in intensity. A loud crash echoed through the clearing, followed by a scream that startled David into leaping up. No sooner did he rise than another sideways lurch threw him to the ground with his legs tangled in the camp chair. He landed with a grunt of pain, then kicked the chair away and scrambled to a sitting position, his hands and feet splayed out to brace against the roiling world.

A rushing roar like that of monstrous waves came from outside, the sound of a sea of trees bending and swaying to the pulsing forces. Realizing that there were a lot of the heavy boughs above made him look up and mutter a quick prayer for salvation. Seconds later, a loud crack, followed by a weighty thump from nearby that made the ground jump. There was nowhere to hide, nowhere to go. He dug his fingers into the tent floor, his knuckles turning white in a futile effort to stop the roiling earth.

More limbs creaked and cracked from the unusual stresses, some with loud reports like small explosions. Branches landed with wet thuds, some near, some far, threatening to bury the entire camp under a leafy green avalanche. Each impact caused David to recoil and forced small moans from his throat.

After ten years, David still mourned his lost mother. But ever since she died, it had been his older sister who gave him comfort in times of need. When the world plunged into chaos, it was to her he cried. "Sally! God, Sally, help me!"

There was no help coming. The only response to his plea was for the world to tilt even further, rolling him out of his braced position and into the side of the tent, which promptly collapsed, smothering him in damp nylon. The table, chair, cot, and various camping items turned into missiles, defying physics and slamming sideways into the fabric. Despite the folds of the tent, the objects pelted his body with painful force as he fought to protect his face and head.

David's heart thudded so hard his ears throbbed with the beat. He fought with frantic energy against the damp fabric that engulfed him. Like a starving beast, the unworldly force tried to drag him toward the jungle. Only the tent stakes, driven deep to find purchase in the always-moist Amazon soil, kept him from slamming into the surrounding trees with murderous strength.

Screams of fear, some of outright agony, came from all around. People, equipment, and hard, sharp branches tumbled across the earth as if magic forces had dumped the camp on a steep mountainside. David tried to scream as well, but the wet cloth tangled about him clogged his mouth and nose every time he sucked in air. He choked and sputtered, fighting to breathe and adding the fear of suffocation to his already overwhelmed emotions.

The silence came so abruptly it took David's addled senses a moment to realize the terrifying motions had stopped. It was difficult to breathe which added to his panic, but he managed to stop the fruitless struggle against the damp cloth that was in effect waterboarding him. Forcing his shaking arms up through the restraining fabric, he managed to push the wet nylon away from his face. This created an air pocket that allowed him to suck in an unobstructed breath.

He lay in the blue cocoon, gasping in air when the first sound broke the silence. The distance was hard to judge, but not far away a woman began crying. Then there were several loud moans a little farther off soon joined by the frantic screams of a man shouting for help in a quivering, tormented howl. The creatures of the jungle added their voices to the chorus of agony, shrieking with a vigor that dwarfed their previous noise. The riot of sound overwhelmed David's already addled senses. Confused, trapped, and scared, he added his own soft sobs to the sounds of misery emanating from the shattered camp and surrounding forest.

Despite the pain from his abused body and the panic of being trapped, his mind became consumed with a deeper, more primal dread of the unknown. How could the world turn side-ways? This could not, could not, could not, be happening. The gray that was his life gave way to a new color, a terrifyingly deep, dark shade of black.

Sally

Sixty odd miles southeast of the North Alabama research camp was Rio Estrada. In the best of times, it was an odd collection of structures that barely deserved being called a town. This was not the best of times. The early light of dawn revealed scattered debris stretching northward from the remains of numerous damaged and destroyed homes. There were a few stone and concrete buildings, and some modular homes and some trailers still standing, but most of the town was comprised of thatched huts that fared badly when the mysterious sideway waves struck in the night.

Falling trees had smashed many of the homes; others collapsed when subjected to the bizarre lateral forces that had swept through the town. Now terrified citizens picked through scattered meager belongings, tended to the injured, or consoled crying children. Many people spent a lot of time staring toward the north, mumbling in terse whispers, "Onda do Demônio."

Sally Morgan sat on the edge of the fountain at the center of the town's small plaza with her head hanging low, feeling far older than her twenty-six years. Her dark-green bush shirt and blue jeans were wet and covered in mud. Around her were a dozen other exhausted people, all of them worn down from a long night spent looking for survivors amid the wreckage.

Myra Hamilton, her best friend, and mentor sat beside her, picking at a plate of military-style reconstituted eggs. Myra was ten years older than Sally and always exuberant and full of life. Not on this morning as Myra's dark-skinned face mirrored Sally's own worried exhaustion. It was hard for Sally to believe they'd arrived yesterday so full of joy over escaping the rigors of camping in the jungle. That seemed like a very long time ago.

Yesterday Sally had managed to talk Myra into coming with her to Rio Estrada for some much-needed rest. Myra had been intent on finishing one of her projects, but the lure of a few decent meals, a hot shower, and a night in a real bed had finally worn down her resistance.

Their mini-vacation had started full of hopeful anticipation. The town's wooden, three-story hotel was old but clean. The building had its own generator, and the air-conditioning worked wonderfully. Even better, there had been plenty of hot water for the showers. Sally had thrilled at the prospect of getting a good night's rest. As much as she loved the rainforest, a dry, soft bed out of the heat and humidity was a godsend.

Now they were far from rested. In fact, they were exhausted and emotionally drained. Their vacation turned into a nightmare when a bizarre earthquake, or whatever the hell it was, had tumbled them out of bed in the middle of the night. Darkness engulfed the town as power failed and confusion reigned. Cries for help had echoed across the small plaza. Sally and Myra stumbled out of the building, groggy with sleep and confused about the situation. Cries for help motivated them to join a group of people heading out to a collapsed house. They then spent the next nine hours clearing branches, digging through collapsed shacks.

At one-point Sally had uncovered a dead woman, then Myra and a local man uncovered another. Both bodies had been crushed then rolled about by the waves. So mangled were the remains they had barely been recognizable as human.

Sally put down her plate of half-eaten food and cradled her face in her hands. "God, I hope David...all of them, are okay."

Myra placed her hand on Sally's back. "I'm sure they are. At least having a tent fall on you isn't as bad as a house, even one made mostly of thatch."

Sally shook her head. "No, but a tree is pretty damn bad, and there are plenty of those around the camp. That's what got that couple last night." She sat back up. "What a mess. Not knowing how they are is making me crazy. Do you think Keith got through to someone?"

Myra shrugged, then managed a half smile and stood up. "Speak of the devil," said Myra, standing up.

Sally followed her friend's gaze to a tall, slim man with salt-and-pepper hair. He wore blue jeans and a black tee shirt and wove his way through the refugees gathered in the plaza.

Keith Anderson and his helicopter had been hired by the Brazilian government to support the research team's mission to reinvigorate the forest. Myra had really hit it off with him when the team had arrived in the Amazon, and now they were pretty close. She greeted him with a hug that he returned with a fierce focus with his eyes tightly shut, before emitting a soft sigh and letting her go.

"Bob's boy died," he said in a gruff, grief filled voice. "Poor little guy's lungs filled with fluid and he drowned. His own damn body drowned him." He rubbed his face. "It really sucks. We thought he might make it after we got that tree off him. But I guess he really never had a chance." Keith looked back at the town hall. "That makes twelve dead, and there's a couple more on the brink. As soon as the weather clears, I plan to take them to Manaus. There's been enough death."

Bob was the assistant manager of the town's biggest employer, an eco-friendly logging camp that specialized in exotic woods. Keith and he had been friends for years. Sally reached up and squeezed Keith's hand, then let her arm drop. He gave her a feeble smile.

Sally pulled out the band holding her dark brown hair in a ponytail and shook it in an attempt to get out some of the water from the intermittent rain. It reached halfway down her back and was thick, curly, and tended to tangle if left loose, a legacy from her Portuguese mother. Her blue eyes came entirely from her father. With a final shake of her head, she twisted her hair back into a ponytail; it was the only way to go in the damp air of the Amazon.

Standing, she looked up at Myra and Keith, both of whom were over six feet in height. She always felt short and dumpy beside her friends, despite being five foot seven and only weighing one hundred forty pounds.

"What about the radios?" Sally asked.

He shook his head. "No go. It's the damnedest thing. The Naval de Brasilia radio, the logging camp, the town's shortwave, nothing is working. All we get is static. Satellite's down, too. No TV, internet, nothing."

Sally let out a slow breath. Leaving David on his own had bothered her some, but she'd told herself he could take care of himself for a change. He was eighteen years old, for Christ's sake. It was getting harder and harder for her to take care of him; she had a life to live, too.

Was he so lazy and unfocused because of their parents' deaths, especially their father's suicide, or was he just a teenager who needed more discipline? Every therapist she'd taken him to had a different opinion, a different way to help him. Sooner or later, David would have to stand on his own. She couldn't babysit him forever, could she? Not that any of it meant much right now with guilt warring with worry to see which could knot up her stomach the worst. Myra sensed her anxiety and gave her a comforting hug. Sally managed a half-hearted smile in return.

Sally turned to Keith and said, "Could the radios have been affected by whatever happened last night?"

Keith shrugged. "Who the hell even knows what happened last night? Some folks think it's a curse or something. Ain't nothin' like it ever been seen around here. Hell, around nowhere I've ever been, for that matter. I've got no idea about the radios."

Myra said, "I felt like I was being pulled, or more like I was falling sideways."

"Yeah, me too," said Keith. "Only, what kind of force pulls stuff? The debris around here looks like it was hit by the shock wave from a bomb or blown by a freakin' strong wind. But that sure as hell ain't what it felt like."

Sally shook her head. "No, it's like Myra said. More like we were falling sideways. But in surges, like invisible waves."

"Onda do Demônio…the Demon Wave. That's what the townsfolk are calling it," Keith said. "As for the radios, the only thing I can think of is massive sun spots or…" his brow furrowed and he glanced at the sky, "intentional jamming."

"Jamming?" said Myra. "Why would anyone jam the radios?"

Keith shrugged. "No idea. Just my old military life making me suspicious, I guess." He glanced at his watch and said, "Come on. Now that it's getting light, you can help me check out the chopper. If everything is okay, I should be able to drop you off at the camp on the way to Manaus once the clouds clear."

Myra nodded, and they began walking along the single paved road toward the river.

Sally paused and looked over the town's small square. The town hall, Catholic church, and the handful of surrounding buildings had fared much better than the huts and shacks on the outskirts of town. However, the hotel, a three-story wooden structure, had a noticeable tilt to it, as though pushed by a giant's hand. A little beyond the plaza, the damage was more pronounced. Everything was tilted, always in the same direction. It really did look like a wave had washed through the town. Huts, small trees, and power poles all bowed toward the north, as though paying homage to an invisible something hidden by tall trees and low-hanging clouds.

A frontier town located deep within the confines of the forest, Rio Estrada had an eclectic mix of residents. The diversity of the community was reflected in the clothing and faces of the people moving about the square, seeking or providing help. Scantily clad local natives mingled with mill workers from a dozen countries dressed in jeans and tee shirts. She'd always heard people came together in a crisis, but this was her first time experiencing such firsthand.

Grit seemed stuck to Sally's eyeballs and it was painful to blink, a reminder that she had only slept two hours last night. The dead she had helped uncover last night and the death of Bob's son didn't help as if she dwelt on them tears would come that would not be the least bit helpful in soothing her abused eyes. Worst was the knot that gripped her gut whenever she let herself think about David and rest of her friends still in the jungle. Nevertheless, as she watched the determined faces of the townspeople in the square, she felt an intense pride. She was proud of herself for not hesitating to help and proud of this odd mix of people for their acts of kindness and tender care displayed toward one another.

At one time during the night, she'd worked next to a woman from a local tribe. The woman had worn only a loincloth and her bare breasts had swung pendulously as she'd labored to move debris from a shattered hut from which came pitiful cries for help.

Not long after, she'd found herself next to a big millworker in blue jeans, work boots and a wife beater tee shirt. His heavily tattooed arms and rough features would have scared Sally had she encountered him in town at night. Soft sobs had come from the debris they'd been working too clear. The man had torn at the wreckage with frantic energy and then wept as he'd lifted a small, limp form from the wreckage. Tears had sparkled on his cheeks. The man had set his jaw in grim determination and hurried toward town with the injured child nestled against his brawny chest. The memory helped dispel a little of the sadness if not the exhaustion. It was uplifting to think of people working so hard to help others. Stretching out her back, she turned and hurried after Myra and Keith.

It was no longer raining as the three made their way down the street, but a clammy mist rose from the ground, and the clouds hung low and heavy. Rio Estrada had come into being in the early 1900's during the Rubber Boon. The town sat on a tributary of the Negro River as far north as one could travel in a moderate-sized barge or boat during the dry season.

The docks, which had been a flurry of activity during the boon days, were the main reason for the town's continued existence. They were built to accommodate the extreme changes in water depth, which varied twenty feet and more between the dry and wet seasons. Now the logging company used them for loading small barges with exotic timber.

"Holy crap!" Myra said as they topped the hill overlooking the river.

"There's no way," Keith muttered. "No damn way."

Sally blinked in surprise and with more than a touch of fear. Before them was another sign of the strange forces that had moved the night. The docks were comprised of three long floating wooden structures that stretched out into the deeper channel of the river. Rusty oil drums provided buoyancy for the docks although in several places those had been replaced with bright blue plastic drums. The docks had been around a long time and proved their hardy construction by riding out the Demon Wave with little damage.

Various small boats and one of the lumber barges hadn't fared well, though. The sight of the barge was the most disconcerting. The vessel was fifty feet long and its battered bow now rested twenty-five feet above the river on the concrete apron where the docks met the shore. The stern sat partially submerged in murky brown water.

Not far away were two large boats that ferried fuel, food, and supplies to river settlements, serving the role of trucks in this sodden land with few roads. Both lay capsized and half submerged. Three smaller boats tied to the center dock were listing badly, and several more were completely underwater.

Branches and debris were everywhere. It looked as though the river had assaulted the high riverbank in a watery version of D-day. Only the high ridge had prevented the river from flowing over the bank and adding to the village's misery.

The three Americans stood on top of the hill staring at the carnage below for several minutes. It was evident no one would be leaving by boat anytime soon.

"What in the hell could do this?" Myra asked in quiet tense voice.

Keith shook his head. "I heard of an earthquake, I think it was in Missouri, that made the Mississippi run backward."

Sally shook her head. "That couldn't have been an earthquake last night, could it? I mean, the trees and stuff all fell in the same direction."

Keith pointed to the high water mark a few feet below their feet. "Man, a little more, and we would have had a flood. That would have really screwed the town over."

Myra snorted. "I would say we were lucky, but after all the crap we went through last night, I sure don't feel lucky."

They watched two people working to salvage items from one of the half-sunken boats for a moment. Other than that, the area was deserted. Tendrils of mist snaked through the wreckage and debris, giving the scene a surreal look.

"Should we go help?" Sally asked, nodding to the people working on the boat.

"Nah," Keith said. "We can do more good at the chopper. I need to make sure the tie-downs held. Makes me nervous. I always tie her down in case a blow comes. But this...?" He waved his hand at the barge.

They turned and walked along the wide, hard-packed dirt road that ran along the bluff overlooking the river. The road was full of potholes and muddy from the heavy traffic and frequent rains. The jungle pressed in on their left, a silent wall of green. They traveled without talking as they picked their way around the frequent water-filled ruts left by logging trucks. After a few minutes, Myra stopped and looked up into the trees.

"Something seems strange," she said in a near whisper.

"No kidding," Keith said with a frown. "So far this is shaping up to be the strangest day of my life."

Sally looked at Myra for a moment before realizing what she meant by something being strange. "No birds," she said softly. "I don't hear any birds. This time of morning they're usually pretty loud."

Other sounds still escaped the jungle: frogs, the distant screech of a howler monkey, insects, but they were nothing compared to the usual greeting of the dawn by the countless birds of the Amazon.

Each day the forest rang with avian songs. The listener's point of view determined if the sounds were melodious or obnoxious, but they were a constant background of sound in the forest. The birds and their incredible array of colors, especially the parrots and toucans, were Sally's favorite aspect of Brazil. Now, not only were their voices missing, not a single winged form was in sight.

Keith frowned and moved to the jungle bordering the road. The foliage grew thick here as smaller plants at the edge of the towering trees fought for light. Pushing his way through the green wall, he looked into the less dense forest beyond and gave a whistle of amazement.

"Son of a bitch," he said, shaking his head.

A rush of dread made her chest tighten and Sally pushed up beside him with a sense of foreboding. It took a moment for her to adjust to the dim light under the layered canopy of the rainforest. Thick mist swirled along the jungle floor, and she detected a cloying odor layered on top of the jungle's usual smells.

As her pupils adapted to the gloom, she could see deeper into the forest as it opened up considerably past the wall of foliage. This was due to the lack of light under the layered canopy of the forest helping restrict the growth of smaller plants. It took a minute for her mind to understand what she was seeing.

The ground was carpeted in brilliant colors. She gasped when she realized the carpet was comprised of the bodies of hundreds of dead birds scattered among the fallen branches, thick vines and thin-leafed ferns that thrived in the lower light. For as far as she could see into the towering trees, bright, sad colors dotted the forest floor. The lifeless forms were pitiful, yet still beautiful even in death.

The pain in Sally's eyes doubled as the pressure behind them spiked. She shook her head in frustration. Her brain wanted to explode from all the emotions rampaging through her head and heart. "Goddamn it," she said, rubbing her face, angry that after the horror of last night, the sight of dead birds was what finally drove her to tears.

    Keith squeezed her shoulder. "Yeah, I know what you mean. I guess this day ain't through gettin' strange. I hope this is it, though. I'm not sure how much more I can take." He pushed past the two women and began striding up the muddy road. "God, I hope the chopper is okay. I really want to get the hell out of here."

Chapter 2

David

After the strange storm, the jungle pressed in on the camp like never before. The endless sea of life that was the Amazon was always a world of mystery, vast and unknowable, but never like this. Prior to last night, the expedition had been more annoying than scary to David. Especially once he'd adjusted to the never-ending cacophony of life and death from the surrounding forest.

However, having been dragged across the loam of the clearing by an invisible force, saved only by the ropes of his tent, made him believe something…out there…desired his death. Not just his death, but the death of all the people in the camp. Even his games had lost their luster, at least for now. The idea of fighting zombies seemed too possible right now to provide the escape he craved.

After the world went mad, which was the best explanation for what had happened during the night that anyone could come up with, the members of the research team struggled through the rain and the chaos to tend to the injured and provide some basic shelter. It took two grueling hours of groping in the dark and the rain to account for everyone and re-erect the Big Tent. Afterward, they spent the rest of the night inside it, huddled together in small groups, exhausted and scared.

The Big Tent was a large musty canvas structure donated to the team by the Brazilian military. It was big enough to keep their supplies out of the frequent rains with enough room for several tables, which they used for eating, meetings, or casual conversations. The Big Tent had fallen in such a way that they'd been able to pull it upright without too much difficulty. This was fortunate, because inside the Big Tent they had food, water, and a place for communal support and shelter.

Most of the other tents had collapsed into twisted heaps that would take a lot of work to untangle. Throughout the darkest part of the night, they'd tended one another's wounds and whispered theories about what had happened.

Twenty-two very well-educated people, and not a one of them had a clue about what had struck the camp. By now, they all referred to whatever it had been as a storm in order to have a label for it.

No one believed it had been a storm though. There was really only one aspect of the night they could agree on—they were all scared. The unknown force had fostered a primal fear even the most hardened scientist couldn't escape. Each person was highly aware of the limitless jungle beyond the tent and its eternal enigmas. For miles around there wasn't a road, a house, or a power line. The extent of their isolation haunted all their thoughts.

The camp was quiet when the muted early morning light began filtering through the clouds and overhanging trees. A quite tainted by muffled sobs that came from the corner of the tent containing Steve Carter. Most of the injuries suffered during the night had been painful, but not life-threatening. Steve's shattered leg was the exception.

The pain from his open compound fracture was way beyond the resources of the research camp to mollify. All they'd been able to do for him was slow the bleeding where jagged bone pierced his skin. People with injuries of this nature were supposed to be in a civilized care facility. However, there was no helicopter to carry him there. Moreover, the radios that would have allowed them to summon help refused to work.

The jungle was also quiet, at least by the standards of previous mornings. Usually the dawn brought the cries of countless birds. This morning, all the birds were dead. Another disturbing fact the team had no idea how to process.

The gray dawn light revealed countless feathered bodies all through the camp and the surrounding forest. The hint of rotting flesh was beginning to join the usual odor of wet decay that permeated the jungle. David dreaded what it would smell like by the afternoon.

Weird as things were, it wasn't the dead birds or unnatural quiet of the forest that disturbed David the most. Rather, it was the sound of Steve's suffering, which had taken on an oddly hypnotic rhythm. Over the last two hours, the pattern had become terrifying and consistent.

After each bout of agonized cries, there was a brief respite as exhaustion drove the injured man into unconsciousness. These never lasted very long, and in a way were worse than his gasping moans. David's tension grew with each second of silence as he waited for the sobs and cries to begin again, as inevitably they would.

Ice coursed up David's spine each time. He fidgeted in his chair, desperate to get away from the noise but with nowhere to go. The sounds made him extremely aware of his own mortality. However, it wasn't death that really scared him, he thought of dying all the time. Pain, especially the kind of pain he was listening too was what he found truly terrifying. David shook his head, as if the motion would somehow change the channel of his consciousness.

Maybe if he tried to focus on the other people in the tent. From the many strained glances toward Steve, it was obvious most of them were as disturbed by the sounds as he was. Few talked and when they did, it was in anxious whispers. Tensions ran high, accentuated by a vocal accompaniment of misery.

The team members sat in three distinct groups, except for David who sat alone, as usual. The group closest to David was the one he always sat near, but was never actually a part of. The gap between them was far larger than the slight distance in seating. These were the undergraduate research assistants, four women and three men, who did most of the grunt work for the expedition. They were only a couple of years older chronologically, but ages older in terms of experience.

David liked to sit near them so he could pretend to be part of their conversations, though only in a voyeuristic sort of way. Their talk was often laced with sexual innuendos that he barely understood. Although he had finished high school, he only kissed a girl one time, and that had been an awkward thing after a junior dance his sister had forced him to attend.

It wasn't that the group was unfriendly toward him, but rather that David surrounded himself with a wall of shyness, self-absorption, and video games. His sister told him they considered him a little odd and much younger than he actually was. Today there were no sexual overtones to their talk. Their conversations were full of fearful supernatural possibilities.

At another table were six men and five women who were also considered research assistants in the academic hierarchy, but were older postgraduates working on their doctorates. Sally was the unofficial leader of this group. If she were here, she'd undoubtedly be sitting with them. Their conversations tended to have a lot of theoretical, logic-based premises, but they were every bit as bewildered and tense as the rest.

The third group was the senior researchers. The assistants called them Gray Hairs, though not all were gray by any means. Each of them had a least one doctorate, and all were well-regarded experts in their fields. They were as confused and scared as anyone, and their experience gave them a deeper awareness of how little they really knew about what had come in the night. They mostly sat in silence.

The conversations, such as they were, stopped when Paul Sanders entered the tent. At first glance, one would be quick to label the tall redhead with thick glasses a nerd. To do so would be correct to a degree, but it was far from a complete description.

Paul had master degrees in physics and biology, but he was also an excellent triathlete. In his late twenties, he already had four patents that generated a comfortable income for him. He and Sally had been friends for several years and had even dated for a while. She'd told David that Paul was probably the smartest person in the camp, even though he hadn't completed a doctorate. In addition to his research, he maintained the camp's radios and computers and had been working on them all night.

After entering the tent, he blinked a few times as his eyes adjust to the comparative gloom. Noticing everyone watching at him, he shook his head and said, "No go on the HF radios or satellite uplink, still nothing but static."

Dr. Robert Allen, a short, rotund man and the expedition's leader, said with a frown, "I'm not an expert in communications, but even I know that's highly unusual, especially the satellite link. Any idea what happened?"

Paul crossed the tent, shaking his head as he walked over to the postgrads. "Not a clue. It doesn't make any damn sense. Several circuits on the radios were burned out. Found the same thing on some of the tablets and laptops. It almost looks like we got hit by an EMP, or something like it."

Dr. Allen gave a confused look. "EMP? As in an electromagnetic pulse? Isn't that from an atomic bomb?"

Paul nodded. "Yeah, the really powerful ones are. There are other ways to do it, but it takes a lot of power to scramble electronics, especially here at the equator."

"What does the equator have to do with it?" asked Heather, a pretty, red-haired graduate student.

"The earth's magnetic field is more stable near the equator," replied Paul. "The northern and southern latitudes have less stable fields that tend to interact with a bomb pulse. That's what causes the energy surge that screws up electronics. If that's what it was, something really big would have had to go off close by."

"Damn," said Dr. Allen. "Did someone nuke the Amazon? Is that what happened last night?"

"Someone may have set off a nuke, but I don't think that's what hit the camp," said Paul. "If it was a nuke, it would have to be triggered at high altitude to generate an EMP of any power. And that wasn't a shock wave that hit us last night."

Heather said, "Well, we haven't heard your theory on it. What do you think it was?"

Paul frowned, took off his glasses, and rubbed his face in thought. "I'm not sure. An explosion would have generated a shock wave and a pressure wave. Sometimes a nuke can generate backpressure, or at least I think it can, due to superheated air rushing upward. Regardless, these would have gone through the camp as two or three separate events, but we were hit by a lot more waves than that. And none of them matched my understanding of how an explosion works. It was more like we were pulled, or the earth tilted on its side." He looked up, gave a sniff, and a half smile. "I know the earth can't tilt, so don't bother pointing that out. I'm just saying that's what it felt like."

David gave a small snort. "Felt more like it turned upside down to me," he said quietly.

Paul's smile widened, "Yeah, you've got a point."

David hadn't intended to be heard and blushed. However, he noticed other people in the tent nodding in agreement.

Dr. Allen said, "So, what do you think it was?"

Paul pursed his lips and drew in a deep breath while casting his eyes over the attentive group. He gave a little, humorless laugh and said, "This is a little crazy, but I think it was a pulsating dimensional rift in space time that allowed a micro black hole to intersect for a brief time with our here and now, causing an intense gravitational anomaly."

Holy crap. This sounded like one his games. *Was Paul kidding?*

Everyone in the tent was looking at each other in confusion except for Heather. She nodded thoughtfully and said, "What...like a wormhole or something?"

"Yeah, something like that," said Paul. "Think about it, have you ever been on a bus or train that took off unexpectedly? I have and nearly busted my ass."

There was a murmur of agreement around the tables.

"That's what last night felt like, only on a massive scale. We know the earth probably didn't suddenly stop, or accelerate. But in physics, gravity and acceleration are basically the same thing. I believe something caused a powerful gravitational field to the north of us. A micro black hole forming and collapsing fits the bill, but I guess a tear in space, or wormhole if you prefer, combined with a high-gravity source like a star or gas giant, could do it."

"Why a micro black hole or tear?" asked Heather, who seemed to be following Paul's line of thought better than anyone else.

"Well, it had to have been something that opened and closed like a tear, or consumed itself as a micro black hole might, or else the gravity surges wouldn't have stopped. Heck, the whole planet could have been torn apart."

Dr. Allen said, "Could that have screwed up the radios?"

Paul shrugged. "Possibly, but I don't know. I was able to scavenge enough parts to fix the radio, but there is some kind of massive interference out there. In fact, one of the boards I fixed got fried again as soon as I turned it on. That means some serious energy is getting pumped out somewhere. It's like an ongoing barrage of EMPs."

"Jamming?" asked Heather.

"That's sort of what it seems like. But we're talking some very serious power, maybe even in the terawatt range." Paul looked up, gestured toward the roof of the tent, and said, "The satellites are something different though. They're line of sight, so even jamming this powerful shouldn't block their signals, and the uplink should be working. But I get nothing on the uplink or the sat phone." His face became grim. "It's...it's like they aren't there anymore."

Dr. Allen said, "So we can't call for help, and we can't find out what's going on." He looked around the tent. "Any ideas on what we do now?"

Paul shrugged. "About all we can do is pray for the chopper to come back soon. Unless someone wants to try going downriver in one of the canoes."

Dr. Allen shook his head. "I don't think we're there just yet. It's at least seventy miles by water to Rio Estrada, maybe more. And it looks like there are a lot of trees down, so it might not even be possible. I guess for now, we wait and hope."

The Big Tent grew quiet again as everyone considered nukes, EMPs and strange gravitational forces in the night. Everyone except David, who fell back under the sad, hypnotic rhythm of poor Steve Carter's suffering, which if anything, sounded more terrifying than ever.

Sally

Sally exited the food line set up by the church with a sandwich and a bottle of water and made her way to the plaza fountain, where Myra and Keith were already eating. They both gave her a tired nod as she sat down. Despite being nearly noon, the plaza seemed to be in twilight due to the low, heavy clouds. A fine drizzle drifted down, but it hadn't deterred most of the town from gathering in the plaza or along the one paved street.

To Sally it looked like some kind of twisted, upside-down festival. One based on sadness rather than joy. The mist and dark clouds made everything seem colorless and gray. The people were clad in shadows with heads hung low. Conversation was infrequent and muted. Most were huddled together in small groups, seeking comfort in this pageant of shock and grief. Instead of music, there was the pitter-patter of water, beating out a melancholy lilt.

"How are they doing?" Myra asked, her voice coming out in a raspy whisper.

Sally had been helping at the church, which was being used as a makeshift hospital and shelter. She knew Myra was referring to the teenage girl with internal injuries and the middle-aged father with a head trauma who were the two in the worst condition.

Sally shrugged and said, "We really can't tell. The local nurse is terrified and doesn't know what to do." She drew in a deep breath and let it out slowly, fighting to keep her tears at bay. "Hell, she keeps asking me what to do, if that tells you anything. What's the news on the helicopter? That's their best bet."

Keith said, "The chopper is good to go." He pointed at the sky with his sandwich. "But we're stuck until this clears up."

"It's not raining very hard. Can't you take off through the clouds?"

Keith nodded. "Yeah, I could. But taking off isn't the problem; landing is. With no radio or weather reports, there's no way of telling if the camp or Manaus is sopped in like it is here. Hell, without GPS, and if I can't see the ground, I doubt we could even find them. It wouldn't be any fun to run out of fuel and have no idea what's below us. Landing in a tree would be a real bad thing. I'm willing to try it as soon as we get a three-hundred-foot ceiling or so. We pretty much have the same problem flying at night, so unless this clears up quickly, it'll probably be tomorrow morning at the earliest."

Sally felt the tears she'd been holding back work free of her eyes. Then the leak turned into a stream. In seconds she was sobbing, her shoulders shaking as she struggled under a torrent of emotions. Grief over the dead and injured weighed heavily on her, but worse was the worry and frustration over not knowing what was going on at camp. She desperately wanted to make sure her brother and friends were okay.

Myra put her arm around Sally's shoulders. "I'm sure they're alright."

Anger welled up in Sally's chest and she shrugged off Myra's arm. "You don't know that! Don't say that! I can't allow…" The anger faded as quickly as it arose. "I'm, I'm sorry. I…I just don't know what to think, how to prepare. To get ready in case…"

"Don't put them in the ground yet, Sally," said Keith. "There's no point in it. We'll have to take this mess as it comes, one step at a time."

"I know. It's…well, my mom died in a tornado. I remember sitting at home when the news about a shopping center being destroyed came on the TV. I didn't link her to the story. They showed the buildings, or what was left of them. She was right there, underneath all that destruction and I didn't even know. Not until she didn't come home that night. Then…then…" She drew in a deep breath, fighting for control. "Sorry I snapped at you, Myra."

Myra extended her arms, and this time Sally leaned into them, the tension fading. She knew her friends were right, but it was oh so much easier to say than to do. This whole thing brought back very bad memories. Sally had a deep sense of foreboding, and no matter how hard she tried, she couldn't shake dark thoughts that something very bad was going to happen.

David
	Sweat streamed off David in the hot, moist air as he struggled to drag his side of the plastic sheet across the uneven ground. It was full of branches, leaves, and dead birds they'd gathered from around the camp. Heather was pulling on the opposite corner of their makeshift sled and getting ahead of him. She stopped yet again to let him catch up. Frowning, she shook her head, which made David's already hot face burned a couple of degrees hotter.
	David was over six feet tall and outweighed Heather by more than a hundred pounds. But while he was huffing, and wheezing, and struggling with every step, she was barely out of breath. In David's video games, he was a superman who destroyed enemies with his mighty strength. Heather's look of disdain was an unwanted reminder of how far apart his fantasies were from reality.
	How had he let himself be "volunteered" to help clear the chopper's landing zone in the first place? *Crap*. Redoubling his efforts, he struggled on. A short time later, he sighed with relief as they reached the line of string Paul had laid out to mark off the landing zone. They began unloading the debris onto the sizeable pile already there. As David and Heather finished, Paul and another research assistant dragged a load up beside them.
	"I just don't understand what happened to the birds," said Heather to Paul, a statement already repeated many times during the afternoon.
	Paul picked up a limp green parrot. "Yeah, so far they're all pretty much the same. I thought we'd see more evidence they had panicked during the anomaly. That maybe they flew into branches and tree trunks. But most of them have no marks, no sign of trauma, nothing. Seems like they all fell over and died for no reason."
	"Radiation?" asked Heather, her voice sounding nervous.
	"Maaybeee, but probably not," Paul said. "I kicked that around with Dr. Allen. Apparently, eggs and baby birds are highly susceptible to radiation, but adults not so much. At Chernobyl, the local bird population was decimated, but that took a couple of years. If a nuke is what knocked out the radio, and if we had fallout, it wouldn't have killed the birds this quickly. We discussed gas, but the energy from last night was an implosion, so gas wouldn't have come out from whatever happened."
	David looked away from the other three and rolled his eyes. He'd

heard this same conversation several times and already knew how it would play out. Everyone knew there was no explanation, but they still wanted Paul's opinion on the matter. For David, the hard work along with all the other terrors of the day had numbed him beyond the point of caring. There were only two things he wanted to know. Where was his sister, and when the hell could they get out of here?

While the others rehashed yet again their theories about birds, black holes, and nuclear explosions, David searched the sky for the helicopter. Where was Sally? *Please God, take care of her.* She was the one solid thing in his life. Ever since their mother had died, Sally had worked feverishly to hold the family together. How would he survive it she didn't come back?

While their father had sunk deeper into depression and alcoholism, she'd become the head of the house, diligently moving them through their daily routines of work or school. For over a year their father had gone through the motions of going to his job and maintained the illusion that everything was normal.

When David was nine, he'd come home from school to find his father hanging in the garage. Things got blurry after that. Somehow, with the help of a lot of counseling, his sister had gotten him all the way through high school. He often resented her constant urging and encouragement, or nagging as he called it, even though a part of him knew he needed the guidance.

She'd been a rock in his limited universe. Only now that he had to face the prospect of her not returning did it dawn on him how much he depended on her. He found himself adrift and very alone. Tears began to form in his eyes, but he shook them off. Sally would want him to be strong. It was something he should have been working on long before now.

"Hey! Look!" yelled the grad student with Paul, an African American named Darrin. He was pointing across the clearing.

David turned around in time to see a bright red-and-blue macaw fly gracefully into the forest.

Heather laughed. "Well, alright then. Some of them made it through."

Paul nodded with a smile. "Or at least they're returning to the area and living."

The clearing began to brighten as sunlight started to leak though the clouds to the west of the field, casting a cheery yellow glow. The tall trees had masked the breaking of the clouds, which now seemed to be moving aside like a giant gray curtain, leaving blue sky in their wake. David noticed everyone smiling as the gloom pressing down on the camp began to lift.

"Maybe now the chopper can make it in," said David.

"Maybe, but not tonight," said Paul. He glanced toward the east, which was still heavy with clouds. "The village is that way. They might make it in the morning."

Heather's face lit up with excitement and she clapped her hands together. She pointed skyward and said, "Hey, there's a plane. Maybe things aren't so messed up in the real world after all."

High to the west, a silver speck stood out against the blue sky. The late afternoon sun spotlighted the large commercial airliner as it slowly crawled through the air. Four bright white contrails streamed out behind it in thick plumes that faded into wispy tendrils. It wasn't unusual for a plane to fly over the Amazon Basin, but today such a simple, ordinary occurrence was reassuring. It served as a bridge from the insanity they were experiencing to the civilized world beyond the jungle.

Heather laughed. "Well, things are looking up. I never thought I'd be so happy just to see a stupid—"

The silver dot disappeared in a flash. The white contrails transformed abruptly from a line into an expanding roiling cloud that burst outward and then down. Little silvery specks drifted across the sky as the main body of the stricken aircraft emerged from the cloud and began spiraling toward the ground, trailing flames and dark smoke. As it fell, David could see pieces break off to make their own sad, forlorn descent to the jungle. The small group watched in stunned silence and after what felt like a very long time, a dull boom echoed across the clearing.

Heather covered her face and turned away. "Oh my God, oh my God, oh my God! What the hell is going on?"

The other three shook their heads with shocked, pained expressions. No one had an answer. David fixated on the smudge in the sky that had once been a passenger plane and felt the worry for his sister turn into a cold, hard knot of fear.

Chapter 3
Josh

"Crap!" said Joshua O'Brian, throttling back the airboat engine as another downed tree came into sight. "We'll never get back at this rate."

The late afternoon sun glinted off the water as the flat-bottomed boat glided to a stop, the bow bumping into the leafy barrier before them. The muscles across Josh's massive shoulders bunched as he squeezed the steering lever in frustration. Some people would say his squat, powerful frame, narrow-set dark eyes and bristly hair made him look like a red-headed ape, but they probably wouldn't say it within earshot of Josh.

Sean Lee, small, wiry, and quick, scrutinized the water beside the boat with care, and then jumped into the calf high water. "Can't be too much further."

"It better not be, or we won't make it back before dark," replied Josh.

Sean gave the chain saw he carried two pulls, and it coughed to life. They had spent many years working together and they made short work of the tree limbs blocking their path. Sean cut and Josh pulled the debris out of the way. In a few minutes, they managed to clear a path through the foliage. The two men climbed back onto the boat, Josh fired up the engine, and with a roar from the huge fan in the back, continued upriver.

Josh was pretty sure Sean was right; the camp couldn't be too far away. It was hard to judge, especially with the GPS and radio not working. That still had him puzzled. However, the failure of the electronics was nothing compared to the crap they'd been through last night on the supply ship.

The weird storm, or whatever it was, had been the strangest thing he'd ever experienced. He kept replaying last night in his head but could find no logical, or even illogical, explanation. The night on the ship would probably haunt him for a long time to come, although a part of him wondered if even stranger times might lie ahead. With the river free of obstructions, at least for the moment, he allowed his mind to drift back to the events of yesterday once again.

===

The day had started well enough. The two men had been looking forward to a break from the unpleasant confines of their jungle base. After an early morning rain, the sky cleared, and they set out in good spirits. The trip was a welcome respite from their otherwise mundane duties.

The camp advisors took turns traveling down the small stream to meet the *Santa Maria*, a grandiosely named one-hundred-foot tugboat the CIA used to ferry supplies they didn't want inspected too closely. Even though the Brazilians were in league with their mission, none of them wanted to attract undue attention. Their efforts wouldn't be condoned by international law. The old tug's rusty hull blended in well with the river traffic, but inside it was well maintained with good food and comfortable cabins.

The trip started with a five-hour trip down a shallow creek that only a fan-driven airboat could navigate at a decent speed. At least riding on the boat was fun. Zipping across the shallow water was one of the best parts of making the trip. The air rushing past always felt good after the stifling humidity of the camp. They took turns steering as they roared across the water, skimming across sand bars and dodging low hanging branches. It gave Josh a sense of freedom that was hard to come by these days.

Captain Larry Fitzpatrick, a tall, very fit gray-haired man, greeted them once they rendezvoused with the small ship. They talked for a few minutes, but there was really nothing new going on in the world. The price of oil was going up, Columbia was still a mess, and some people in the Middle East had blown up a bunch innocent people for some cause none of them understood.

Once the airboat was secure, they dumped their belongings in a cabin and settled into the galley with a few beers to watch the World Cup.

Around midnight, during the closing minutes of a game between Brazil and Mexico, things started getting weird. One second the TV showed Brazil pressing down the field and the next there was nothing but static.

"Son of a bitch!" yelled Sean. He had serious money riding on the game. Grabbing the remote, he began punching buttons with no luck. "Wouldn't you friggin' know it?"

Josh laughed. "Calm down, dude, it's probably jus—"

The boat lurched and leaned sideways, as though it had been struck by something. However, there hadn't been a sound of anything hitting it, just the sudden motion. Very odd, and odd usually meant trouble.

"What the hell?" said Josh. He got up and headed for the narrow gangway leading to the top deck with Sean right behind. Even without any sound, Josh feared the lurch had been from something ramming into the small ship. *Had the sound been muffled somehow? Maybe on purpose? Are we under attack?* In his line of work, it paid to be paranoid.

However, there was no sign of attack as he emerged from the gangway. Something had happened though, as the crewmembers were walking along the ship's railing and looking down at the water.

They were calling out to one another, "Nothing." "Nothing here." "All clear over here."

The Santa Maria lurched again and rolled. This time, water sloshed past the small ship as the stern swung around for no apparent reason. The Negro River, the largest tributary to the Amazon, was over a mile across along this part of the channel and the water normally flowed at a gentle pace west to east. Now the current was rushing from the southern shore toward the north, pulling the ship with it.

The crewmembers exclaimed in fear at this unexpected change in the river. *How is this even possible?* As the small ship swung around, the anchor chain groaned in protest. Then the anchor lost purchase on the river bottom, and the ship jumped northward. The anchor must have snagged on something else as the vessel stopped with a jerk, knocking Josh to his knees.

The ship tilted down in the stern, as though they were sinking. But his eyes told him the small ship was more or less on an even keel, certainly not as far down in the back as it felt.

The world righted itself, and the river surged back in the opposite direction, pushing the craft southward and pivoting it around the anchor chain. Water sloshed over the side with a hissing sound, it seemed for sure they were going to capsize. However, the ship shuddered upright as water flowed off the deck. No sooner had they stabilized than another weird tilting sensation hit, and the river rushed back toward the northern bank as more water rushed over the *Santa Maria*'s deck.

Again and again the world tilted as surges of rushing water pushed, pulled, and twisted the boat, sending more waves crashing over the deck. As the tug struggled to remain upright, one of the crewmen lost his grip. With a terrified scream, he disappeared into the now frothing river. The men exchanged desperate, ashamed looks but no one made an attempt to help the poor soul, lest they be swept over as well. None of them really had a choice in face of the wild tempest sweeping around the ship, but guilt was plain on their faces.

Josh was amazed at the toughness of the small vessel. All he could do was hold on and watch helplessly as the life-and-death struggle raged between the river gone mad and the Santa Maria. He found himself cheering the tugboat each time it fought its way upward. Somehow, despite being sluggish and heavy, the ship managed to rise from the water again and again. "Go baby! Go!" he yelled at the boat.

An eternal eight minutes after the first lurch roused them from the galley, the surges stopped. The river continued to rock the boat with white-topped waves coursing back and forth across the channel like fuming beasts awakened from a sound slumber. The Santa Maria easily rode these less-angry waters, though now with a slight list.

Staggering to his feet, Josh check on the airboat and was surprised to find it still securely lashed to the deck, although half full of water. He then joined the men searching for the lost crewmember. They spent the rest of the night calling out to him, sweeping the water with searchlights, but to no avail.

The roiling waves had calmed, but the radios and TV still gave nothing but static. Even the radar showed nothing but white haze with each sweep, which did nothing to mollify the men's frayed nerves.

Dawn arrived with low clouds and tendrils of mist, obscuring the northern shoreline with a haunting curtain of white. The exhausted men gave up the search and collapsed on the deck in an uneasy sleep, fearful of being trapped below if the strange forces returned.

Not long after dawn, Josh and Sean set out for base. The strange events of the night proved to be only the beginning. Oddities continued as they began traveling back up the small creek to camp, which was now a jumbled mess of fallen trees, broken branches, and dead birds.

They had to stop repeatedly to cut and move tree limbs to clear the narrow channel leading to the base. The dead birds acted as fuel for a wild feeding frenzy along the shallow stream and made most stops a harrowing experience.

Caiman, distant cousin of the crocodile, were everywhere. Several times when the boat had to stop, Josh could hear the large reptiles grunting and snorting as they feasted on the unexpected bounty of delicate, colorful morsels.

The promise of easy food drew other predators as well. There were jaguars, piranha, and anacondas in abundance. They had to keep a sharp lookout as they progressed up the small tributary. So far, they'd been lucky. The worst injury had occurred when Sean got a nasty, quarter-sized hunk taken out of his calf by a piranha. The frequent tension-filled stops transformed the normally enjoyable airboat ride into a grueling, nine-hour journey that seemed would never end.

===

At last, Sean called out over the airboat's motor, "Thank God! I see the camp."

Josh nodded as the rough-hewn log steps leading uphill from the river to the base came into view. The team's second airboat was tied up beside the steps, and it appeared someone had cleared away some of the fallen trees in the immediate area. However, no one was in sight, which was a quite odd. The airboat was loud, and someone should have heard it and come to meet them. He throttled back the engine and let the craft glide to stop beside the other boat. It was half full of water and sat low in the river. With a frown, Sean hopped out with a line and tied the boat to a protruding stump.

The two men glanced at each other while putting on their gear. Full military harnesses and belts heavy with ammo pouches, canteens, and other essentials were standard issue here at the camp. Sean picked up his M16, chambered a round, engaged the safety, and slung the weapon over his shoulder.

Josh watched him and then nodded and chambered a round into the massive pistol he preferred. He didn't carry a rifle; this was supposed to be a safe area. But he never went anywhere without his pistol, save maybe and airport. "Always be prepared," the moto of the Boy Scouts and special forces the world over. They warily began climbing the steps leading up the hill that overlooked the river, expecting trouble.

When they crested the hill, it was immediately obvious the camp had suffered from the same strange forces they'd experienced on the Santa Maria. There were numerous downed trees around the edge of the clearing. The log structures used for live-fire drills were noticeably askew, but most were still standing. Tents and equipment were scattered haphazardly around the large field the Brazilians had picked for this crazy scheme.

Some effort had been made to restore order, as there were several piles of carefully stacked equipment and supplies.

Josh's eyes swept the area. The field was roughly square and about two hundred yards on a side. The stream at their back ran along one side of the field, and the boundless jungle bordered the other three sides. Everything sat in silence, all empty, all still.

Sean unslung his rifle and cradled it in his arms. "Something's up. Where is everyone?"

Josh nodded and let out a long, slow breath. "Yeah, somethin's up alright. Damn, I'm getting too old for this crap."

Sean mustered a smile. "You say that every year."

Josh snorted. "This time I mean it. After this contract, I'm done."

"Yeah, you say that every year, too," Sean said with a dry chuckle. "But what do we do now?"

Josh shrugged and studied the camp, feeling every one of his forty-two years. He looked wistfully back down the hill at the airboat. Something told him they should turn around right now and get the hell out of Dodge.

The mission was almost over. Why did crap always seem to hit near the end of a tour? It never failed. They were in the process of training the third and supposedly last batch of so-called "Columbian Patriots". Once trained, they'd be off to fight the Russian-supported drug lords who now controlled Columbia. There had never been any love lost between Brazil and Columbia. The unexpected success of Columbian communists in taking over the country had been a big surprise though, and tensions had rocketed. In response, the Brazilian intelligence agency, ABIN, had enlisted the help of the CIA to begin undermining the new government.

Whoever dreamed up this mess was way above Josh's pay grade, but that had been the case ever since Afghanistan. This group of Columbians was the worst yet. They were little more than murders and thieves, and he shuddered to think what they'd do to propagate their civil war when they went back.

However, he'd served with the other six CIA advisors for a long time. They'd all been Rangers together before becoming CIA Special Liaison Operatives. He couldn't leave without finding out what happened to them. While he had less and less use for crazy politicians and their schemes, he had a strong sense of loyalty to his comrades.

Several shots rang out, echoing across the clearing from the far tree line and causing both men to duck instinctively. More shots followed, swelling into a roar as dozens of rifles began firing simultaneously. Josh drew his pistol and glanced at Sean, who responded with a quick nod. They set out across the field in a crouch, each of them instinctively scanning different points of the field. No one was in sight, the shots coming from a wide arc of jungle. The gunfire began to slack off into sporadic pops. The participants and reason of the fierce firefight stayed hidden in the shadows of the jungle.

A dark, thrashing shadow along the northern edge of the field drew Josh's eye just before twenty or so Columbians burst into view. Every man's face was etched with fear and they sprinted with frantic energy across the clearing. Their running had a surreal look. The men's legs moved in a rapid, pumping motion, sometimes splashing through and slipping in mud. But the sound of their footfalls were lost against the roaring hiss from the jungle, making it seem they ran in silence. Three of the terrified men tossed away their rifles, and a moment later the rest did the same. Escape was the single focus of the entire group. But what the hell were they escaping from?

Josh moved into their path, his hands out, and called in Spanish, "Stop, what the hell is going on?"

The men ignored him, only a few even glancing in his direction. He managed to grab one of the men as he rushed past. The man struggled frantically, desperation evident in his wide, terrified eyes. Despite Josh being a hundred pounds heavier and far stronger, he had to struggle to hold on to the panicked Columbian.

Josh shook the man and yelled, "Where are the others? What's going on?"

Only a semblance of sanity came to the man's face as he looked at Josh. He stopped struggling and in a hoarse voice said, "The devils have them! They take the trees! The devils have the trees!"

The moment of lucidity passed as panic flooded back into the man's face. With desperate strength, he twisted free of Josh's grip and resumed his headlong flight across the field. In moments, he disappeared over the hill heading for the stream.

Sean came over and whispered, "Oh man, oh man, oh man. What was that about the trees?" He gestured toward the stream with his chin.

"Those guys are assholes, but they ain't cowards. What could have spooked them that bad?"

Josh shook his head and turned back toward the jungle. The shooting had stopped, and a deep silence again settled across the field, broken only by a breeze rustling the trees. The urge to turn around and get the hell out was even stronger now. Something very bad was going down here. But he couldn't do it. He had to find the rest of the team. He drew in a deep breath, gripped his pistol tightly, and resumed his cautious advance across the field. After a brief hesitation, Sean followed.

At the edge of the field, a crude log fence, more of a brush heap actually, separated the camp from the jungle proper. The fence was comprised of trees and foliage cleared by the long-gone farmer who'd piled it up in an attempt to deter some of the forest's inhabitants from raiding his field.

For the most part, the jungle grew right up to the barrier in a tangle as smaller plants fought for light not available in the deeper forest. Slash and burn farms such as the field had once been tended to leach the soil of nutrients, making an oasis of dirt in the midst of the jungle for years after they were abandoned.

The two men stared intently into the shadows at the edge of the field but Josh couldn't see or hear a thing. Sean held his rifle tensely across his chest. Josh fingered the safety on his pistol, as though combat was imminent. There were no clear threats to justify the reaction other than the silence was deep and ominous; not even a buzzing insect could be heard. Very unusual.

Josh cupped a hand to his mouth and yelled, "Hey! Steve! Mark! Bob! Are you guys all right?"

There was no reply. Josh's heart beat a little faster. Damn it, this was supposed to be a training mission. A snort pushed its way out of his nose. How many times had he heard that line? It rarely played out that way. With a scowl, he started walking slowly along the crumbling fence while peering into the silent jungle.

"If this is an attack, the camp is wide open." He glanced back at the field. "There's a lot of high-dollar equipment and supplies sitting out there for the taking. Why ain't they busting in here?"

Sean opened his mouth to reply but snapped it shut when a faint noise pierced the silence. A soft, hissing crackle came from deep in the jungle. Sean cocked his head to one side, listening with intense concentration. "Is that a fire? That might be what ran off the Columbians."

"Then why all the gunfire? And where is everyone else? And a fire sure as hell isn't a walking tree."

Sean's eyes reflected puzzlement as he shook his head with a sigh.

They stood staring into the jungle for several long moments. A growing part of Josh's brain told him he'd done enough, that he'd satisfied his obligation to the team and it was time to run. The rational side of his brain asked, from what and to where? He'd learned long ago that running usually killed more men than actual combat.

The need to understand what they might be up against held him in place now as much as his obligation to the rest of the team. The fact that the others hadn't come out of the jungle by now made him pretty sure they weren't going to come out at all.

The strange sounds from the jungle grew louder, going from a crackling hiss to a continuous series of cracks, pops, and crunches. Josh tried but failed to pinpoint exactly where it originated. The noises seemed to come from everywhere along the entire length of jungle.

They stopped and crouched behind the fence where it pulled away from the jungle and studied the dense foliage twenty feet away. Sean kept swinging his rifle back and forth, looking for targets.

Josh watched him for a moment and then shrugged and placed his pistol in its holster. If a hundred men with automatic rifles hadn't stopped whatever was making the strange noise coming toward them, he couldn't imagine his pistol being of much use. There was a growing chance they'd need to run like hell in a few minutes and he didn't want to lose it. Besides, while no quick-draw expert, he could pull it out pretty fast if he needed it.

Sean's eyes darted around nervously and he gripped his rifle so hard his knuckles were white. "Should we go back to the river?" he asked in a husky whisper.

Josh looked back at the camp. It was hard to believe those damn Columbians would panic like that. They'd been scared out of their wits. There were only two boats, and Josh seriously doubted they'd still be there. "Not me. Go ahead if you want. I gotta see what this is all about. And maybe we can still find the team."

Sean nodded but didn't look convinced. However, he stayed at the brush wall and continued peering into the jungle.

The cracks and pops became louder and louder, now a constant roar that made Josh's heart thump hard in his chest. He'd never heard anything remotely like it. It sounded like the jungle was being ripped apart.

A dark shape burst from the jungle in front of them, heading straight for the fence. They ducked as the thing skimmed over the barrier and thudded down right behind them. Josh whirled about in time to see…something, take an impossible leap, and then another, before bounding out of sight among the clustered logs of the practice field.

"What the hell was that!" screamed Sean, spittle flying from his mouth and sticking in unheeded white flecks to his lips.

Up and down the length of fence, other similar shapes emerged from the jungle, all moving with incredible bounding leaps. They were fast and vanished from view too quick for the mind to grasp their strange alien silhouettes. Josh struggled to categorize the creatures but failed. This added to the weirdness of the things as they disappeared over the hill, leaving behind a vague image of dark bear-sized shapes with too many legs.

Mad screeches erupted from the jungle and both men twisted back around toward the tree line. A mass of knee-high creatures erupted from the wall of foliage, coming directly for them. It took Josh a moment to realize it was a whole troop of red-faced monkeys bounding wildly across the ground. They surged like a red-and-orange wave over the barrier, ignoring the two men in their haste to escape the source of the hissing and popping coming from the forest.

More animals began to burst from the forest up and down the line. Monkeys, a jaguar, a large group of tapers, and other creatures Josh couldn't identify, though at least they had the right number of legs, all running for the river, desperate to be away from the jungle.

After the exodus of animals, Josh resumed staring at the wall of jungle. The late afternoon sun and deep shadow under the massive trees continued to mask the source of the noise. Then a sliver of light appeared deep in the brush and began expanding with fearful speed, moving and flickering along his entire field of vision. It looked like the jungle was melting away. *Maybe it is a fire.* The light seemed to flicker like one, but… Josh's mouth fell slowly open.

"My God!" screamed Sean. "What is that?"

Josh didn't attempt to answer. Something was indeed destroying the jungle, and it was no fire. The crackle and pops came from trees and brush being ripped from the ground. Fear and surprise sent a pulse like an electric shock up his spine. The light, now spilling through the widening gaps in the jungle, outlined dark, massive shapes. Josh wiped sweat from his eyes and strained to see, but the thick undergrowth at the tree line made it impossible to make out details.

A small rubber tree to their left groaned for a moment and then surrendered to whatever assaulted it with a loud ripping sound. The tree slowly rose with more moans from tortured wood as the roots fought vainly to hold the tree to the ground.

The tree pivoted out of the way, revealing a massive dark shape covered in scales and spikes. It had to stand over twenty feet high, nearly as tall as the tree itself. The shape and tree vanished into surrounding trees, all of which were now shaking and groaning in wooden protest.

Josh heard a strangled gurgle and glanced over to see Sean's face contorted in fear. His lips were stretched tight over his teeth and flecked white with spittle. Josh had been with Sean through some terrifying times during their long, violent careers, but he'd never seen such a maniacal mask of raw terror on the other man's face.

Another creature jostled past the first. If anything, it was even taller. Two huge flat black eyes were the distinctive feature, their shape of gave the creature a fixed, evil stare. The next oddity, besides the gargantuan size, were a plethora of spikes and antenna, which protruded from all over the head. It had a short muzzle with a fleshy opening in the shape of an O. The head swiveled slowly, like a praying mantis, as it surveyed the mass of undergrowth and fledgling trees before it.

It was built like a centaur of a nightmarish size. The upper torso was vaguely man-shaped, only huge and scaly, with long, powerful arms. The bottom looked a little like an elephant but at least twice as big with spikes resembling huge rose thorns sticking out all over. It stood on four massive legs and the two upper arms were equipped with powerful though clumsy-looking three-fingered hands tipped with long black claws.

"Oh my God, oh my God, oh my God," mumbled Sean, his face white. His body shook, and more sweat than the heat called for ran down his face, like he was freezing and burning up at the same time.

Josh gripped his arm and pulled him back from the barrier. Sean stumbled a few steps and then followed as if in a trance to one of the log structures a little farther from the jungle.

Sean's reaction was almost as terrifying as the sight of the creatures, but at least his friend's panic kept Josh from thinking he'd gone crazy himself; otherwise he wouldn't believe what he saw. As the jungle melted away, Josh pulled Sean up and got him moving again. They retreated behind another cluster of logs about forty yards from the fence. The two men watched the ongoing destruction with slack jawed awe.

Whitish-brown fluid erupted from the round opening of one of the creature's muzzles. It came out in a lumpy stream, expanding and congealing as it settled like a huge web over a section of the brush wall. The arms tightened and flexed with what had to be incredible strength as it pulled the whole mass upward with one heave.

Josh noticed small gleaming eyes from some frightened animals peering out of the foliage, their hiding place now a trap. All along the field, the last vestiges of jungle disappeared under the assault of hundreds of the behemoths. As the ripping and popping noises faded, the two men were left facing a line of gigantic creatures across fifty yards of open ground. They formed a solid, silent wall, staring straight ahead with their huge, evil-looking eyes.

The silent standoff lasted but a moment. Josh shook his head and gave up trying to make sense of what he was seeing. It was time to get out of here. Hell, it was way past time. He rose to a half crouch and began backing away. Without warning, Sean emitted a maniacal shrill scream and swung up his rifle.

"Are you crazy?" Josh shouted as he grabbed for the weapon.

Sean glared at him with blind, mindless fury, his panic and fear pushing aside all rational thought as he wrenched the rifle from Josh's grasp.

Josh grabbed for the weapon again, yelling, "We gotta get out of here!"

While Sean may have not been in his right mind, there was nothing wrong with his combat reflexes. As Josh reached forward, Sean smashed the butt of the rifle against Josh's head with blinding force. Josh fell heavily to his knees, the world spinning out of focus. After a short fight to stay upright, his mind gave up and he fell face first onto the muddy ground.

He was dimly aware of Sean's hoarse animal screams as the rifle chattered away in full auto.

He always has been a hotheaded little bastard. Things then grew very black and time lost meaning.

Chapter 4

Josh

Josh woke to a rumbling noise in his ears and a noticeable vibration under his back. With awareness came remembrance, and fear. Energy rushed through his battered body and he jerked upright, wincing in response to an intense stab of pain that shot through his head. Forcing himself to ignore the pain, he looked around, trying to regain his bearings.

In response to the pain, he dabbed at his head with care where Sean's rifle had struck and found a large bump that left a sticky substance on his fingers. It was hard to focus on his hand and he stared stupidly at it for a moment before realizing the sticky stuff was blood. Nausea clutched his stomach and throat with every movement of his head. The world kept trying to spin, pulling his head to the side. It took an effort to keep from falling over again and it was hard to concentrate.

Besides a blistering headache, the first thing to penetrate the fog in his head was that his feet were tied together with some kind of white scratchy stuff. The next thing he noticed was that a rough rock wall on his left, embedded with pipes and glowing blues rods, slid by at a steady pace. A moving wall? That didn't seem right. How could such a mass be moving? After a few moments of pondering this strange situation, it dawned on him that he was the one moving. Despite the pain and disorientation, a rising urgency to move coursed through him.

His vision refused to come into focus, making it difficult to understand what was going on around him. As Josh managed to piece together the blurry images, he found that for the second time that day he had reason to doubt his sanity. He sat on what appeared to be a huge conveyor moving through a large tunnel. Stark, electric-blue light radiated from rods intermixed with pipes of various sizes implanted in the rock walls and ceiling.

The conveyor was stacked high with an assortment of trees, brush, and animals, all coated to varying degrees with the web-like stuff binding his feet. Visibility was limited due to the debris, a situation that made Josh very uncomfortable. There was a distinct, low hum punctuated by a loud mechanical squeal that sounded like an old bearing in desperate need of oil.

The air was cooler than the jungle and smelled of uprooted plants and broken branches. There was also a sweet smell that made Josh think of cookies. Of everything, this smell was the most disconcerting. It made for an odd mix with the cloying odor of death coming from farther up the conveyor. It was a challenge to get his hands to go where he wanted. His first swipe actually missed his chest. *Crap.* The skin around his eyes crinkled in concentration and his hand moved with exaggerated slowness to his combat harness, then his belt, and finally his pistol and knife. Everything was still there, which was a bit of a surprise. Still moving slowly, he clumsily drew out his survival knife and began sawing at the stuff holding his feet together.

The material was tough, but his well-honed knife cut through it with only a little effort. Although it wasn't sticky now, it clung to his pants where it had dried like old tape. He cut it off as close as he could and left most of the residue on his fatigues. He moved his legs gingerly to loosen stiff joints. In spite of the dizziness and confusion, it was pleasing to have a least won this small victory. He was about to try standing when he noticed the material that had been wrapped around his legs was attached to a large white form. The web-coated mass was man-sized and had a familiar pair of boots sticking out of it.

"Sean?" he said, crawling over to the bundle. It was evident that the bundle did indeed contain Sean. It was also evident there wasn't much point in calling out again. Josh let out a sigh as he surveyed the corpse.

The white substance covered Sean's head and shoulders. His friend's ever-present M16 was plastered across his chest. The odd position of Sean's arms, no doubt broken and still clutching the rifle, indicated the amount of force with which the stuff must have struck. Right below the rifle was a gaping hole surrounded by blood that glistened purple in the harsh blue light.

Josh remembered how the creatures had slung their bundles onto the spikes protruding their bodies. Evidently, they'd been sprayed with the web stuff together. Like the brush pile, back at the base, one of the creatures had tossed them onto the back of another creature, and Sean had caught the spike.

"Stupid ass," Josh said, shaking his head. "Of all the times to lose your shit. We probably could have gotten away." He placed his hand on the man's head. "Hell of a way to go, brother. But I gotta feeling I may be joining you pretty soon."

His hand rested on Sean's head for only a moment, and then the smells of death invaded Josh's awareness, making him refocus on his situation. Losing friends had happened to Josh on more than one occasion, most often in the midst of a dangerous situation. It tended to be thing for those in special ops. You learned to move on because you had too. If he lived long enough, he would mourn for Sean latter.

It took some effort to struggle to his feet. The strain of concentrating on trying to balance brought on an even worse wave of dizziness. To keep from falling, he had to stop, bend over, and place his hands on his knees. His head spun and he choked back vomit, sucking in air with slow, deep breaths.

After a couple of minutes, the spinning eased and he slowly stood upright. The harsh light sent sharp stabs of pain through his left eye and deep into his brain, making him squint and blink rapidly. Little by little, the pain eased and he began to think more clearly.

Where the hell is this conveyor going? Where indeed? Nowhere good for him. The dead smell drove realization and triggered a fresh wave of fear. Being on a large conveyor carrying a mass of dead or dying things was not good. He looked around with desperate eyes, seeking a way off. A loud crash pulled his attention back down the conveyor's direction of travel in time to see a large tree flick up and then down, followed by the foliage and white bundles a few dozen yards ahead of him.

"Oh crap," he muttered and turned to run. In a few steps, he ran into a mass of interlocking branches blocking the way. He tried pushing through but only managed to entangle himself. A moment later, the belt carried him over the edge and he fell, clutching a tree limb that offered no support whatsoever.

He landed with a grunt on top of a huge pile of white bundles, leaves and brush. This broke his fall but gouged and scraped him, leaving painful abrasions on his skin. The mound shifted as he floundered for purchase. It was a struggle to fight back panic as he began to sink into the leafy surface.

More debris cascaded down on him. More bundles, trees, and God knew what else landed on him, and the harsh blue light faded to a dim green gloom. The sounds of heavier objects hitting nearby gave evidence of how quickly death could find him here. The smell of decay and sickly-sweet chocolate chip cookies were much stronger in the pit, making breathing a chore as bile again rose in his throat.

Josh thrashed upward, part climbing and part digging through the branches, leaves, and white bundles toward the diminishing light. In the shifting mass around him, he fought upward in near darkness. He'd almost reach the light, only to have more brush and trees or dead animals pour down from the conveyor. He grabbed onto a body, not realizing what it was until a dead, staring face came within inches of his own. Recoiling in surprise and horror, he thrust it away.

The fear of being buried alive churned through his mind and gave frantic strength to his struggle. Branches slapped at him, snagging his clothes and tearing his flesh as though the trees were trying to grab him, to hold him in place, to entomb him.

Another body tumbled into him, the face that of a Columbian from the camp. The other man jerked, saw Josh, and latched on to him like a drowning man. Both of them began to sink deeper into the pile. Each time Josh pried the man away, the terrified Columbian would grab him somewhere else.

The world turned a darker green as more debris landed on them and they slipped further down. "Let go! Let go!" Josh yelled. "You're gonna kill us." With fear-fueled anger, Josh slammed his fist into the other man's face.

The Columbian grip weakened for a moment, but with a desperate wail wrapped his arms even tighter around Josh's waist.

"No! No! No!" Josh screamed. There was no way Josh could save them both. Anger surged through him at the man's panic, but so did pity. Tears ran down Josh's face as he drew back his fist and hit the man again, then again and again. At last the Columbian let go with a sound between a moan and whimper.

Josh twisted and shouted in Spanish, "Climb man, climb for your life!"

The Columbian, his face a bloody pulp and crying like a child, curled into a ball and sank back on the leaves below. Josh started to reach a hand out to the man, but before he could make a move, the Columbian disappeared into the green darkness as the light surrendered to the onslaught of falling debris.

With a snarl of frustration Josh turned and leaped upward, once more fighting toward the fleeting light. On and on, up and up, Josh struggled. His arms and legs were now impossibly heavy. His breath came in ragged gasps and his head was a mass of pain. At times he wasn't even sure which way was up; he just kept fighting toward the light. Several times, a shift in the mass would drop him back and he felt all was lost. Time lost meaning; his sole existence became an endless struggle through a world of leaves, branches, tree roots, and white bundles. Finally, he scratched and clawed onto the trunk of a huge tree, and nothing more landed on him.

Clinging to a thick branch like the gunnel of a lifeboat, still gasping for air, he looked around the pile, finding it hard to believe the world had stopped its relentless effort to bury him. Relief was fleeting though. A low rumble arose from deep in the pit and, as impossible as it seemed, his heart began thudding even harder in his chest. *Shit, being on top of the pile isn't safe; no, not safe at all.*

He looked up into a large, domed chamber. The light was too bright, too blue, and too harsh. The end of the conveyor was high above him. It protruded from one side of the domed ceiling of the chamber. The top of another tree protruded over the edge of the belt overhead, poised to fall next. Josh eyed it nervously, but decided it was the least of his problems right now.

The pit was maybe two hundred feet across and God alone knew how deep sat in the center of the domed cavern. A wide ledge boarded by a low wall ran all the way around. On his left, about a hundred feet away, were several trees that had interlocked into a pile. The top of one tree slanted above the others, reaching up the side of the pit almost to the low wall. If he could climb over to the pile, the tree might give him a way up to the ledge.

He began making his way across the debris. The going was rough, better suited to a monkey than a man, but at least crap wasn't falling on him anymore. Another rumble from below was followed by a massive lurch that reverberated through the entire pit and nearly sent him plunging down. His tired arms found the strength to keep from falling and he resumed the awkward journey. Nearly at the end of his endurance, he reached the interlocking trees. He paused for a moment, shaking his arms out to get fresh blood to his trembling muscles, an old rock climber trick, and forced himself to reach out, grab the rough bark, and pull himself up.

The climb was tough on his battered body. However, after a few painful minutes, he succeeded in reaching the ledge, which proved to be a walkway bounded by the low wall that circled the huge pit. He swung up and over the barrier and lay gratefully on the solid surface, thankful to be alive. His body was scratched, bloodied, and bruised. His head hurt and his muscles were empty of strength. His mind still whirled with fear and confusion.

The faces of Sean and the Columbian he had been forced to abandon swam into his consciousness and made his heart hurt as well. But sorrow over the men's death began to fuel a new emotion. As he lay on the hard surface sucking in air and regaining his composure a smoldering anger started to burn in his soul.

"You didn't kill me, you sons of bitches," he muttered to the ceiling. "And by God, I'm going to make you wish you had."

The only reply was more deep rumblings from the depths of the pit.

The city of Manaus, Central Brazil

The light of dawn revealed dark smoke rising above the city of Manaus from dozens of raging fires. Situated in north central Brazil at the junction of the mighty Amazon and Negro rivers, Manaus was famed for its deep-water harbor that could serve ocean-going vessels despite being over one thousand miles inland. The city was home to over a million people with a highly industrialized economy and a large international airport. The only real city for nearly a thousand miles in any direction, it was an island of civilization surrounded by a vast green sea of jungle. However, today it burned as columns of black smoke darkened the sky.

Throughout the morning, without warning, aircraft, both large and small, exploded from unknown reasons and crashed into the city like flaming missiles. Massive radio interference scrambled communications and prevented frantic air traffic controllers from warning off approaching planes. No satellite communications were available to talk to distant airports from which the planes came. For many long hours, aircraft arrived with pilots confused by the static coming over their radios and the black torrents of smoke obscuring the city and the airport. Here, in the depths of the Amazon Basin, there was nowhere else for the planes to go. So one after another, they descended from the east, burst into flames, and fell in burning heaps onto Manus's homes and buildings.

In the midst of the carnage, countless acts of bravery took place.

Sadly, there were also acts of cowardice, looting, and even violent robberies. Such situations tend to bring out both the best and worst in people. As dawn tinged the thick black smoke with orange, most of the populace huddled fearfully in their homes, trying to hide from the death and destruction raining down on their city.

Others stumbled through the smoldering ruins, crying out for missing loved ones. Still others fought the fires and tended the wounded. Many more lay dead or dying, buried among the rubble. Sirens screamed, babies cried, and mothers sobbed. Around public buildings, scared and angry crowds gathered, demanding answers no one had.

At one scene of devastation, Major Marcus Antinasio, senior officer for the Brazilian marines stationed at Comando Naval de Manaus, took off his hat and wiped his face. His dark eyes smoldered with suppressed rage along with a touch of fear as he surveyed the still-burning wreckage of the Air France jetliner that lay crumpled and scattered before him.

The smell of jet fuel clung to the air. His men were digging frantically as a woman screamed in pain somewhere, hidden by smoke, rubble, and the deep shadows of the early dawn. God alone knew how many had died here. Moreover, this was just one many aircraft that had fallen into the city. It was like the September 11th World Trade Center attack times ten or twenty or more. There were so many crash sites that it was hard to tell how extensive the damage was, but Marcus knew it was very, very bad.

"What does this mean sir?" asked Lieutenant Nelino Pereira, Antinasio's second in command. The man was a head shorter and heavier than his commander, but his face held the same mixture of anger and fear. "Are we at war? Is there a revolution?"

Antinasio shook his head. Everyone was asking these questions. Drawing in a deep breath, he said, "It's hard to imagine a war starting here in the middle of the Amazon. As for revolution…" He shrugged. "I suppose the jamming makes that a possibility. However, it would take a major power like China or the United States to kill the communication satellites. The worst part is we don't have a clue how these aircraft are being shot down, much less who is doing it. If terrorist were on all these planes… Well, that is hard to imagine." He looked at his watch. "The general's aid said he would call at eight. I'd better get back to the base."

The drive to the base was a heartbreaking one. Marcus loved this city. He'd been born and raised here and was thrilled when given command of the patrol boat base. To see Manaus burn, the people awash with terror and agony, tore at his soul.

When Marcus answered the phone a short time later, the connection wasn't great, but at least it provided an avenue of communication. Many had thought maintaining a landline in the age of satellites to be a waste of money. Now it was proving to be a very good investment.

Even with the poor connection, he could hear the tension in General Juan Julis Fernando's voice. The general commanded the Central Amazon District and had been a friend and mentor to Antinasio for many years.

General Fernando got right to the point. "Marcus, we're pressed for time. I know the basics of your situation and I know things are rough there. But I have an important mission for you."

"A mission, sir? We have thousands of dead and wounded in the city. My men are spread thin now. We need help! I can't spare any men for a mission."

"I know the city needs help and I'll get some there as quickly as I can. But there is much more going on than what's happening in Manaus."

Marcus frowned at the phone. He'd wondered why his calls to headquarters hadn't generated a quicker response. "I haven't heard much news, sir. Information here has been tough to come by."

The phone line crackled with static. "I can well imagine. I'm having a difficult enough time here. I know this is not a secure line, but you need to know a few facts that we do not want shared with the public at this time."

"Yes, sir?"

"First, the two dozen or so aircraft reported down in your area are only the tip of the iceberg. We have fifty other commercial airliners with flight paths through north central Brazil that have been reported past due and missing. The Manaus air force base reported losing four helicopters and three fighters trying to conduct patrols. All other aircraft have been grounded."

Antinasio hadn't heard this. Infrastructure damage had knocked out most of the phones. Where cell towers still worked, the phones didn't due to powerful interference. He hadn't been able to contact his counterparts at the airbase. He gave a small grunt of surprise.

General Fernando continued, "The massive interference you're experiencing is causing communication problems for the entire northern half of the continent. The source of the interference has been located." He paused. "It has been determined to be centered approximately three hundred kilometers west of Manaus."

"In the heart of the jungle?"

"Yes. That's why Manaus is completely without radio. Radio communications improve as one gets farther away and are nearly normal along the coast. Your patrol boats are the only assets in the area that can get there in a reasonable amount of time. I need you to track down this interference. We believe it's more than a coincidence that aircraft are going down in the same general region."

Marcus sat down and stared at a map on his wall of the Amazon. "Yes, sir. It might take a few hours to pull my men in from the crash sites and load the boats."

"I understand, Major. In addition, I want you to go into the area ready for trouble. However, your main objective is to get me information as quickly as possible. If you can stop the interference or destroy whatever is killing the planes, do it. But do not risk your ability to get information out. We must understand what is going on in the jungle."

"Yes, sir."

"And Major, there's one more fact I think you should know." The General's tone sounded odd.

"Yes, sir?"

"Satellite transmissions—you're aware we've lost that avenue of communication as well?"

"Yes, sir."

"We've been in contact with our consulate in the United States and learned... Well, all the satellites in orbit, every one of them, they are gone."

A cold shiver went down Marcus's back. Their inability to link to any satellites from Manaus made him suspect some had been destroyed, but all of them? He stood, moved to his window, and looked up at the cloud-filled sky. "I'm...I'm not sure I understand, sir."

"Something has destroyed every satellite that orbits the planet, including the new International Space Station, the Chinese and Indian space stations. The whole world is in a panic."

"What would it take to do something like that?"

"No one can tell us that, but it's an incredible technical feat. This situation has really complicated communications and travel. There's no GPS, no weather information, and long distance communication is relying totally on land and undersea phone lines. It's no big stretch of the imagination to tie the satellites to whatever is causing this interference. Be very careful, Marcus. Take your best men and as much firepower as you can, but speed it of the essence. Get me some information."

"Yes, sir. Goodbye, sir." Marcus slowly put the phone down as he continued to stare up at the cloudy sky. The blue sky and the darkness beyond had become a strange and hostile place where planes died and men's most advanced technology disappeared. After several long moments he shook his head and set out to gather his men.

Chapter 5

Sally

Sally gently pulled the restraining strap over the stretcher holding the semi-conscious form of the teenage girl and snugged it down as much as she dared. The girl had a broken collarbone, ribs, and right leg, which she'd suffered when a large tree had crushed her home the night before. The urine in her catheter bag had a distinct pink tint. The injuries made securing the girl for the helicopter trip a heart-wrenching process as she moaned at almost every touch. However, it wouldn't do to have the poor thing fall out of the stretcher in the event of turbulence.

The other patient, a middle-aged man, had a severe head trauma and hadn't made a sound all morning. The nurse at the clinic was amazed he was even breathing on his own and didn't hold much hope for him. Sally double checked everything and nodded to the nurse, who was hovering nearby. The woman gave her a half smile and exited the cabin.

Keith stood at the front of the helicopter, rubbing his chin and staring up at the early morning sky. Heavy clouds drifted by, as though trying to mask what had been a clear dark blue an hour earlier. Before dawn, the stars had been unobstructed and sparkled so bright you could see by their light. Not long after she and Keith had started checking out the chopper and loading it for flight, the clouds began to creep back in.

Sally stepped through the loading door, walked over to him, and looked up as well. The sight of the clouds made her clench her teeth in frustration. "Well, what do you think?" She asked hopefully. "Are we still a go?"

Keith glanced down at her, raised one of his eyebrows briefly, and then looked back up. "I'm willing to go, but I'm not wild about it." He pointed south, where the sky was noticeably clearer. "At least we can bail out that way in case this cloud cover is higher than I think it is. Or if it closes back in around the town. There are several logging camps along the river. We should be able to find a place to put down if we have to."

"Maybe we should wait," said Sally, even though her stomach clenched at the words. Her brother's safety continued to haunt her. Taking a boat upriver to the camp had proven to not be an option. The surge of water that had damaged the docks had also done a lot of damage to the small boats stored along the waterway. It would be quite a while before anything larger than a canoe would be available to make the trip.

Keith looked down at her tense face and smiled. "Don't worry, I'm mostly just being paranoid. I've found that being a pessimist is a good policy when it comes to flying in the Amazon. I'm a bit nervous about not having access to weather reports and navigational information. But we should be safe enough. Besides—" he nodded to the nurse who was fidgeting nearby. "She made it pretty clear we need to get our patients to a hospital pretty soon if they're going to have a chance. We'll make it. And I believe, with a little luck, we can still manage to stop at the camp to check on your brother and the rest of the team."

"Hey!" Myra's voice rang out. She was approaching with a sizeable group of townspeople, including the mayor and Lieutenant Goulart, the commander of the local Naval de Brasilia post. "Are we going?" she asked in her heavily accented Portuguese, no doubt for the benefit of the crowd since her command of the language was limited.

"Yes," said Keith. He continued in fluent Portuguese, "I need to do a final preflight check and we'll head out."

The townspeople all looked relieved. It was a good sign that after so many tension-filled hours, something positive was finally happening. In addition to getting the town's two most seriously injured citizens to help, Keith and his helicopter were viewed as a lifeline to the outside world. Smiling, the mayor and Goulart shook hands with Keith and gave him folders to deliver to Manaus. Most of the other villagers also had messages they asked Sally and Myra to deliver for them. After the brief flurry of message passing and goodbyes, the small crowd moved off, and Keith began his final check of the helicopter.

Sally scrambled into the passenger compartment and settled into a rear bulkhead fold down seat situated between the two stretchers. She checked both patients one final time and then buckled herself in. Myra climbed into the copilot's seat on the left side of the chopper, put on a headset, and buckled in as well. A couple of minutes later, Keith climbed into the pilot's seat. He began flipping switches, and a low whine came from overhead.

The overcast continued to break up over Rio Estrada, though it still hung low and heavy to the north. To the southeast, the sun cast bright shafts of light through the clouds, painting them a bright pink and orange. The air was hot and heavy. The term sauna was often used to describe the Amazon, especially after a rain, and no term fit it better. Sweat ran down

Sally's face, neck, and torso, making her bush shirt cling to her back.

As the helicopter's rotors began turning, they sent a merciful breeze wafting through the cabin. At first, the moving air could barely be felt, a soft tickle across damp skin. The whine got louder and turned into a dull roar accompanied by the thump, thump of the spinning blades. The breeze increased and became a swirling rush of air that made loose strands of hair dance around her face.

Sally put on her headset, and the noise abated considerably. The thumping tempo increased still more, and the blue-and-white Bell 206 Jet Ranger gave a slight lurch and then lifted smoothly into the heavy air. Once airborne, Keith kept the helicopter low over the trees and swung them in a wide turn toward the east.

As the chopper rose, dozens of smiling upturned faces waved up at them. It made Sally happy to bring a little hope to those below as they worked to restore their damaged homes. She waved back and gave a couple of fist pumps that elicited even bigger smiles.

They lifted higher and she frowned at the scars left by toppled trees and flattened homes around the small town. She'd always found Rio Estrada an interesting town if not a quaint one. It was an odd mixture of Spanish stucco houses, rough-hewn wooden shacks, and straw huts interspersed among meandering footpaths. Everywhere she could see people worked on damaged homes or moved debris. It was heartwarming to see the townspeople putting their lives and town back in order.

They soon left Rio Estrada behind and Keith headed them out along the river, staying low to avoid the lingering clouds. Sally watched the jungle rush by as they skimmed the treetops. As usual, she found the vastness of the rainforest amazing. Sadly, wounds and scars were visible, especially this close to the village. Farmers left dead patches when they set fire to stretches of land to clear it, called slash and burn farms. While she knew the local Indians were only trying to provide for their families, it broke her heart see the damage they caused.

The slash and burn method had worked fine for over a thousand years. It would still if there were fewer people. Now however, between new settlers, loggers, and mining, the damage didn't have time to heal. It would take years, even decades for the orange scars to regrow into a healthy forest. The Amazon environment was far more fragile than most people realized. Mostly due to the cycle of seasonal flooding that leeched nutrients from the soil. Trying to find ways to make the forest more resilient was the primary reason she and the University of North Alabama research team was here. What was needed was a biological solution to reconstituting the depleted soil. The team had great hopes for finding a solution, but many locals believed the effort was doomed to failure.

An odd, dark cloud bank came into view on the left side of the aircraft, drawing her eyes from the forest. Sally studied it, trying to understand why the shape caught her eye. The cloud looked remarkably solid, rising up from the jungle and merging with the overcast sky, growing more indistinct the higher it went. It didn't look right for some reason. It seemed more like a mist-shrouded mountain than a cloud. That was ridiculous, of course; the nearest mountain was over five hundred miles to the west. And yet...

The mist continued to thin, a white veil growing sheerer by the moment. A small gasp escaped Sally as the helicopter broke free of the clouds and the shrouded object was revealed. *It is a mountain! But it can't be.* Her chest constricted, squeezing her heart. Her senses reeled as her mind warred over what she saw versus what she knew. Time seemed to slow as her brain struggled to process too much conflicting information. Sound, smell, touch...her other senses faded from awareness as the vista before her consumed her complete focus.

A mountain vista that could have been cut from the most rugged part of the Andes rose white and tall from the green jungle. The helicopter was cruising two hundred feet above the treetops below. The jungle stretched into the distance in a wavy green carpet. There was no telling how far away the mountain was, no sense of scale for size and distance. But it rose for what had to be thousands of feet. The base was miles wide, narrowing to a half-mile wide column of white granite that jutted skyward like a rocky bone. At the very top, an obelisk-like spire rose onward, the top of which was lost in the clouds.

A second peak came into view behind and to the left of the first, not as high, but it stretched even wider. The areas hit by sunlight were dazzling bright in the morning sun, like gray snow. In contrast, across both mountains, the shadows were deep and dark. The shadowed outlines of smaller spires and peaks marched northward into the distance. Thrusting up from the jungle wasn't just a mountain, but rather an entire range of mountains. The sight of the white, gray, and black vista standing in stark contrast to the deep green of the surrounding forest was surreal.

The Andes, a thousand or more miles to the west, were known for rugged, steep mountains. *Could the helicopter have been transported so far somehow?* As impossible as that seemed, it was no more impossible than an entire mountain range appearing overnight. However, she felt certain the latter was closer to the truth of it. The Andes were a young and rugged mountain range, but not as rugged as these. The gray-white wasn't snow; it had a yellowish tint and seemed dirtier. Only the intensity of the early morning sun made it appear so white. These mountains were otherworldly, as if from the moon, bright and dazzling, but alien, sinister, and foreboding at the same time. The white was more the color of old bone, only…not.

How, how, how…? Sally felt reality was coming unraveled. Where…? Impossible. But…? Am I going insane? Am I? Am I? No! *Well, maybe.* If she accepted what her eyes were telling her, then… *What could it mean?*

She shuddered. Be it illusion or be it real, at that moment Sally knew her life would never be the same. Keeping her gaze fixed on what lay beyond the window, she loosened her seat belt, leaned forward, and reached out a trembling hand to touch Myra's shoulder.

Myra was absorbed in her journal and responded to the touch with a frown and an annoyed, "What?" Seeing Sally's expression fixated beyond the window, her frown deepened and she turned back around to look out her own window. Myra's jaw slowly dropped open. Confusion showed on her face as thoughts came, were analyzed, and discarded in rapid succession. After a moment, the older woman said in a hoarse, tense voice, "No way! No friggin' way."

Hearing the odd statement in addition to the strain in Myra's voice over the headset, Keith glanced over and then focused beyond her out the window. Shock washed over his face. He shook his head and leaned over Myra, as though getting a fraction closer to the window would help him grasp the impossible manifestation. If by so doing, he could pierce the magician's trick behind what appeared to be a mountain. No trick. The shape refused to disappear and instead became sharper and more distinct as the helicopter cleared the last wisps of cloud.

Whatever was out there, Sally found solace in the knowledge her friends saw it, too. The sun shone bright on the peaks, twin monoliths thrusting upward, immense white fangs rising from the verdant green of the forest, silhouetted against a crisp blue sky. The image so solid and real her spinning brain had to accept that mountains now existed where none had before. Her friends had a mixture of fear, awe, and bewilderment on their faces that must mirror her own. All of them clearly struggled to understand the appearance of what amounted to a new landscape, an altered world. Time lost meaning and they sat in frozen silence, senses transfixed on what lay beyond the windows.

The helicopter gave a violent lurch.

"Damn," came Keith's voice over the headset, "I think something hit us."

Then time began to move very fast.

The window by Myra exploded inward, along with her head, in a spray of sharp plastic, bone, and blood. Keith screamed in agony as his body jerked from unseen impacts. Sally screamed in terror, shaking her head in desperate denial of what was unfolding in front of her.

Shafts of sunlight pierced the cabin as holes appeared in the door to the right of the window. Something hot and burning kissed Sally's cheek. She cringed back in her seat, fumbling and tugging at the seat belt in a frantic effort to cinch it tight even as Keith slumped over and the chopper lurched violently to one side. Flashes of green and blue swirled outside the passenger door window as the helicopter spun and rolled over.

At their low altitude, it took only seconds for the stricken aircraft to drop into the forest. With a dull crunch, it slammed into the trees. Leaves and small branches of the upper canopy absorbed some of the impact, though far from all of it. Only slightly slowed, the helicopter sliced downward. More crashes resounded as the rotors fragmented and the bent and broken fuselage smashed against ever-larger branches. Everything happened too fast for Sally to comprehend.

Now nothing more than metal and momentum, the chopper lurched down through the layers of the rainforest canopy until it came to a violent stop between two huge, close-growing mahogany trees thirty feet above the jungle floor.

Pieces of metal, plastic, branches, and various bits of unrecognizable material continued to clatter-clack down through the foliage. Monkeys and other animals that made their home in the canopy screamed in rage and fear at the violent intrusion.

The helicopter's battered frame groaned in protest as it slowly wedged itself between the thick branches. The rain of debris continued with more thumps and clatters, taking a long time to come to a stop. The animals fled for their lives, still screaming as they ran. The monkeys stayed the longest, voicing their protests with howls and screeches. After a few minutes, they grew tired of the fruitless yelling and scampered off in a sudden, mass rush to find a new home, leaving silence in their wake, a silence broken only by soft, yet hysterical sobs of a hurt, confused, and terrified woman.

David

Even at night, the inside of the Big Tent was hot and humid. The canvas sides were rolled up in a vain attempt to catch any stray breeze that might find its way through the jungle, though the surrounding mosquito netting rarely stirred. The sound of insects and frogs, combined with the camp's small generator, provided a steady buzz of noise beyond the tent. Steve Carter was quieter now, though on occasion he uttered soft moans as he struggled with a rising fever.

Two light bulbs lit most of the interior space, although shadows lurked in the corners. But these shadows were nothing compared to the darkness in each person's heart as he or she pondered a suddenly transformed world. Not long after dark, Darrin had seen another plane disappear in flames and fall from the sky. David was in near panic and prayed frequently that his sister hadn't suffered the same fate.

"So there's a war? Or terrorists?" mumbled Heather, her eyes red from crying.

"It's got to be something like that," said Dr. Allen. "One plane could have been an accident, I guess. But two? The thing is, why here in the middle of the Amazon? It's not exactly a political hotspot."

"Could it be the Columbians?" Darrin asked. "There is a lot of craziness going on there right now."

"The Columbians have enough problems in their own country," said Paul. "I can't imagine them picking a fight with Brazil."

Heather frowned and shook her head. "And even if that explained the planes, what about the gravity thing, and the radios, and the birds?"

"I'm pretty sure the birds died because of the anomaly, one way or another," said Dr. Sharon Hauptman, the team's senior biologist. "A lot of them obviously flew into trees...or were pulled into them. It's easy to determine what killed these since they were busted up pretty bad. But that was nowhere near all of them. As for the others, I did necropsies on five of them from different species and they all had extensive coronary hemorrhaging. It's like the gravity distortions made their hearts pop. Basically, I think they died from fear, or at least partly."

David remembered how his own heart had hammered in his chest the night before. In hindsight, he was amazed his heart hadn't popped as well. "Why just the birds?" he asked. "What about other animals?"

Dr. Hauptman shrugged. "I can think of several reasons. Birds are fairly delicate compared to most animals. Plus, there may be dead animals in the jungle we haven't seen yet. The birds show up because of their bright colors. Maybe other animals are out there that have blended in to the foliage and we just haven't come across them."

"Screw the birds!" Darrin said. "We've got planes falling from the sky and you guys are worried about a bunch of stupid parrots? What the hell are we going to do if the chopper doesn't come back?" He stole a glance at David before continuing in a softer voice, "What if the chopper got shot down, too?"

David's heart lurched as his worst fear was voiced aloud. Paul looked at him, his concern obvious. David glanced around the tent to find the people around the tables looking at him. He realized everyone must have the same thought. He felt tears well up as the tight control he was maintaining began to slip.

"I think it unlikely they got shot down," said Paul, his eyes locked on David. "There's a big difference between a high-flying airliner and a helicopter. They're probably still at Rio Estrada. If something bad were happening, they wouldn't try taking off. Hell, if that's the case, Sally and Myra have probably found a boat and are cruising up here right now."

David wiped his tears and gave Paul a feeble smile. It wasn't much, but at least Paul's words loaned hope that his sister was okay.

"Still," continued Paul, looking over the rest of the team, "we need to consider what to do if the chopper doesn't show up in the morning."

"What do you mean?" Dr. Allen asked. "What can we do?"

"We've still got the canoes. Some of us could take Steve to the village and make sure help is coming for everyone else."

"You're nuts," said Dr. Allen. "It must be at least seventy or eighty miles by water. This is the dry season and you know what thrives in that tributary, don't you?"

"Yeah," said Paul. "Piranha. The villagers warned us about them."

"*Pygocentrus nattereri*, red-bellied piranha," said Dr. Allen. "The worst kind, and the dry season is when they're the most aggressive. If you roll one of those canoes and start splashing around, that could be bad news."

"Come on, Robert," Paul said with a skeptical look. "You know they aren't as bad as those stupid movies show."

"No," replied Dr. Allen. "Sharks aren't as bad as stupid movies show, either. Nevertheless, they kill and maim people every year. With the water low, the piranhas are jammed together and food is scarce, so it doesn't take much to make them swarm. And they're not the only bad thing in the river."

"So what the hell do you want us to do? Wait until Steve is worse? By then it might be too late." Paul turned to Heather and said, "You were just checking on him. What do you think?"

Heather glanced in the direction of Steve's tent and said, "He's getting pretty bad. He has a definite fever and his leg is really red. I think it's infected."

Dr. Hauptman nodded in agreement. "He needs help pretty soon. I already fear he may lose that leg. If we wait too long, well…"

"Yeah, I know we need to get him some help," Dr. Allen said. "But I'd hate to lose someone else. I'm telling you, going down that river is cra-"

"I'll go," said David. Paul and Dr. Allen both looked at him in surprise. He said more loudly, "I'll go; I need to find my sister."

Dr. Allen's eyes showed concern, but he shook his head. "I really don't think you would be a good choice. I mean, it would be a rough trip."

"I want to go," David said. "I need to go!"

"I'll take him," said Paul. "He can ride with me. Who else is coming?"

"Damn," said Dr. Allen with a thin smile. "How did we go from 'if we send someone' to 'who will be going?'" He shrugged in resignation. "Well, I'm too damn old." He turned toward the grad students. "Are any of you feeling adventurous?"

"I'll go," said Heather.

"Yeah, me too," Darrin said. "I want to get as far away from this place as I can."

"Okay then," Paul said. "We'll give the chopper a little time in the morning. But if they don't show up by 9 o'clock, we'll head out."

David took in a deep breath, trying to loosen his suddenly tense chest and shoulders. He was glad for the chance to go find his sister. But he's also moving way beyond his comfort zone. A shudder ran through him at the mental image of flipping the canoe and being savaged by thousands of tiny, razor-sharp teeth.

God, what was he thinking? He opened his mouth to say he'd changed his mind. That Dr. Allen was right and he'd wait at the camp. Fear of the river warred with the desperate need to find his sister. After a few moments, his resolve firmed with the knowledge that Sally would want him to be strong. He needed to grow up. That was what everyone kept telling him.

By focusing on his sister, he managed to quell his panic, if not his fear. David prayed silently for the strength to make the trip. After a quick glance at Paul, Heather, and Darrin, he said another prayer that he wouldn't let the others down along the way.

Sally

Sally didn't actually lose consciousness after the helicopter went down. However, her touch with reality was so sketchy afterward that the difference was a moot point. At some point after the crash, she must have freed herself from her chair harness, although she could not remember doing so. There was a fuzzy remembrance of checking on her friends, of bouts of hysterical sobbing, and of lying down in a clear spot amid broken plastic, metal bits, and sticky fluids that didn't bear thinking about. After that, she'd cried for a long time, transfixed by the gory mess that had been Myra hanging limp in the seat above. Now it was dark. Thank God for the dark. Darkness masked the world and the horror all around her.

The darkness allowed her rational mind to surface, and Sally's world slowly came into focus, even though a part of her fought against the process. Reality was something she didn't want to face. There way too much pain there. Insanity beckoned, offering a journey free of the pain and ending in merciful oblivion. She thought of her mother's smiling face and it brought comfort her for a moment. If she died now, would she see mother? That would be very nice.

Visions of her mother's funeral swam out of the darkness. Images of standing by the grave, color gone from the world, her father's despondency, and the lost, confused look on David's face all danced through her mind's eye. There was no sanctuary in these thoughts—why did they come to her now?

The visions brought other pains, long buried. The pain of learning about her mother's death. So random, so pointless. Her heart hurt at the sudden remembrance of how her close-knit family of four had transitioned into three strangers overnight. More pain when three became two a year later. The day she'd come home to an empty house and instinct had taken her to the garage.

Was that day worse than when Mother died? Maybe. Or at least a different kind of bad. That day in the garage had left a heavy burden on her young shoulders. She'd never forget walking into the hot, musty building and finding her brother sitting stone-faced in an old kitchen chair, staring at Father hanging from a rafter. David hadn't cried, hadn't spoken, and didn't eat for four days. Sally had cried enough for both of them though.

After Father's funeral, David came back some, but was never the same. Life became very complicated and very hard. Overwhelmed by a burden she was far too young for, a burden for which she saw no end, she'd gone to her mother's grave. There, kneeling in the damp grass, it seemed her mother had reached out and soothed her battered soul. She'd found strength there, found connection, and made a promise. A promise she knew her mother would want and one Sally needed to make to keep going. She'd promised to take care of David and remain a family, no matter what.

"David!" she yelled and jolted upright in the cramped corner of the canted helicopter. Pain stabbed through her side. "Shit!" she gasped, falling back and panting like the wounded, trapped animal she was. As the waves of pain subsided to a dull throb, Sally focused on David. He needed her, dammit, and she wasn't going to let him down. In a way, she needed him too. She needed an anchor to keep from losing her mind.

Remember the promise. Remember they had to be a family and families took care of each other. This became her mantra. Death or insanity, neither was an option. She couldn't allow them to be. An old promise made long ago was her life raft in the storm. Though tears still flowed, her mind began to calm.

"That which doesn't kill you..." she muttered, realizing the true meaning of the phrase for the first time. During that terrible time after Father's death, she'd found the strength to rise above the crushing sorrow and move forward, not for herself, but for her brother and, in a way, her mother. She must draw on that same strength now. She gave a quick prayer that it would be enough.

Think, she told herself. *I'm going to survive this. I'm going to find a way to live.*

"How?" a small, little-girl voice from inside asked. Panic boiled up when there was no immediate answer.

She began gasping in air, wincing with every breath. "Think!" she shouted angrily. "Think, damn it. There's no one else to do this for you. How bad am I hurt?" she said in response to the pain. That seemed like a good place to start.

She gingerly felt her aching side. Probably some broken ribs; badly bruised at the very least. But she had no way to tell how severe it was. It sure as hell hurt and made movement very difficult. At this point, she could only hope there were no major internal injuries. Moreover, while it hurt to breathe, it wasn't unbearable. She took this as a good sign.

She felt the helicopter shake and roll with a gentle swaying motion and realized it must be lodged in a tree. *Great*. No surprise really, but it would definitely complicate getting out of this hellish prison. She forced the helicopter's location from her mind and focused on her immediate surroundings.

What next? Check on the passengers.

Light, she needed light. She remembered a flashlight mounted somewhere. *On the wall?* She looked around and saw a small red light winking out of the darkness. Yes! She slowly leaned over until her fumbling fingers located a cylindrical object. It flashed to life when she pulled it free, the beam illuminating the horror of Myra's shattered skull. The older woman's head had been snapped around so that her eye, partway out of its socket, was staring blankly into the rear compartment. Sally flinched and swung the light away, suppressing a sob as the barriers she'd erected threatened to fail. She shut her eyes and breathed deeply, getting herself under control.

After several long moments, she calmed back down. Myra would want her to be strong, to get out of this, to keep her promise. She couldn't allow her friend's ruined face to shatter her hard-won self-control. Steeling her mind and heart, she opened her eyes and pointed the light directly at Myra.

Fresh tears streamed down her face. However, these were tears of loss and sorrow, not panic and terror. Cleansing tears over the loss of a cherished friend. "God, Myra. What a mess. I'll try to keep it together." With a final soft sob, she turned the light away and shone it around the compartment.

The helicopter lay on its side, the main passenger door facing the sky. The air was heavy and reeked of sawdust, aviation fuel, blood, and voided bowels. Holes spangled the walls from whatever hit the chopper. Odd bulges were visible in the fuselage. No doubt from impacts with tree limbs on the way down through the canopy. Sally sat on what had been the left wall behind the pilot's seat. The two patients they were carrying to Manus were strapped to the floor, which now her new wall, directly in front of her. Myra and Keith were beyond help. But what about these two?

Gasping with every movement, she eased forward and up until she was in a sitting positon. This brought her face level with the young girl's. The man was on the higher side of the floor-now-wall. It didn't take much of an examination to see he was dead. The flashlight beam revealed bloody holes along his side from whatever had pierced the helicopter. The girl, hanging from the straps on her gurney still breathed, however. Sally loosened the straps slowly and, bit by bit, managed to lower her. She tried to make the girl as comfortable as possible, although the teenager never made a sound. Having done everything she could think of, Sally slumped back with a soft grunt.

She began exploring the space around her with the flashlight. The back section of the helicopter was littered with boxes and small bundles, the camp's supplies that were the original reason for the trip to Rio Estrada. She began to investigate, ignoring splatters of blood, moving very slowly due to the pain and an acute awareness of the helicopter's ongoing motion. In short order she found water, food, and a first aid kit. She drank, ate a candy bar, and swallowed half a dozen Tylenol.

These small victories helped boost her morale a bit. "Okay, Myra. You always said I was tougher than I realized. I sure hope you were right." She leaned back against the wall of her prison and closed her eyes. "God, please let her be right."

Marcus

In the dark hours of the morning, Major Marcus Antinasio stood on the rear deck of his patrol boat looking out at the river with a simmering mixture of anger, sadness, and fear. The searchlights of Patrol Boat Group 31, dazzling against the black waters, revealed the carcasses of thousands of dead birds. The muddy waters masked individual forms, but the multitude of brilliant colors undulating in the river's sluggish current made it plain what floated before him.

The small, pitiful bodies covered the river for as far as the lights could reach. Beyond the direct light, in the deeper darkness, pairs of slanted red coals surrounded the boats, glimmering reflections from the unblinking eyes of dozens of caiman, the crocodiles of the Amazon. Gurgles and grunts made haunting echoes off the water. The sound from the blackness of the reptiles feasting on the unexpected bounty provided a grisly soundtrack to the birds' demise.

Marcus was angry because he felt certain the destroyed aircraft and mysterious interference were connected to the dead birds. He didn't know how, but it was hard to believe it a coincidence. Here was yet another crime to lay at the feet of whoever was behind this. His sadness came from the loss of what he considered the most beautiful part of the rainforest. The birds, with their beautiful plumage and merry songs, flittering from tree to tree, had always brought magic to the jungle. A very different sadness from what he'd felt at Manaus, but it added another layer of pain to his already heavy heart. The fear came from the sheer number of dead birds, and more importantly, the unknown force that had killed them.

Marcus looked up from the river and surveyed the sleek boats of PBG 31. The faces of his men, crowded along the gunnels and lit by the glow reflected back from the lights, showed their fear and anxiety. Many of them cast glances at their commanding officer, seeking guidance and reassurance. Drawing himself up, Marcus squared his shoulders. "Set a good example," he muttered under his breath.

Lieutenant Pereira was carefully examining the carcass of a parrot pulled from the river. When they'd first come upon the mass of dead birds, panic had nearly engulfed the men due to fear of a chemical attack.

Birds were notoriously susceptible to poison gas and Antinasio's small command, while well equipped, didn't have provisions for that type of threat. Marcus held his own fear tightly in check. If he wavered, the already nervous soldiers might break and began speeding back to Manaus. His men were officially considered marines, but in reality, they were closer to being a police force tasked with patrolling the rivers in the region. They were brave enough, but the idea of an invisible choking death roiling across the river could strike terror in the staunchest heart.

"What do you think?" Marcus asked in a quiet voice.

"I don't know," replied Lieutenant Pereira in the same low tone. "If it's a chemical agent, why would anyone release it way out here? Surely not only to butcher birds."

Marcus took off his bush hat and ran his hand over his close-cropped dark hair, then slapped at a mosquito braving his bug repellent for a quick meal. *Should we continue?* The dead birds floating in the water were another reminder of the strangeness of their situation. Instead of finding answers for the general, they now had more questions.

So far, they'd traveled nearly three hundred kilometers along the twisting river, moving at a reckless pace in response to General Fernando's urgent order. From what he could determine without GPS, in a short distance, they'd have to leave the boats and set out cross country. This was a prospect Marcus wasn't the least bit happy about. While he loved the jungle, he knew from experience it was best to admire it from the river.

There were many ways to die in the Amazon, none of them pleasant. However, the general's instructions were clear, so what choice did he really have? Moreover, someone had to answer for the death and destruction in Manaus. They couldn't turn back now. Taking in a deep breath, he looked up at the still-dark sky and then released the breath slowly while he counted to ten.

Turning to Pereira, he said, "It'll be light in a few hours. Get us away from these birds. Then we'll moor and wait for dawn on the boats. Pass the word to leave the machineguns behind and load up on extra food, bug repellant, and water purification tablets—it may be a long trip."

The other man frowned. "Are you sure it's wise to leave the heavy weapons behind, sir? There's no telling what you'll run into out there."

Antinasio gave a small shrug and nodded. "I know. But it can't be helped. There's no telling how far we have to travel, and food may be more important the bullets. God, I hope so anyway. Besides, if over one hundred men armed with assault rifles can't deal with whatever we encounter, a few machineguns would probably make little difference. Have the boat crews man the watch, and order the rest of the men to get some sleep. I want everyone as fresh as possible before we head into the jungle."

Come dawn, fog lay across the river. Languid tendrils drifted over the water, probing the riverbank as if seeking entrance to the forest proper. The mist was a bright white in the early morning sun, making the gloom under the trees seem even darker in comparison. Marcus studied the shadowy tree line with more than a little trepidation. He hated taking his men into the depths of the rainforest.

The local Indians spoke with awe about the mysteries of the vast sea of life that made up the heart of Brazil, even though they spent their entire lives amidst the towering trees. Today the jungle seemed even stranger than ever, primarily due to what was missing—the usually riotous sound of birds. Plenty of other noise came from the wall of vegetation, however. Here in the early dawn, the night hunters still prowled as the day hunters first emerged.

The sounds seemed deeper and more threatening without the music of the birds to mollify them. In addition, there were unknown and likely malevolent forces loose in the forest, lurking just out of sight. Tension grew among the men as the boats neared the wall of vegetation.

Lieutenant Pereira, who Marcus had selected to stay behind to command the boats, walked up and said, "We're ready to put you ashore, sir."

Marcus surveyed the surrounding boats, nodding in satisfaction at finding those already unloaded were anchored well away from shore. "Hopefully this won't take long. Keep your men alert."

Pereira nodded. "Be careful, sir. The jungle is dangerous enough without…well, whatever is causing all this."

Marcus noticed the anxious faces around them, studying their officers' actions. He flashed a smile and grasped Pereira's shoulder. "Don't worry, Lieutenant," he said loud enough to carry to the men. "We're Patrol Group 31, tough enough to chew through the jungle with our teeth. Better for whoever's out there to be careful of us."

Pereira smiled back encouragingly, but his only reply was a slight nod.

They had to duck low-hanging branches and vines as the patrol boat approached shore. A moment later, it struck the bank with a gentle thump. Marcus leaped through the opening in the wall of foliage cut by the advance party and onto the soft loam of the forest. Plants grew in matted layers along the river's shore, fighting a savage battle of survival to reach the light.

It had taken the lead platoon nearly an hour of hard work to hack their way through the tangled mass bordering the water. Marcus hurried through a dim green tunnel, mindful that snakes and poisonous spiders were prone to hide in the thick cover. It took another hour for the rest of PBG 31 to unload from the remaining boats and follow.

Once clear of the initial wall of vegetation, there was comparatively little undergrowth. The layered canopies of tree limbs caused a perpetual twilight in the forest proper, choking off the bulk of the vegetation. This didn't mean there was no growth, however. Other plants like ferns and ropy vines thrived in the dim light between the towering tree trunks. This limited visibility and would make for slow going.

Marcus surveyed the area and found it hard to believe there were over one hundred men gathered among the trees. The soldiers' camouflage was designed to blend with the terrain. It was good for fighting, not so much for keeping track of a large group in rough country. He prayed he wouldn't lose anyone during the trek.

Lieutenant Jeronimo Viana, leader of 3rd Platoon, walked up to him. Viana had been born in the jungle and lived there with his family until his seventeenth birthday. They'd run a less-than-legal logging business until his father had been arrested. A big, hulking man with a reputation for being tough, Viana was the best leader Marcus had at moving men through the jungle. Under his tutelage, the men in his platoon had developed a reputation in the Brazilian marines for their ability to live and navigate in the forest. For this reason, 3rd Platoon would lead the way.

Viana saluted and said, "We're ready to go, sir." He pointed to a tree where the bark had been hacked away, revealing light-colored wood. "I have men blazing a path. Trees will be marked on both sides so we can find our way back to the boats."

"Very good, Lieutenant. Lead on."

With a few yells, the men set off through the jungle. Marcus took off his hat and wiped his brow. The still air among the trees seemed at least ten degrees hotter than on the river and felt thick in his lungs. One could almost taste the soupy air, which was heavy with the reek of rotting birds, decaying wood, damp mold, and other rich but unidentifiable aromas.

The hollow thump of an axe striking a tree echoed from up ahead. A slow but necessary task if they were to find their way back. He could see only a dozen of his men moving among the trees and foliage. Thick tree trunks and ropy vines hid the rest. All the men carried heavy packs loaded with food, a one-man tent, mosquito netting, water, and ammunition. They'd be lucky to cover ten kilometers a day. This was not going to be a pleasant journey, no matter what they found along the way.

Amazon Harvest

Chapter 6
David

The trip down river from the university camp to Rio Estrada was hot, uncomfortable, and at times, terrifying. The sweat plastering David's blue polo shirt to his back came from fear as much as the heat and humidity. His hands ached from grasping the paddle far harder than the dip-stroke-lift action of moving the canoe downstream required. Paul, sitting in the back, did most of the work anyway. His muscles were strained from more than the work of paddling; he was iron tense from fear. It was hard to believe his body could sustain the level of tension he felt. What if he couldn't? There was still a long way to travel. He couldn't remember ever being so scared.

Caiman, with their huge jaws and sharp teeth, were everywhere, feasting on the multitudes of dead birds in and along the river. The large reptiles watched the travelers pass with yellow, menacing eyes. They didn't attack, but their silent stares served as a constant reminder that any mishap in the unsteady canoes could end very badly.

Felled trees, the victims of the same forces that racked the camp, stretched well into the riverbed in many places, their dying branches still leafy and green. The small group was fortunate the tributary flowed wide during the wet season. As the water receded during the dry season, it left extensive mudflats in its wake. With the higher bank to the north, such flats tended to lay to the south of the meandering stream, keeping the bulk of the trees clear of the water.

They'd been on the river for several hours and the sun was high and hot when they rounded a sharp bend to find the water boiling red before them. The bend led the river through a rise in the land. The banks on both sides rose and narrowed. The river current picked up speed, and David felt a breeze caress his face. Any pleasure it would have otherwise given him was cut short with the realization that they were now going pretty fast, and that a large tree lay directly across the channel ahead.

Working with Sally had forced upon him a certain degree of knowledge about the local trees, far more than David ever wanted. But identifying the tree before them would have been easy anyway. If there was one tree people asked about upon arriving in the Amazon rainforest, it was the Kapok tree. This was primarily because it was the tallest tree in the forest and had a massive, distinctive root system.

This one was a true monster of its kind. Something had eaten away a good portion of the Kapok tree, from roots to lower branches, which had weakened it and was no doubt the main reason for its collapse. From the two hundred feet of destruction leading from the right riverbank into the jungle, its fall must have been spectacular. Smaller trees had been turned into kindling by the impact. Now the giant tree was sprawled across the waterway with the upper branches partway up the north bank. This left the higher side of the channel choked with branches while the right flowed under the main trunk with maybe three feet of clearance.

The water churned pinkish-white around the branches and for most of the way across the channel. A hissing roar could be heard coming from ahead, and rapidly growing louder.

The frothing water and hissing sound puzzled David. *Damn, is the current that fast?* It didn't look right somehow. The flow of water didn't seem fast enough to account for such a boiling froth. And why was the foam pink?

"Oh my God," said Heather with a slight quiver the carried over the hiss of the water.

"Piranha," said Darrin from the front of their canoe in a husky, fear-laced voice.

The narrowing channel and mass of branches from the fallen Kapok tree had captured the bodies of thousands of dead birds. Piranhas were in a feeding frenzy, driven wild by the blood in the water and the thrashing of their fellows. The roiling water was tinged pink with silver-and-red flashes so close together it was impossible to make out individual fish.

Several caimans on the south bank watched them pass. Though a feast was near, even the fearsome reptiles didn't dare enter the water when the piranhas were in such a murderous state. With their unblinking eyes and crocodilian grins, they almost seemed amused by the scene.

"Back! Paddle backward," yelled Darrin.

"No!" shouted Paul. "Too late. Go forward!" He dug his paddle deep into the water and heaved, driving them onward. "Go right! We can make it underneath."

David had already started to back paddle. The canoe wobbled and lurched sideways.

"Forward, dammit, go forward," yelled Paul. "We're more stable going fast."

David obeyed, even though fear gripped his heart at the idea going into the flashing pink, silver, and red froth only feet in front of them. The tree trunk stretching across the way was still twenty feet away. He stroked once, then twice, and the canoe surged forward, due way more to Paul than David.

Then they were in the midst of the piranha. A dreadful cadence began as a hundreds of flashing silver-and-red streaks slammed into the bottom and sides of the canoe. The impacts of the crazed fish were strong enough to be felt through David's aluminum seat.

As they neared the tree, the thumps became even more intense. The gap between the right bank and the entanglement of branches to the left was only six or seven feet. Paul was aiming closer to the bank where the tree was higher above the water.

Steve, laying swaddled in a thin sheet in the bottom of the canoe, had been still and quiet all morning. There was no telling if the fish hitting the boat disturbed him or maybe it was bad timing. But he screamed and then started convulsing. His unexpected, violent motion rocked the canoe back and forth. David and Paul were caught off guard as the vessel pitched sideways. They very nearly capsized. Water, feathers, blood, and several thrashing piranhas splashed over the gunnel. David jerked away from the roiling water and nearly flipped the canoe in the other direction.

"Sit still! Sit still!" yelled Paul. He dropped his paddle on top of Steve and grabbed the sides of the canoe to steady it, fighting both Steve's convulsions and David's panicked efforts to avoid the water.

The canoe continued forward at a brisk pace, unguided, and thumped hard into the right bank, knocking David off his seat. One of the piranha that had splashed on board slithered past him in the shallow water at the bottom of the canoe. Only its lower half was in the water as the thrashing tail sent it skimming about, sharp teeth gnashing as it sought something to bite. David yelped and scrambled back onto his seat, rocking the canoe even more.

Heather and Darrin passed them, paddling hard. As they went by, Heather locked eyes with David, fear carving lines in her face that were far too deep for such a young woman.

With a visible effort, she tore her eyes off them. From her place in the back of the canoe, she picked her target carefully. Her arms and back flexed through her blue tank top as she dug her paddle deep into the water for one last stroke.

"Now," she yelled. She and Darrin ducked down.

The other canoe glided under the tree, jerking with a wooden *chunk* that came when the back tip of the canoe hit the trunk, and then they were gone.

Seeing Heather's fear didn't help quail his own. However, the brief contact did permit some reason to pierce his terror, enough for him to realize his panic was making the situation worse. This helped him find enough control to sit still, though spasmodic trembles shook his limbs despite the effort.

The front of the canoe had cut deep into the mud of the right bank. The sluggish current pushed them around by the stern, making balancing even more difficult. As they swung around, Paul had to let go of the gunnels to grab the tree. He grunted with the contact, then grunted more as he clutched the end of a broken branch and used his knees and midsection to counter Steve's thrashing.

Paul seemed to hold the canoe upright with sheer force of will. David stayed still, though it required more self-control than he knew he had. Every lurch threatened to send them into the frothing water.

With a final loud moan and shudder, Steve quieted.

Paul stared at him for a long moment, and then shook his head. "Okay, get ready. When I let go, get down."

David eyed the piranha still thrashing in the several inches of water in the canoe and started to tell him to wait.

The words barely formed when Paul said, "Now."

Paul ducked, and the tree slid over him as the canoe pivoted on around. However, it was still stuck on the bank. Paul placed both hands on the tree and pushed. The front of the canoe sucked free of the mud. They scooted free and drifted backward. The tree seemed to rush toward David, forcing him off his seat and into the bottom of the canoe. One of the piranha snapped at his hand as he pushed himself back up into his seat with terror driven strength, nearly slamming his head into the tree as he went under it. In seconds, they were clear of the tree, going the wrong way. The water still churned around them, but much less than on the other side of the tree.

With determination on his face, Paul snatched up his paddle and bellowed, "Back paddle!"

David's shaking hands were white-knuckle tight around the paddle and his arms didn't want to move, but he forced himself to do as instructed. Still going backward, they picked up speed and pulled free of the piranhas' frenzied red boil. The river became shallower and the canoe scrapped on gravel, then they were clear.

Heather and Darrin had pulled ashore a short distance away on a sandy flat in the middle of the river. Both of them were looking at them with relief on their faces. Paul and David continued backward until they grounded beside the other canoe.

"Out," Paul snapped to David. Glancing at Darrin, he said, "Come help me hold Steve. Heather, David, dump this crap out of the canoe."

Paul and Darrin lifted the injured man as gently as they could, and David and Heather turned over the canoe. Reddish-brown water, mangled bird parts, and three large piranhas splashed onto the sand.

The fish flopped with frantic energy, their jutting, tooth-filled jaws snapping as if they didn't realize there was nothing for them to bite but air. David recoiled from them and shuddered. Paul came over and kicked the fish into the water. The piranhas streaked off upriver, following the flow of blood back to the dead birds.

"Why did you do that?" Darrin asked. "Should have let 'em die."

Paul shrugged. "Why not? They're just doing what they do."

Darrin snorted but didn't say anything else.

Sorrow showed on Heather's face. "This is all messed up. I've never heard of so many piranha schooling in one place. And we're quite a ways up river."

Paul nodded. "Yeah, the bird kill really kicked something off. Predators and scavengers will have a field day. The blood in the river will pull them in from miles away."

"Yeah," Heather said. "So what happens when all the easy food gets eaten?"

No one said anything. It would pay to proceed very carefully though. As if they weren't already.

After a brief rest, they wiped out the bottom of the canoe, made Steve as comfortable as possible, and set out once more down the river. David trembled off and on for an hour after they left the sand bank behind.

Sally

Small scratching noises woke Sally, and she shifted uncomfortably in the cramped confines of the helicopter. The smell of her friends' rotting flesh assaulted her senses, and she pulled the alcohol-soaked kerchief up over her nose with a grimace, blinking her eyes to get them to focus. Muted daylight from the late afternoon sun filtered through the trees, lighting the cabin with a dim green glow. The scratching grew louder and was soon joined by clicks and clacks. *What's that?* she wondered as she became more alert. *A monkey?*

The sound was hard to pinpoint, but it seemed to come from outside. A dark shadow moved over her, accompanied by the sound of plastic fracturing with a crunching sound. Her gaze zeroed in on movement right past Myra's ruined head. She choked back a scream at what appeared to be a huge greenish-black spider prying at the window.

No, not a spider—it had too many legs. She wasn't sure if it was dangerous, but it certainly looked like it could be. The thing had a small head in proportion to a lumpy body that was maybe a foot long and nearly as wide. At least ten long legs were scratching and probing around the window frame. The two longest appendages were tipped with wicked-looking claws, but she couldn't tell for sure where they originated from the body. Huge eyes and a cluster of antenna dominated its head. There was no sign of a nose or mouth. It began prying at the seam along the window frame with its claws.

It was strong, too. The window gave a groan and then separated from the frame. The window was made of heavy plastic that cracked and split rather than shatter, sending thick, heavy chunks down on Sally. After removing the window, the spider-thing slipped through the opening and scrambled onto Myra's corpse. Another one dropped down from somewhere above to take the first one's place. The motion drew Sally's attention beyond the window and she cringed at the sight of dozens, hundreds, more of the things swarming all over the trees above.

She tried to lie absolutely still, but shivers ran through her body, rattling the debris around her with soft crunching sounds. Her breath came in short gasps, sounding loud and intrusive in her ears. The spider thing half-stood, half-clung to the back of Myra's seat, swiveling its head in a slow, steady motion like a security camera, taking in the helicopter's interior.

It spent several long moments staring at the aircraft's controls and instruments. The way it moved was more machinelike than animal. When its emotionless gaze fell on her, terror made her throat constrict. After an eternal minute, the eyes moved on toward the back of the helicopter. The head stopped several more times, taking in the various objects and bodies. Then it jerked into motion and scuttled back through the dislodged window. With a flurry of long scrabbling limbs, accompanied by a riot of clacking sounds, all the other spider things followed it from sight.

Whatever the creatures had been, they were like nothing she'd ever seen or heard of in any of her studies. Something told her they weren't of this world. *Ten legs or more? They couldn't be.* There was no proof, but her heart told her they must have come from the mysterious mountain they'd seen moments before the crash. Tears began to flow down her cheeks as she hugged herself tightly, ignoring the aches of her battered body. Her mind revolted at her impossible situation. *What in the hell is going on?*

David

It was dark when, at long last, the docks of Rio Estrada came into view. A single light flickered bright against the night on the ridge above the docks. Thousands of insects swirled around it, black shadows that cast dancing sparkles across the water. The illumination barely reached the end of the docks jutting into the river. The long wooden piers bobbed with a slow rhythm as small waves lapped against the barrels on which they floated with a faint slurping sound. Dim as the light was, there was enough to show the wreckage of a long barge and several overturned small boats, giving the scene a sad and forlorn look. Other than the light, there was no sign of life.

The four exchanged nervous glances at the sight of the destruction around the docks. It was obvious that whatever had ravaged the camp, birds, and trees along the river hadn't spared Rio Estrada. They headed for the left-hand wharf, which was shorter and lower to accommodate smaller boats. David kept fidgeting with nervous energy, twisting and turning in his seat as they drew near.

"Take it easy," said Paul. He stretched out and grasped a cleat to tie off the canoe. "It would suck to make it this far and then get dumped in the river."

David forced himself to sit still, though his gaze roamed the ridge above, looking for any sign of people or reassurance, but found neither. The only motion was the fluttering of countless insects around the single light. It seemed to take forever to tie off the canoes. Once Paul was satisfied they were secure, he and David scrambled onto the rough wooden dock.

Heather studied the dock which was three feet or so higher than the canoes and shook her head. "I think we'll need some help to get Steve up there."

Paul nodded. "You guys stay here. David and I will go find someone."

Heather and Darrin gave quick nods in reply. Heather climbed onto the dock and then sat and braced her feet on the side of Steve's canoe to keep it steady. "Try to make it quick," she said in a tired voice. She plucked at her blue tank top. "I'm in serious need of a shower, a hot meal, and some sleep."

"Amen, sister," said Darrin. He sat beside her, sprawled back on the dock, and placed his feet on the canoe as well. "But at least we're out of that damn canoe. My back is killing me."

David and Paul walked up the wooden ramp from the pier to the concrete apron near the top of the ridge. David was puffing before they were a third of the way up. The two were about the same height, but Paul was slender and athletic, whereas David was large and dumpy. They walked past the bow of the barge, which rested on the cracked concrete and looked like a huge stricken animal in the flickering light. A small, corrugated steel building housing the town's diesel generator sat beyond the barge, shrouded in shadows. The machinery emitted a faint hum while it worked to provide Rio Estrada's modest power needs. The sound quickly faded as they trudged past it. When they reached the top of the hill, David had to stop and place his hands on his knees to keep his head from spinning.

Paul said, "Man, you're way too young to be so out of shape."

David was too winded to reply. After a few moments, he stood and they began walking into town.

The entire length of Rio Estrada's sole paved street stretched for three blocks from the ridge to the fountain in the center of the small plaza. Lining the first two blocks was an assortment of wooden and tin structures.

Most of the establishments were stalls where locals displayed whatever they could grow or craft in hope of selling something to barge crew or mill workers from the docks. The only real buildings—two bars, a restaurant, and a general store—were easy to identify, as they had windows. Meager lighting came from small lamps suspended from wires over the two intersections where dirt roads met the paved one. The lamps had metal shades to protect them from the frequent rains. They cast weak, yellowish light, which was further dimmed by multitudes of swarming insects. Along the street, every stall and window was dark and silent. At the far end, a light shined out of their line of sight somewhere in the plaza casting a faint glow over the small fountain.

Paul looked at his wrist comp and frowned. "It's only seven o'clock. I would've thought the bars at least would be open. I wonder where everyone is?"

David shrugged, still sucking in air, albeit at a slower pace.

The quiet was eerie walking down the street. Their footfalls echoed back from the buildings on either side. The silence was broken when they entered the plaza by singing coming from the large church on the left side of the town square.

Two lights framed the church's double doors, each set in antique basket-like covers. The stained-glass windows over the doors glowed with multicolored hues. The Office de Naval next door also had a light glowing from inside, a faint illumination leaking through drawn blinds. The courthouse, hotel, medical building, and three small shops that completed the square were all dark.

Paul pointed to the two-story wooden hotel. The structure had a distinct tilt to it. He said in a soft voice, "The restaurant is closed, and the hotel looks like it's about to fall over. So much for finding Heather and Darrin a shower, meal, and bed. C'mon, let's go see if we can find someone in charge." He headed toward the Office de Naval.

The office was locked, and banging on the door drew no response.

"I guess everybody's at church," said Paul. "Funny, I don't remember the people here being that devout. Something strange is going on."

"Maybe it's a holiday or something."

Paul shrugged and led the way to the large double doors set deep in a stone arch. Missionaries had built the church during the height of the rubber rush almost a century earlier. It was by far the grandest building in Rio Estrada with a tall spire, stained windows, and a large sanctuary. There were several connecting buildings that served as a rectory for the priest, a small nunnery, and classrooms for the town's only school. The sprawling complex made up one-half of the town's plaza.

The front doors were locked, which was very unusual for a church with mass underway. With a puzzled look at David, Paul rapped on one of the heavy wooden portals.

The singing trailed off, leaving the plaza in silence. That was really weird. Like the entire congregation was concerned about who was at the door. David and Paul exchanged nervous glances, this was getting stranger and stranger. Maybe they had been better off back at the camp.

After a long pause, a series of clunks came from the door, and it opened with a soft squeal about a foot. An old gray-haired man with a close-cropped beard wearing a brown robe peered out at them, his face betraying extreme nervousness. Behind him, two dark forms shuffled about, whispering in tense tones.

The old man said in Portuguese, "Who are you? Are you from the mountains?"

Paul stepped back from the door and said to David, "You're up."

David nodded. While he didn't speak Portuguese as well as his sister, he was comfortable with the language. His mother had come from Portugal and after she died Sally had insisted they speak it on occasion to honor her. As with most things in his life, he'd gone along to keep his older sibling from nagging him to death. And once again he was glad he had. On the other hand, would Sally have gotten permission to drag him into this mess otherwise?

"Uh, um, no mountains," he said. "We came from the river. We have an injured man and need help."

The old man's eyes lit with recognition. "Ahh, you are from the university team? Are you not? Paul?"

David shook his head and gestured toward his companion. "No, this is Paul. My name is David. Do you know my sister? Sally? Is she here?"

The old man pulled the door open the rest of the way. Behind stood two men, both armed. One was skinny, dressed in the uniform of a Brazilian marine, and carried an assault rifle. The other was much larger and dressed in blue jeans and a stained gray tee shirt. He looked very jumpy and cradled a shotgun.

The old man said, "I'm Brother Lorando. Your sister was here earlier, but she and her friend left with Keith Anderson in his helicopter this morning. They were supposed to be going to your camp and then Manaus."

David emitted a big sigh at the news. He slumped, deflating almost if the exhalation was air leaking out of his soul.

Paul understood enough to get the gist what was said. He reached out and gripped David's shoulder. "Sorry, man. Don't worry though. I'm sure she'll be okay." A frown crossed his face and he nodded to the men standing inside the door. "Ask him what's up with the guns? Also, did he say something about a mountain? There's no mountain anywhere near here."

David asked Paul's questions in a leaden voice, beyond caring right now. Brother Lorando shook his head and said, "You didn't see them? The mountains appeared from nowhere. They're white, well, mostly white. Brother Arruda says it's a sign from God, but Father Sardenberg fears it's demonic. We were praying for guidance. The whole town is here."

David relayed this to Paul, who shook his head and said, "There can't be any mountains. We were here a few weeks ago and we would have seen them." He scratched his head in thought. "Well, whatever has them all so scared will have to wait for morning. Ask him about getting some help and finding us a place to sleep."

David nodded and in the same leaden voice, asked the brother about getting people to help carry Steve up from the canoe. The old man nodded and hurried into the church. David was exhausted; only the drive to find his sister had kept him going thus far. Even so, he suspected dreams of his sister perishing in a fiery crash would make sleep difficult that night.

David's sleep was every bit as poor as he'd feared. Images kept flooding through his head of his sister's agonized face as the helicopter exploded like the jetliner over the jungle did. He could almost hear tearing metal as visions of it going down in flames danced across his closed eyelids. They twisted his stomach and made his eyes ache.

Other things also haunted him. What was he going to do without

Sally? Where was he going to go? He had no job, he sucked at school, and... Well, what else was there? Tears came and dripped down his cheeks at the unjustness of it all. First, his mother, then father, and now his sister...all taken from him.

A bitter thought surfaced, a part of The Memory. An old wound. His father hadn't actually been taken. Father had killed himself, abandoning David when he'd needed him most. Unfair, unjust, and unforgivable. It wasn't until near dawn that he'd exhausted his tears and drifted off into an uneasy slumber.

The church put them up in a large common room used for everything from wedding receptions, to church meals, to funerals. Over the last few days, the room had seen far too many of the latter for such a small town. About fifty people were sharing the space, all of whom had lost their homes during the strange pulling wave storm. The room had dividers that could be slid in place to separate the room for men and women. At night, everyone pitched in to set up rows of cots. In the morning, the partition was pushed back and the cots were stored and replaced with folding tables for the day.

The sound of moving furniture intruded on David's troubled sleep. Blinking his eyes to get them to focus, he struggled to his feet, still groggy from a restless night. After a few moments, his head cleared enough for him to remember where he was and why. Depression settled over him like a dark cloud.

He noticed that the cot he was on was one of the last one still set up and several people were eyeing him with annoyance. Dragging himself up, he took the bedding off the cot and folded it. He went to the bathroom to clean himself as best he could, which wasn't all that great since there was no shower, only a small sink. Then he put on a fresh pair of blue jeans and a dark green tee shirt that had Zombie Battle Master on it. Thus refreshed, he went to look for Paul, Heather, and Darrin. They weren't in the hall, so he trudged through the church nave and out into the plaza.

The early morning sun was hot and bright, making him blink while his eyes adjusted. Heather and Darrin sat on the edge of the fountain, staring off into the distance. Paul was sitting cross-legged on the ground in front of them at a little table, writing in a notebook. David plodded over to them. Heather and Darrin glanced at him, nodded, and then returned to staring into the distance. David followed their gaze to the huts and trees that made up the northern side of the plaza, then to the tree line, and finally to the huge mountain, make that mountains, beyond.

A huge hand seemed to clutch his chest, forcing out a gasp. Fear fought to overwhelm his misery, a poor fight for his heart regardless of the outcome.

"Mountain," he mumbled. "No way."

"Yeah. That's what we said. But there it is," said Heather. "Just like the townsfolk said it was last night."

"And we thought they were all crazy," Paul said, still focused on whatever he was working on at the table.

"Well, maybe they are. Us too," Heather said. "I for sure know it wasn't there when we first got here a few weeks ago. I keep expecting it to disappear, like a mirage. But it ain't even wavered."

"Too impossible to be real, yet too real to be impossible," said Darrin. "We've been staring at if for a half hour, and I still can't really accept it."

"It doesn't look right, does it?" said Heather.

"What? Like a mountain that appeared out of thin air should look a certain way?" replied Darrin.

Heather frowned. "No, not that. I mean the color. It looks like it's covered in snow, but the color isn't right."

"Granite," said Paul. "Not snow. I don't think it's been there long enough to accumulate snow. But the peaks may be high enough once the rainy season starts."

David sat down next Heather and joined the others in staring at the mountain. Paul stopped writing, got on his knees, and moved the table. Underneath the table was a string tied off at both ends with small rocks. Paul carefully aligned one of the table legs next to one of the rocks, sat back down, and began fiddling with a plastic triangle and a ruler.

David nudged Heather and said, "What's he doing?"

Paul answered. "I'm trying to estimate how far away it is." Satisfied with the table and triangle's position, he carefully sighted down the ruler at the mountain. He nudged the ruler, aimed down it like a rifle, nudged it some more, and then squinted down it again. "Hmph," he muttered. "Good enough I guess." Getting on his knees, he looked down where the ruler intersected the triangle.

David noticed that the triangle had numbers along the edge and realized it was a square. This brought back bad memories of trigonometry class at school. One of his many academic failures.

Paul wrote down his findings and whispered something to himself while he worked over an equation. "The big peak is about twenty-two miles away, give or take. If the slope holds reasonably steady, the base would be maybe eighteen from here. The other peak is at least twenty-seven miles away."

"Damn," whispered Darrin. "Those things are frickin' huge."

Paul scratched his head with the ruler for a moment and then braced the square upright on the table.

"What are you doing now?" asked Heather.

"I should be able to estimate the height now that I have a distance," Paul replied, his face flat on the table as he lined up the ruler. "This will all be pretty rough, but …"

"I know, I know," Heather said with a grimace. "'To measure is to know,' per Lord Kelvin, your hero."

Paul stood and began scribbling on the pad again. "Yeah, though calling him 'my hero' may be a bit of a stretch. But do you have any idea what this means?"

David tore his eyes away from the peak and said, "I don't know, the end of the world maybe?"

Paul hesitated and looked up at the peak. "Hmmm. Well, let's hope not. But if those gravity spikes come back…well." He shook his head. "There's nothing we could do about it anyway. But this—" he pointed with his pencil at the mountain, "—this is pretty damn amazing no matter what. It's an unprecedented event in human history."

David shook his head and glanced around the plaza. The townspeople were hurrying about whatever business they had with their heads down, turning occasional fearful glances toward the enigma towering above the forest. Paul seemed to be the only one swept up in the excitement of scientific discovery. Everyone else was just scared shitless.

"Son of a bitch," muttered Paul, looking up from the notebook with a shocked expression. "Nineteen thousand feet!" He frowned. "Give or take a thousand or so, but still, that's one damn big mountain. The tallest in South America is only twenty-two thousand."

"That's just great," said Heather, her sarcasm unmistakable. "We already know it's a big friggin' mountain. How did it get there? Isn't that the question?"

Paul raised his eyebrows. "Well, yeah. But that might take a while to figure out. So we start with what we can." His expression glazed over as he looked at the peak. "We need to go there."

Heather put her hands on top of her head and gave Paul a withering look. "Are you crazy? Planes are falling from the sky, we're cut off from the world, no radios, and the chopper is God knows where, and you want to go to that damn mountain?"

Paul nodded. "How else are we going to find out how it got there? As you said, 'that's the question.'"

"I only want to find my sister," said David. "If I still have one," he finished in a whisper.

Paul gave a small start. "Yeah, of course."

"You don't sound too sure," said David. "Can we go back to the camp?"

Paul looked grim and shook his head. "Well, the villagers told us most of the boats are damaged. And even if they weren't, there aren't many that can handle the shallow water upriver from here. Plus, it may take some work to clear out that Kapok tree we went under. I think was might be stuck here for a while."

"Then let's take the canoes."

Heather walked over and put her arm around David. "I know you're worried, but it would take at least two days to go back up river in the canoes. What if we missed them again while we were on the river? I'm sure she's safe—heck, they're probably headed back here by now."

David snuffled and blinked back tears. "You don't know that. I want to go back and find her. Or… at least find out what happened.'"

Paul said, "No, we don't know for sure. But going up and down the river won't help. Besides, we need a powerboat to make the trip feasible. In the meantime, the best thing for us is to stay put and wait."

Darrin frowned, snorted, and said, "Not me. The priest said a tug and barge docked this morning and the captain offered to take Steve back to Manaus. He said he'll put in word for me to go along to take care of him. If you guys are smart, you'd come, too. The main river is supposed to be a big mess. There may not be another barge or boat for quite a while." He pointed toward the mountain. "And I for one want to get as far away from that thing as possible."

Heather gave Darrin a dirty look and said to David, "Don't worry, Paul and I will stay. The guys at camp need help, too, so we'll keep trying to find a boat."

David nodded, grateful for Heather's support. However, he didn't blame Darrin for wanting to leave. In fact, if not for his sister, he'd be on that boat, too. In addition to being scared, he was sick of the heat, humidity, uncomfortable beds, and never-ending supply of bugs. The trip downriver had been terrifying. Despite his brave talk, he knew he couldn't face an even longer trip upriver paddling against the current all the way.

As much as his sister annoyed him, he'd love to get one of her lectures about now. All those times he'd shrugged off her efforts to prepare him for the world. It hadn't seemed important then. Now it seemed much, much too important. Was it too late? What would he do if she…? It hurt to even frame the question.

Darrin said, "How do you know she's not in Manaus herself? Isn't that where they were taking those patients?"

"All the more reason to stay here," said Heather. "It's like when you were a kid and got lost in the supermarket. My parents always told me the best thing to do is stay put and wait for them to find Me. If you keep running around, you're most likely to make things worse."

"I never got lost in a supermarket," Darrin said. "I think you're crazy."

Heather gave him another dirty look, but didn't say anything.

"Besides," said Paul, "I heard the barge is already crowded with villagers heading out of town. The only reason Darrin got a slot was to take care of Steve."

David rubbed his eyes as he fought back tears. "I don't know what to do. God, I just want to find Sally and go home."

Heather gave David a gentle hug, smiled, and said, "Like Paul says, the best thing we can do is wait here where it's safe."

David looked up at the mountains looming in the distance and wondered how safe they really were, but didn't say anything.

Chapter 7
Daniel
USS *Bataan* Amphibious Ready Group, Mid-Atlantic

First Lieutenant Daniel Johnson placed his hand on an overhead pipe as he exited the USS *Bataan*'s main conference room. A habit he'd developed to keep his head safe from such obstructions. His six foot, five-inch frame was ill-suited for the confines of the warship. After four years as a Marine, he'd identified most of the places that posed a danger to his skull. Not all of them were in the ship.

The military built things of hard metal for average-sized people, and he still got painful surprises on occasion. Some of the men behind him smiled at the sight. Daniel was one of the biggest men on the ship, which, in addition to his piercing green eyes, was in direct contrast to his strong Asiatic features. The traits were a result of mingling his father's Norwegian ancestry with that of his Japanese mother.

Once out of the traffic flow of junior officers and senior noncoms, he caught the eye of a tall slender black man with graying hair and motioned him over. Gunnery Sergeant Lewis Stevens had served with his father and had been in Daniel's life to some degree for as long as he could remember. Together they were the command team of Marine Expeditionary Unit 22's Light Armored Recon Platoon.

Daniel had no doubt his father had pulled some heavy-duty strings to get such a gifted noncom assigned to his platoon. That his father thought he needed such handholding annoyed him a little, but also pleased him. His father was not a man known for expressing terms of endearment. Going to the trouble of getting Stevens assigned to his unit was probably the closest thing to a declaration of love his father had ever made, such as it was.

Daniel led the way outside and leaned against the ship's railing. Overhead, the flight deck crowded down on the walkway, but it was still higher than the ceilings inside. He always preferred being outside the ship whenever possible. Gunny Stevens joined him and stared out at the passing ocean.

"Well, Gunny," said Daniel. "What do you think?"

Gunny shook his head. "Sounds like a lot of crap piling up without any real information." He turned around and leaned back against the rail. "Sounds like we need to repaint the Pigs."

The platoon's Light Armored Vehicle 25Es, or LAVs, had been painted tan and brown for a NATO exercise off the coast of North Africa. They were commonly called Pigs by their crews, most of whom were younger than their vehicles. But the machines were reliable with a reputation for being tough, so there was a love-hate relationship between the Pigs and their crews.

Now the entire *Bataan* Amphibious Ready Group was turning around mid-Atlantic and speeding for the jungles of South America. This should make the tan-based camouflage pretty much useless. Green was the traditional color for the region.

Daniel nodded. "Yeah, I guess so. Well, we should have plenty of time. Sounds like we're at least ten days out. I guess there's not much else we can do until we learn more."

They were silent for a time, watching the water rush past. Several hundred yards away, one of the *Bataan*'s escort ships sent up sheets of white spray as its bow cut through waves, the vast emptiness of the open sea beyond it. After a few minutes, Gunny looked over at Daniel's profile.

Daniel knew the older man was watching him and braced for the inevitable question.

Finally, Gunny said, "Are you still thinking of getting out when this deployment is over?"

Daniel's head dropped, then he turned with an annoyed look. "Yeah, for the hundredth time. That's what I plan to do."

Gunny shook his head. "Your dad sure ain't going to like that. Colonel had high hopes we might make a real Marine out of you."

Daniel's annoyed look faded and he looked back out at the ocean. "Come on, Gunny, you know I'm not really cut out for this."

Gunny snorted. "A man can be cut out for anything if he wants to be."

"Yeah, maybe. Bottom line is, I don't want to." He turned back to face the sergeant. "Look, I did all the tough guy stuff my father wanted. Football, Marines, Recon. Now I'm ready to try going my own way."

Gunny shrugged. "Well, everyone's got the right. But don't kid yourself, son. You could make a damn fine career out of the Marines. You have potential if you set yourself to it."

"No thanks. You can tell my dad the Marines aren't for me."

The older man laughed. "Me tell him? No way, that's your job.

And I bet it'll be real interesting when he finds out."

"Yeah, I know," said Daniel with a sigh. "It's not something I'm looking forward to. But when this deployment is over, that's it for me."

"Okay," said Gunny. He leaned on the rail and gazed out across the water. "In the meantime, I'll just keep trying to make a decent Marine out of you."

Sally

The sun shone green through the layers of leaves above the helicopter. The muted glow was enough to rouse Sally from her disturbing dreams and back into the nightmare. The one where she was in a small metal room trapped with her dead friends. It was hard not to get lost in terror with the sights and smells of the dead and dying right in front of her. She moaned and then gagged as a wave of death-stench assaulted her nostrils. The smell triggered an overpowering urge to escape. She had to get away from the horrible smell.

Gagging, she lurched upright. Too fast! Pain blazed from her side, forcing her back with a gasp. No use. It wasn't the first time panic had forced her into movements her body wasn't ready for. She made herself breathe slowly, through her mouth, getting her emotions under control.

The smell was always bad, but sometimes it was worse, depending on how the wind flowed around and through the fuselage. Holding her breath, she fumbled for alcohol from the first aid kit, doused her kerchief with it, and wrapped it back around her face. It didn't help much, but it was better than nothing.

During the night, strange sounds had echoed through the jungle for several long hours. She pondered what they could have meant. The noises had started as a hiss and then grown to a crackling roar. For a time, she could swear something huge and terrible had been right outside the helicopter.

The roar had consisted of a cacophony of snaps, pops, cracks, and booms blended into one terrifying deluge of sound. Then it had faded away into the night. Was the noise linked to what had happened to her, with those weird creatures, with the mountain? There was no way to tell from her prison. It was one more item to weigh on her heart and soul. Strange and scary things were afoot in the world, going on all around her, and she was isolated and helpless.

Despair settled over her like a shroud. To be free of this nightmare, she'd have to get moving. But she couldn't move, at least not enough to climb out of the shattered helicopter, much less down the trees that held it. She'd tried to cling to the hope that someone might come to help, the hope had faded with the hours. Besides, there was almost no chance of anyone finding her, even if someone was looking.

No, she'd have to do this on her own. But... She tried leaning forward, slower, and not as far. It hurt, but it was better than yesterday. While upright, she slowly twisted back and forth, testing the limits of her pain. Even this small victory gave her confidence a little boost.

"I think it's better, Myra." She moved a little more. "Yup. Getting better. Still a long way from being able to climb out of here though." Frowning, she looked up at her dead friend. Despite her mangled visage, for some reason, Sally drew comfort from her friend's face. Funny what you could find comfort in if you got trapped and scared and were all alone in a crazy world.

"You always said to take it one day at a time, one step at a time. That's the way to get things done."

Leaning back with a soft sigh, Sally pulled out a breakfast bar from one of the boxes stored in the back of the cabin and nibbled on it, forcing down each bite with a grimace. It took all her willpower not to gag, but she had to eat, to get her strength back.

She stared past Myra's ruined face at the trees and sky beyond, trying to ignore the flies crawling in and out of the gaping mouth. Time moved very, very slow as the clouds moved in and it began to rain. The water turned the cracked windshield of the helicopter into a shifting green abstract painting. The sound of water dripping through the broken windows made a soft pitter-patter on the shallow pool that had formed on the aluminum beside her. The frequent rains were a godsend, as she'd been able to flush much of the blood out of the cabin. It had helped a little with the smell. A little.

The teenage girl hadn't shown any sign of waking, and her pulse was a weak flutter in her neck. "I think she's going to die. I don't have any IV bottles. Dehydration will get her if nothing else."

One more thing to be depressed about. Another reason to feel helpless, powerless. She was in a perfect storm of depressing things. Time was a horror-laced boredom. Despite her efforts to ignore Myra, Sally's gaze kept returning to the shadowy form of her dead friend. Was it crazy to find comfort there despite it being a grotesque facsimile of the one Sally cherished? Probably, but what the hell.

"I don't know why I keep talking to you, Myra. The sound of my own voice maybe?" She forced down another bite of the breakfast bar. "I wonder if anyone is looking for us. No? Yeah, I guess not. With no radios, nobody in Manaus is even expecting us, are they?"

"No one," said Myra in a raspy voice.

Sally jumped and studied Myra's face. Had she heard that? The helicopter creaked in its wood-and-leaf prison, and she gave a nervous chuckle. *Just the wind.* She gave a small chuckle of relief.

After a few minutes, Sally said, "Still…somebody will try coming down the river from the camp, don't you think? They won't sit up there forever. Probably Paul. He'd be really up for that sort of thing. Once he gets to Rio Estrada, he'll start looking for us."

"Nobody," said Myra as the helicopter creaked and moaned.

This time, Sally's chuckle had a hard edge to it, forced and strained. That had really sounded like Myra. Then she shrugged and the tension eased. What if it was? Mountains appearing from nowhere, impossible eleven-legged creatures, getting shot down in the jungle… What the heck, why not a talking dead friend? *It's better than being alone, isn't it?* A cold shiver traced up her spine. Maybe not. Was she going crazy? Was she already?

Did it matter?

"So, you're going to talk to me, are you?" Sally studied Myra's one gloomy eye. "What should I do now?"

"Get out."

Sally shuddered. That was Myra for sure. Soft, hoarse…but? "Myra? Is that really you?"

There was a long pause. Tree limbs scraped the aluminum hull. Sally relaxed, and then Myra's voice came, "No… Yes."

I am going crazy. Sally sat in silence for a long time, listening to the moans and groans of the dead aircraft, and the rasps and scrapes from living trees. Death and life. *That's me, in a world between life and death. I'm both and neither.* The sounds were so forlorn, making the quiet seem more pronounced, sadder. As if she needed something else to make her situation more dismal. She knew she should stop talking to Myra. Right now, while she had enough reason left to wonder about her sanity. But if she kept talking? A soft moan from the sad wind sent fresh chills through her. It was too quiet and too loud at the same time.

"Well," she said in an effort to battle the soft sounds of silence trying to engulf her. "I sure hope David is okay."

"Lazy...useless."

"Come on now, you shouldn't be so mean. David isn't lazy. Not really. It's just...just that ever since he found Father... Well, you know. Something hasn't been right with him."

The moan and scraping and Myra repeated, "Lazy...useless."

"You have to stop criticizing him, or you'll make me angry. I know you think he holds me back, but I made a promise. And a promise is a promise. Let's talk about something else."

"Talking stop," Myra said.

Sally's head drooped. "I know, you're dead. I can't talk to you. God, am I losing it or what?"

Myra replied with a soft, rattling, windy chuckle. "Yes."

Sally's tears flowed and her eyes ached. "I know. But I don't want to stop talking to you. You're all I have. Nothing is making any sense."

Myra's tone was serious. "Live... Get out."

"I'll try. I'll try. But not yet. I hurt too much. And please, don't go, not yet."

"Talk," said the raspy moan.

They talked throughout the day. Every word helped her heart but wounded her mind. Reason shouted at her to stop, but not talking to Myra was beyond Sally's ability. She'd never felt so helpless and alone. Time passed very slowly.

Marcus

Early morning mist greeted the men of Patrol Boat Group 31. Steamy tendrils rose from the ground and drifted through the trees and around the tents. The air didn't move much this deep in the jungle, blocked by mile upon mile of interlocking trees. The only force stirring the mist was the gentle cascade of water dripping down from the layered canopy overhead. The rain made a steady pitter-patter as it fell.

Men stirred in the muggy twilight, eating, packing, talking in low voices, and preparing for another day's trek through the otherworldly environment of the forest. The jungle was quiet away from the river. Marcus heard occasional cries in the distance, one he recognized as a jaguar's scream of triumph. Insects buzzed, but the soft drone was sucked up by the heavy air. The sounds of falling rain and men packing their equipment were much louder. The lack of singing birds roared in the comparative silence.

Marcus looked at his watch and shook his head. It was well past sunrise, but if not for the luminous dial, he doubted he could see the hands. He'd forgotten how dark the heart of the rainforest could be, especially when there was cloud cover. It made for short days and would further slow their progress. This trip would take a very long time unless he risked traveling in the dark by flashlight, a venture he dreaded undertaking. But he felt an intense pressure to hurry. They were moving too slow. The desperate importance of finding out what was happening in the heart of his country was a heavy burden.

Lieutenant Jeronimo Viana appeared out of the mist. His hulking, poncho-shrouded form transitioned from an indistinct gray ghost to a solid body as he approached. A moment later, Antinasio's other two platoon leaders, Lieutenant Dante Campos and Lieutenant Henrique Gale, walked out of the mist and joined them.

"Any idea how far we've come Jeronimo?" asked Marcus.

"Not really, sir. Somewhere between ten and fifteen kilometers."

Lieutenant Campos, a slender man of medium height, shrugged. "Not too bad, sir."

Marcus frowned and shook his head. "Too slow. Too damn slow by far. If we don't do better today, we'll need to travel late, by flashlight."

Campos looked down, "That would be very dangerous, sir. Very easy to lose someone."

"I know. Believe me, I don't want to do it. However, time is critical. Anything may have happened since we left Manaus."

Viana turned and looked off into the jungle. "We should be getting close, sir. It's hard to tell without GPS. But we had a good fix on the source of the interference from the river. I'd guess we're within ten kilometers."

"Half a day," said Lieutenant Gale in a nervous voice.

"Half a day," repeated Marcus in a near whisper. Louder, he said,

"Very well. Jeronimo, please get the trailblazers moving. We have a lot of ground to cover yet."

The next two hours dragged by as the men of PBG 31 moved through the dripping murk. Under the layered canopy of the forest, there wasn't enough light to support a thick layer of undergrowth. Nevertheless, trees died and branches broke. They fell to the ground in contorted angles, huge, rotting wooden carcasses, creating walls propped up by their living neighbors. Heavy vines and occasional ferns grew between these random walls and more than made up for the lack of plant growth most people associated with a jungle. These combined to make the forest a confusing maze and slowed the soldiers' march.

They'd covered about three kilometers when shots and a scream echoed through the trees. Marcus froze as more shots and another scream reverberated through the gloom. The men around him also froze, looking about anxiously with their rifles at the ready.

Thrashing ferns and running feet indicated someone, or something, was fast approaching. Several men tensed and brought up their rifles.

"Hold!" yelled Lieutenant Campos. "Hold your fire! At ease."

The men relaxed, but only slightly. No one was ever at complete ease in the depths of the rainforest, even less so after hearing shots fired not far away.

One of Viana's men, Private Julio Arente, emerged from the trees. "Major Antinasio," he called out. "Major...? Sir, where are you?"

"Here," responded Marcus. The private glanced in his direction and trotted over to him.

Julio Arente was small, dark, and slender. Marcus knew him to be much stronger than his slight frame suggested, as well as fast and agile. He was nineteen and had joined PBG 31 last year. Marcus had met him two years ago in Manaus at a recruiting event for the local high schools. Julio had told him then of his intention to become a Marine. So far, he had been a very good one.

"Major," Julio said, his chest heaving as much from excitement as exertion. "Lieutenant Viana needs you right away."

"What is it? What happened?"

A look of confusion crossed Julio's face. He shook his head and said, "Things, in the trees, thousands of them. They killed Ernesto and

Juan. Lieutenant Viana wants you to see."

Confused and fearful for his men, Marcus nodded and gestured for Julio to head out. After signaling the rest of his men to hold their places, he followed. The young private led him through the foliage at a rapid pace, moving with an athlete's grace. They traveled a couple of hundred yards before they came upon Lieutenant Viana, who was leaning against a rubber tree, peering around it toward a small stream. As Marcus approached, Viana glanced back and silently pointed at another large tree on the opposite side of the watercourse.

Two bodies were sprawled beyond the edge of the stream, underneath the tree. The sight of two of his men lying face down in the mud, their bodies contorted and covered in blood, caused Marcus's chest to constrict.

"Oh my God," he said in a soft, shocked voice.

Several black shapes were scattered on the ground around the soldiers. The tree they were under seemed unusually dark, much more so than its neighbors did. It stood black against dark gray. In the dim light, it took a moment for him to realize that the darkness on the tree was moving, as if the bark was shifting with its own volition. It took a few more seconds for him to realize the tree was covered with a mass of…things.

Black, lumpy, multi-legged creatures a little over a foot in length, excluding their legs, covered the tree. He couldn't make out much detail in the dim light. However, there had to be thousands of them clustered all over the trunk and going up out of sight in the overhanging branches. Shadows shifted in dark variations as the creatures crawled around and over one another with soft clicking sounds.

"My God," he whispered. "What are those?"

Viana shook his head and whispered, "I have no idea. Ernesto and Juan were on point. They must have just crossed that stream when something happened. I don't know if they were attacked or if one of them panicked and began firing. No one actually saw them go down. By the time we got here, we found them like this. Sir, I was barely able to restrain my men. They want to see if they're still alive. But these beings might be linked to what's going on and I thought you should see this first."

Marcus nodded. "What's your plan?"

Viana gestured to the right where the bulk of his men waited; hiding in the foliage in a line facing the tree, all of them had their rifles pointed at the mass of creatures and waiting to fire. "Sir, with your permission, whatever they are, I plan on killing them. All of them if we can."

Marcus frowned and almost said no. Then anger swelled in his breast as he studied the forms lying in the mud. If there was any chance they still lived, they had to get over there.

He nodded and said, "Very well. You were wise to wait though. Despite the situation, we need to take some pictures first. The general will no doubt want to see this."

He pulled out his phone, made sure it was set for low light conditions, and took a dozen quick shots of the sprawled soldiers, the tree, and its strange inhabitants.

As he finished, Viana asked, "Do you think they're part of what's going on out here?"

Marcus shrugged. "I don't know. However, whatever these things are, they're like nothing I've ever heard of. Anything strange could be important." He put away his phone, wishing it could connect to…well, anywhere. However, with the interference, it hadn't even worked in Manaus, much less here in the jungle. "Very well, Lieutenant, you may execute your plan."

Viana saluted, then turned, and called out, "Sergeant, prepare to fire on my signal."

There was a rustle up the line as men clicked off safeties. However, even as Viana raised his arm, the mass on the tree began to flow upward. With a clicking and rasping from the jostling of thousands of scaly bodies, the creatures rapidly flowed up the trunk. The treetops rustled and shook as the mass traveled from tree to tree. It was hard to tell which way the things were going and for a moment, Marcus feared they'd drop down upon them. However, the sounds faded as the mass moved away, scurrying through the canopy to the east. In a matter of moments, the surrounding treetops were vacant.

Antinasio and Viana looked at one another for a second, and then Viana turned and stepped into the open.

Marcus said, "Be careful."

Viana nodded. With a quick glance to verify his platoon was still in position, he motioned Julio to accompany him. The two men moved cautiously from the shelter of the trees, stopping every few steps to scan the canopy above. They splashed across the stream, and Viana gestured upward with a few words to Julio. The private nodded, stopped, and looked up, searching the shadows above for signs of movement.

Viana went over to the two prone men and kneeled down beside them. A second later, he stood and called back across the stream. "Medic! Quickly! Ernesto is still alive."

Three men emerged from the brush and hurried over. Marcus splashed across the stream right behind them. The platoon's medic rushed to Ernesto's side while the other two spread out, joining Julio in pointing their rifles at the treetops.

Marcus hesitated a moment, surveyed the scene, and then walked over to the men lying in the mud. As he drew closer, he saw that one of the men's neck and chest had been torn to bloody shreds. Marcus knew him well.

Corporal Juan Assino was only twenty years old with an even younger wife he was very much in love with. Juan had beamed when she'd accompanied him to a cookout last summer. Marcus sighed. Juan was the first man he had ever lost on a mission. A shiver went up his back with the premonition he might not be the last.

The other man, Private Ernesto Lassender, moaned with pain when the medic began wrapping up a long, ragged tear in his shoulder.

The medic looked up and said, "He has lost a lot of blood. But he has a good chance. He will need to be carried back to the boats."

Viana smiled and said. "Don't worry Ernesto. We'll take good care of you."

"Hang in there, Ernesto," Marcus said. "You'll be home in no time."

Ernesto smiled back weakly and the thumbs up sign.

Marcus turned and squatted by the contorted body of a nearby creature. He drew out his combat knife and probed at it. Purplish fluid oozed from a hole in the hard scales. Using the blade, he flipped it over. A bullet had passed completely through it. The thing's proportions were all wrong, violating any sense of what he would expect to find.

First, it had a lopsided body that was thicker on one side. Next, it had eleven legs arranged in a jumble of different lengths. It looked wrong to his eyes, different from any creature he had ever seen or even heard of. Two of the legs had long, sharp claws covered with red. No doubt, it was blood from one of his men.

He shuddered with revulsion but forced himself to continue. If he had to find something to compare it to, an oversized tick came to mind, though the misshapen creatures would make a tick seem positively appealing in comparison. It had a small head with huge eyes. Antennae or horns of different lengths protruded from all over the head and body at random angles. He could not find any sign of a mouth or nose. He stood and counted the other plate-sized bodies. Five of them lay under the tree; none showed any sign of life. *Thank God for that.*

"Wrap two of these up," he said, nudging one of the tick-things with his foot. "We will send them back to the base. I fear General Fernando will not believe us otherwise."

A short time later, Marcus dispatched a runner with one of the tick things and a hasty report. They had left two-man relay posts strung out on the trail behind them to help speed any messages. Nevertheless, it would still take almost twenty hours for his report to reach General Fernando—about ten hours for the message to reach the patrol boats and another ten hours by boat to Manaus. For one used to instant information flow, it was a slow, painful way to communicate. There would be no help if they needed it, a sobering thought.

He assigned four men to carry Ernesto out of the forest. The trip would take at least four days. Counting Ernesto, the death of poor Juan, the messenger, and the litter detail, he had in effect lost seven men. Another dozen was strung out behind them in the relay posts. PBG 31 was fast losing combat power, and they had not even located the source of the interference.

He gazed down at Juan's body for several long moments. Should he have it carried out now? It would mean losing four more men from his dwindling command, just when he might need them most.

The idea of burying the man here, in the ravenous jungle, saddened him a great deal. He had never lost a man before and felt strongly that Juan should be taken home and be buried by his family and friends. However, to send four more men away now could put others at risk if they ran into further trouble. Setting his shoulders with determination, he decided it would be best to leave him here. Sentiment could wait; they had a job to do. He must be strong, for his men and his country.

"Sorry, Juan," he said under his breath. "We will come back for you and take you home to your wife." He glanced at the bodies of the strange creatures nearby. "If we are able." In a louder voice, he said, "Lieutenant. Have this man wrapped in his tent and bury him here. Mark the grave well. We will retrieve him after we complete our mission."

They buried Juan, and Marcus held a brief ceremony. He choked up a little at the end. The faces of the company reflected deep sorrow and more than a touch of fear under camouflaged bush hats. All of them could not help but consider their own mortality in a different light as they stared at the grave. After Marcus finished, the soldiers maintained a long silence that even the jungle seemed to respect.

"Alright, PBG 31," said Marcus. He did not raise his voice, but the sound of made several of the men jump. "Time to head out. We have a job to do."

The men moved almost as if they were in a trance at first.

Then Lieutenant Viana's voice barked. "Hop to, 3rd Platoon. You know the drill."

This broke the spell and in short order, the company sorted itself out into their traveling formation and resumed the trek toward the source of the mysterious interference. The men now moved with more caution. Everyone looked up frequently, scanning the canopy for lumpy black shapes with sharp talons. There was less talking. The sounds of chopping from machetes blazing the trail ahead echoed through the forest with a haunting cadence. Juan's death weighed on the men's spirits, adding to the fear and tension of their already difficult trek.

Amazon Harvest

Chapter 8
David

A grunt of frustration escaped David as he watched his game avatar die a horrible death. The games he relied on to block out the world, to hide in, had lost their luster. The escape he craved was not there, and he very much wanted to escape. Recent events were driving a seismic shift in his life, forcing him to consider a future that was unimaginable a few days ago. Now the games just did not satisfy his needs.

One of his favorites had him trying to escape zombies by running through obstacles in a jungle. At first, it had been cool. It had been a release to slip into the make-believe world and escape his troubles. Then the game began to seem silly, especially after the canoe trip yesterday. No one would try to do the things the dude in the game did. It was impossible to maintain focus, and the zombies kept catching him.

However, it was far worse when the game was too real. After giving up on the zombie game, he had tried a first person combat game. However, he when he found himself shooting down a helicopter with a rocket launcher, he had nearly lost it. Images of Sally flashed into his head as the game aircraft went down in a fiery mass. It was too close his fears about his sister. He dropped the tablet as if it was white hot. With a sigh, he put the tablet back in his pack. At least The Memory wasn't nagging him, even without his games. Apparently being scared and worried out of your wits tended to refocus your emotional triggers, but it wasn't worth it.

The church had set up an awning in the square to provide shelter from both the rains and the sun. David had it to himself right now. The townspeople shunned it during the day, probably because the mountains were hard to ignore from any of the six tables. Most of the town avoided looking at them as much as possible. Their existence violated what people knew to be true. The sight of the two bone-colored peaks rising over the jungle was haunting and disturbing.

David was not thrilled with the view himself. However, at least there was a breeze here, which was more than could be said for the interior of the church. River traffic had been disrupted, and the barge carrying diesel to Rio Estrada was late. This had forced the town to cut off electricity during the day to conserve fuel. This meant the church didn't even have a fan to stir the heavy air, much less light, or air conditioning.

Without his games, the mountains called his eyes—the towering peaks were impossible not to look at, especially the tallest one. Yet despite the magnetic draw, the scene could not hold his mind, at least not totally. While he stared at the large peak, his mind went 'round and 'round. His sister, the mountains, his future, his life, his mother, and his father all zipped through his brain in succession, and then started over. Nothing was making any sense.

  Thoughts of his father stayed the longest and hurt the most. As bad as his father's hanging had been, it was not what damaged David's spirit the most. Rather, it was the knowledge that his father had left when David when he really needed him. His mother had been taken, which was terrible, but she did abandon him. Father had left entirely on his own. If David wasn't worthy enough to keep his father, then was he worthy of anything? Was he even worthy to go on living? Maybe not, but the idea of dying scared the hell out him.

  Now, with Sally gone, if he didn't want to give up on living, he would have to start taking care of himself. But he didn't know where to start. Solving problems and taking action had never been his thing. Sally had always been there to guide him. It was something he had taken for granted. Most of the time it was guidance he hadn't even wanted. Now he missed it, and her, with all his heart.

  Should he talk to Heather? She was only a couple of years older than he was. However, she really had her act together, or at least she seemed to. She had said something about helping him figure it out, hadn't she? The problem was he had a hard time talking to women other than his sister, especially pretty ones. And Heather was certainly pretty with her long auburn hair and flashing green eyes.

  Forcing his eyes away from the mountains, he looked across the plaza where she was working with Paul on his latest contraption. She wore tight green shorts and a loose gray shirt, intently studying the screen on a laptop. The shorts were a bit distracting.

  Why did girls like to wear such tight clothes? It for sure did not make talking to them any easier. The idea of going over to her was both appealing and terrifying. She had always been friendly, but probably due to his sister more than anything she felt toward him. Could she help him find a direction? Maybe give him some idea where to start? At least asking her would be a start in a way. Due to his father, he tended to trust women over men, but if she had no useful advice, then maybe Paul would help.

The rig Paul and Heather had set up was composed of five small TV satellite dishes, each hooked up to a smart phone. These, in turn, were hooked up to Paul's laptop. The satellite dishes had window screen mesh taped around them in the shape of expanding cones. Paul had dragged David all over the village to help beg for materials from the locals. People looked at them like they were crazy. But it hadn't been all that hard to get a dozen of them since none of it worked now that the mountains had arrived.

Heather had been almost as enthusiastic as Paul over the setup in the square. Despite her derisive comments about it being a waste of time to learn more about the mountains, she would not have been pursuing a degree in science if she hadn't been drawn to the same 'need to know' as he. They had labored all morning while David tried, and failed, to get into his games.

Near noon, the priest who had greeted them last night, Brother Lorando, exited the church, blinked, and headed across the plaza to Paul and Heather. He wore a long brown robe despite the heat. After they all smiled and nodded cordially, he said something to them in Portuguese. Heather and Paul looked at one another in confusion, and then Heather waved for David to come over.

David walked over and said, "Greetings, Brother Lorando."

"Ah, David," the brother replied with a smile. "I have found a man with a boat that may get you upriver."

David relayed this to the others.

"Awesome," said Paul. "Let's go check it out."

The priest led Paul, Heather, and David out of town, through the forest, and down the ridge to a ramshackle hut on stilts beside the river. The man he introduced them to was a hard-looking character. Tall and burly with arms and neck covered in tattoos. His face had a perpetual scowl that made David nervous. When he learned who they were, however, his face lit up with a big smile that, to some extent, softened his features.

Raul Carlos Santos hailed from Columbia. He came to Brazil three years ago to escape the turmoil at home. He smiled as the priest introduced him to the three North Americans. After shaking their hands, he nodded to David and said in passable English, "You sister, I worked wir her and the tall black laady the night of the Demonia Wavees. I will glad to help you if

I can."

David nodded with a half-smile. If they could get back to the camp, at least he would know if Sally had made it that far. "When can we leave?"

Raul frowned. "Uh, I sorry, but only take one. My boat is small and the river it not so deep dis time of year. And, umm, well, you too beeg."

David's shoulders slumped. It was not the first time he had heard that.

Paul said, "How about me?"

Raul looked him up and down and nodded. "She would be best," he said, twitching his finger toward Heather. "But you do. No baggage. Water, food, chainsaw, gun. That all. If way is clear, maybe bring one, maybe two back. But we not know till get there."

"What about the tree?" said Heather.

"Tree?" said Raul.

"Yeah, that might be a problem," replied Paul. "There's a Kapok tree across the channel about halfway to the camp."

Raul ran his hand through his thick, black, unruly hair. "Kapok tree. Dey very beeg. Better bring special equipment." He went into the shack and came out holding a hand-cranked wood drill and several sticks of dynamite.

Paul chuckled. "Special equipment?"

Raul nodded. "Kapok go kaboom. No problemo. Trees fall on water often. I blow dem up all da time."

Paul said, "Sounds like a plan to me. Can we leave today and make it by dark?"

"No problemo," Raul said with a wave upstream. "She ready to go. If we gonna go, best go now."

A little way upstream, behind some brush, a small, four-seat, gray aluminum boat floated near the shore tied to a tree stump. The rear of the boat sat low in the brown water, weighed down in back by a big motor mounted to a large wooden two-blade prop in a cage. The boat did not have a raised seat like the ones David had seen in movies of the Everglades. Instead, the motor and fan swiveled on a gimbal mounted on a platform where the back two seats would have been. A long pole with a throttle lever on it protruded from the motor between the back seats.

"Okay then." Paul placed his hand on David's shoulder. "Don't worry. We'll be there and back before you know it." He turned to Heather and said, "Well, the rig should be working. Those readings are probably for real. I'd run those tests we talked about before saying anything though."

Heather nodded. She was no electrical engineer, but her major in biological engineering gave her an understanding of basic electronics and physics.

Raul stuffed the drill and dynamite into a duffel bag sitting by the shacks door. Hanging underneath the shack was a large red chainsaw. He pulled it off its hooks, checked the gas tank, and nodded. Then he picked up the duffel bag and headed for the boat.

Paul chuckled softly. "Well, this guy don't mess around."

He waved at the three staying behind, turned, and followed Raul. In a few minutes, the men were seated and the boat untied. They shoved off from shore. Raul started the motor and with a roar and another wave from Paul, they headed upriver and out of sight.

Brother Lorando led them back to the square. He accepted their thanks with a smile and a nod and walked back to the church.

Heather frowned and headed for the array of window-screen-wrapped TV dishes, cell phones, and the laptop. Everything was as they had left it. The villagers didn't want any part of the researchers' mumbo jumbo.

"What did Paul mean by 'the readings are probably real?'"

Heather shrugged and said, "We aren't sure what we're picking up. Give me a minute."

Heather bent over the screen on Paul's laptop. She pulled up a menu and entered some data. A graph appeared. Frowning, she entered a string of numbers and then studied the graph. She pressed a key, and four other graphs came up. Shaking her head, she looked toward the jungle and huts that made up the north side of the square.

"What's the matter?" David asked.

She jumped at the sound of his voice, then smiled and ran her hand through her sweat-dampened hair. "Nothing, just trying to figure out what these readings mean."

"What, these graphs on the laptop?"

She nodded. The screen had five active graphs, all of which

showed jumping wavy lines. One graph didn't change much; the wave on it was flat-lined at the top, occasionally spiking downward a fraction. The others were near the bottom of their depicted graphs, jumping up about a quarter way up the scale from time to time.

Heather tapped the maxed-out graph and said, "Well, this is from the mountains. Something over there is putting out some serious wattage. It's like one continuous lightning bolt that never stops. Though, if I'm reading Paul's scale right, it's even stronger. Like, crazy strong. Powerful enough to screw with FM and cell phones, which are not very susceptible to interference. Even lightning usually doesn't do that."

"So you're trying to figure out how strong it is?"

She shook her head. "No, that's pretty clear. No clue how the signal is generated, but… Well, the thing is…"

David could hear the tension in her voice. "What?"

"Well…" She tapped the maxed out graph again. "This one is easy." Then she touched the other four in turn. "These…well, at first we thought it must be interference from the really big one. But…But that doesn't make sense." She pointed at the dishes. "Those cones Paul set up should be effective at making those dishes directional. But when the big one dips down, at least as down as it ever goes, these other four go crazy. It's like these others are timing their signals to the big one, like they are communicating."

A cold chill went through David. "Like there is more than one out there."

Heather nodded. "Like there are a whole lot of ones out there." She waved her arm to encompass the entire north side of town. "Like, from all over out there."

"Oh crap."

She looked out at the jungle with worried, nervous eyes. "Yeah, oh crap is right. I'm not sure, though. I really wish Paul were still here. He thought we should tell the priest, or those naval guys."

A panicked yell caused both of them jump. A local Indian boy of about eleven, wearing only a loincloth, burst out of the trees in front of them running as if the Devil were right behind him. "Help! *Lastra afue! Democias!*" he yelled in a mix of Portuguese and one of the local Indian tongues. "Devils have the trees!" the boy screamed in Portuguese as he raced past them toward the Naval de Brasilia office.

110

Villagers in the square looked up in confusion. Many of them glanced at the mysterious peaks rising above the trees with apprehension on their faces. The boy reached the office, fumbled with the door a moment, threw it open, and rushed inside. His next words were unintelligible, but the terror in his voice carried outside. People began drifting toward the office, anxious to hear what strange new event may be afoot. David met Heather's eyes and saw his fear mirrored in her deep green irises.

"Come on," said Heather. "We'd better see what's up." They walked over to the office and joined the small crowd trying to listen to what the boy was saying.

After several minutes of the boy babbling loudly in two languages, a man's voice shouted in anger. The door to the office banged open, and Lieutenant Goulart stormed out looking flustered. The sight of the small crowd outside caused him to stop and he gave an angry glare at the people who had gathered around the office. The boy, crying and blubbering, followed him out, bumped into his leg, and sank to the ground, his face in his hands.

Goulart looked down at him, his face warring between frustration and pity. "Can anyone make sense of what this boy is saying? He is talking crazy."

David did his best to translate for Heather what was going on.

A middle-aged woman, followed by a girl of about thirteen, slid through the crowd. She kneeled beside the boy, grasped his chin, and stared into his eyes. Then she enfolded him in a protective hug.

"Do you know this boy?" asked Lieutenant Goulart.

"Yes. He belongs to a small group of Yanomami Indians northeast of here."

"Well, he is talking crazy. Something about demons attacking his family, killing his dog, and carrying off trees." Goulart touched the side of his head and raised his eyebrows. "Is there something wrong with him?"

The woman frowned. "No. The tribe converted to Christianity and his family usually attends mass the same time I do. He is only now learning Portuguese, but he has always seemed very bright and polite."

The girl kneeled beside the boy and leaned close. After listening to him mumble for a moment, she said, "He says things are carrying off the trees, huge things. And other, smaller demons are everywhere." The girl had a worried expression as she addressed the Brazilian officer. "I only understand a little of his language, but I think something very bad has happened."

Goulart scowled. After a moment and with obvious reluctance, he said, "Well, I guess I'd better get out there and check it out."

Heather nudged David. "Tell them. Tell them about the signals."

David shrank back, shaking his head. Heather gave him a withering look. Reluctantly David nodded and said in a quiet voice, "Uh, there's something you need to know." No one paid any attention. Heather nudged him again. A flash of anger went through him and he said much louder, "Excuse me! There is something you need to know."

The people in front of him jumped at his tone and turned toward him. The other villagers also focused on him, most with frowns. With annoyed murmurs, the group began to move and back away to clear a path to Goulart. Once a lane was open, the officer glared at him.

"What?" the Brazilian said. "What do we need to know?"

David took a half step backward, looked at Heather for encouragement, and then stammered, "We've picked up some signals coming from around the village. There seems to be something moving out there. Things that may be part of the mountains."

The townsfolks' annoyed expressions transformed to ones of fear in a ripple around David. Some began praying while others whispered to one another with glances at the strange pile of equipment in the square. Many of them scanned the plaza in all directions as if expecting a beast from hell to leap into their midst at any moment. David could see the fear building in the crowd; he felt it building in himself.

Lieutenant Goulart yelled, "Be still!" The crowd quieted as he stepped closer to David. "What do you mean? What things are moving around the village?"

The man's intensity made David flinch. After another tentative glance at Heather, he said, "Uh, the signals we picked up…" He wasn't sure how to explain and looked helplessly at the equipment beside the fountain. "Um, maybe I should show you."

Goulart nodded and gestured for David to lead the way. All the people in the square followed them over to the equipment and crowded around. "Get back," snapped Goulart. "Give us some room!" He turned to David. "Show me what you mean by signals."

With occasional help from Heather, he described the nature of the equipment and the signals. As he talked, the people behind them mumbled and fidgeted.

It seemed to David that the four weaker signals were peaking higher now than they were before. Did this mean whatever was out here was getting stronger? Or…even worse, closer? His already knotted stomach clenched even tighter.

Goulart nodded when he finished, his eyes following the arc scribed by the shielded satellite dishes. "Can you point these two," he said, gesturing at the two outside dishes, "further away from the mountain?"

"No problem," said Heather when David translated the request. She picked up the poles holding the dishes and turned them so that they faced ninety degrees away from the mountain. Then she, David, and Goulart gathered around the laptop.

The two images recording information from the dishes did not change. If anything, the one on the left, now pointing west, was spiking even higher.

Goulart tapped the screen and said, "What does this mean? Why is this stronger?"

"Whatever is to the west is either getting stronger, or closer," Heather said through David.

Goulart nodded to where the woman and girl were still consoling the boy. "His tribe lives northwest from here." He drew in a deep breath, rubbed his chin, and stared at the mountains.

The townspeople behind them began moving away, breaking into small groups and having animated discussions. A lot of them headed for the church or hurried away from the square. David wondered how many were on their way out of town. Although, with few to no boats available, there weren't many places they could go.

Goulart turned to one of the villagers still lingering nearby. "Go to the docks and get Corporal Luiz," he commanded. The man gave a quick nod and ran off. Goulart turned to three large men whose clothing marked them as being from the lumber mill. "I need you to get your guns and meet me here in ten minutes. Can I count on you?"

The millworkers glanced at one another, and the one in the middle nodded to the officer. He set off at a jog with the other two following close behind.

With a nod to David and Heather, Goulart stalked back to his office.

Heather nudged David and said, "You should ask him if we can go along."

David gaped at her. "Are you crazy?" He pointed at the laptop. "Something is going on out there, and I want to stay as far away from whatever it is as possible."

Heather shook her head with a frown. "Stay away where? In case you hadn't noticed, those signals are coming from all around Rio Estrada. Where do you think we can go?"

"Well…" David eyed the laptop. "I don't know. But I sure as heck don't want to get any closer to whatever is doing all that. Maybe we should go to the river and get our canoes."

"And go where? Paddle to Manaus?"

David snorted. "No. But we passed other villages on the way. We could go to one of those."

Heather said, "Those villages were on the Japura River. It's at least as far to there as it was coming here from the camp. Besides, what about Sally? If the helicopter comes back, they would never find us."

David shrugged. "Yeah, I guess you're right. But that doesn't mean we need to go heading off into the jungle."

In front of the Naval de Brasilia office, Lieutenant Goulart was organizing the men he had sent for. A young soldier in uniform, obviously Corporal Luiz, joined him. Both men had military-style rifles. In addition, the three millworkers had returned, carrying hunting rifles, with eight others holding shotguns or pistols. Goulart nodded in approval as he greeted the newcomers.

An old, faded red farm tractor rumbled up the street towing a large flatbed trailer. When the tractor reached the group of men, the engine chugged to a stop, and Goulart walked over to talk to the driver.

Heather said, "There are a lot of men with guns. That will probably be the safest place we could be."

David didn't feel that way at all. "Nope, no, and nope. Not going to do it."

Heather sneered at him and snatched up her backpack from beside the laptop. "Fine. You stay here. I'll go. Not knowing what is going on out there is driving me crazy."

The idea of Heather going off and leaving David alone was very disconcerting. As she began walking across to the trailer, he fidgeted in indecision. *Damn, damn, damn.* With a sigh of resignation, he shouldered his own backpack and hurried after her. "Hey," he called out. "Okay, you win."

Heather turned with a triumphed smile. "All right! I knew you would. Don't worry; I won't let anything happen to you."

Her ability to manipulate him angered David. It was what his sister liked to do. When she didn't flat-out him order him around, of course. But what else was he going to do? He already felt desperately lonely, and Heather was the only person who might give him guidance. To avoid further conflict, he stared down at his shoes and nodded. Heather's assurance of safety did not comfort him in the least. In fact, he felt scared as hell.

The trailer was made of a metal frame sitting on four wheels, two on each side set close together. Wooden planks made up the bed. It sat low to the ground, a little over knee height to David. There was a chest-high wall on the front, but not on the sides. Instead, metal poles stuck up every few feet all around its twenty-five-foot length.

Goulart and Luiz leaped on and stood holding onto the wall at the front. An older man joined them and pointed toward a dirt road leading out of the plaza between a small group of trees and a large thatched hut. More men piled on behind them, sitting cross-legged on the wooden slats or on the side of the trailer with their feet dangling inches above the pavement. There were fifteen armed men on the trailer, though it still had plenty of room. A few seconds later, the old, hard-worn tractor chugged to a start with a coughing rumble and a cloud of smoke.

Heather gave David's arm a tug and said, "Come on." She trotted over to the rear of the trailer and sat down next to a metal pole set in the center.

David hesitated, and she frowned at him while motioning for him to join her. "Man, oh man, oh man," he said under his breath. He jogged over to her and sat down on the other side of the pole even as the trailer lurched into motion with a soft squeal. Lieutenant Goulart frowned at them for a few long seconds and then shrugged and went back to watching the road over the front wall of the trailer.

The tractor lumbered off the concrete of the town square onto a narrow dirt track. Its tires made a crunching sound as they rolled along, kicking up an occasional rock or clump of mud. It took a few moments for the old reddish tractor to pick up speed, but soon they bounced along at about twenty miles per hour. David and Heather had to hang on to the metal pole to keep from being bounced off the back. The trail wound back and forth through huts, wooden shacks, and an occasional old mobile home.

Most of the huts showed damage from the strange storm and villagers were working on many of them. A few of them waved, but most only stopped and stared with concern on their faces as the trailer full of armed men rumbled by.

David had not been outside the square during his previous visits and was surprised at the number of people working in only loincloths, both men and women. A group of women and girls carrying bundles on their heads were forced to the side of the road by the tractor's passage. None of them wore anything but strings of beads above their waist. Several of them waved, but all David could do was gawk.

Heather punched him in the arm.

David felt as though he had been caught with porn in church.

"Uh," he said, his face turning red.

"Yeah, 'uh,'" she replied with a smile and a shake of her head. "It's not polite to stare. Around here that's how a lot of folk dress."

"Yeah, I know. It's just that in town you don't see so many…"

She snorted. "Yeah, I know what you don't see so many of. This is the Amazon, you know. Now mind your manners."

They met several more groups of local men and women coming up the road, all similarly dressed. The villagers had to move into the tall grass and brush lining the road to let the tractor and trailer chug past. There were more than a few frowns, but most smiled and waved albeit nervously when they spotted the guns. David kept his gaze firmly fixed on people's faces and waved whenever a reply was appropriate.

The huts thinned out as they traveled and they were soon bouncing along under the layered canopy of the forest. The road became narrower and more rutted, forcing the tractor to a crawl. A shriek made David jump. It was followed by a chorus of screams that grew louder and louder. The trees all around them shook with loud rustling sounds. David ducked down and peaked around the edge of the trailer, searching for the source of the commotion.

"Wow!" yelled Heather over the commotion. "Have you ever seen so many monkeys?"

Hundreds of primates filled the trees around the trailer. All of them screamed furiously as they hurled themselves through the forest canopy, going in the same direction. A direction opposite to the one the tractor was traveling. Howler monkeys, spider monkeys, capuchins, and more that David couldn't recognize were all rushing through the forest.

What do they know that we don't? He turned to Heather and said, "Man, this is not good, not good at all."

Heather glance at him in confusion and then stared past him into the forest beyond. "Oh my," she said.

They were deep enough in the trees that the scant opening proved by the road had not fostered the usual riot of competing vegetation along most roads. They could see quite far and what they could see did not help settle David's nerves.

A host of animals were rushing toward them, all headed in the opposite direction the tractor was traveling, back toward Rio Estrada. Tapirs, wild pigs, capybaras, anteaters, a feral water buffalo, and even a jaguar passed in quick succession. Predators and prey ran together, ignoring one another in their attempt to escape. But to escape what? A fire? Or something else, something David was quite sure he did not want to encounter.

The tractor lurched to a halt, the trailer making a clanking sound as it grated against the tow coupler. The men began talking in tense tones about the animals, which David translated for Heather.

The old man with the Naval de Brasilia officers yelled and pointed up the road. David and Heather stood and peered along the side of the trailer to see what was happening. The road ran straight for a long way here. Perhaps two hundred yards ahead, three women and two men in loincloths were running toward them for all they were worth. The men on the trailer looked at one another and fingered their weapons nervously.

As hard as the men and women were running, it only took a few seconds for them to reach the tractor. One of the women stopped beside the trailer while the others skirted it and kept going. She pointed back the way she had come and yelled in Portuguese in a shrill voice, "Demons! The demons carry the trees. They take everything. There are still people back there, please, help them, help them!" Then she turned and chased after the others as fast as she could go.

David told Heather what the woman had said, but it wasn't really necessary. The terror had been evident in her panicked voice. Goulart and the rest of the men exchanged nervous glances.

Lieutenant Goulart said over the noise, "Demons carrying off trees? That is what the boy said."

"Why would demons want trees?" asked Corporal Luiz. "That does not make any sense."

Goulart rubbed his chin and said, "She said there were people up there. People who need help."

"Something bad is going on up there," said the old man who had been guiding them. "You saw all the animals." He waved his arm at the surrounding forest. The flow of animals had diminished considerably, but monkeys still rustled by overhead, and an occasional tapir or small brocket deer bounded through the trees.

Goulart had a grim expression. "Bad or not, we must go help if we can." He swept his gaze over the men in the trailer. They fidgeted, but after a few moments, one by one, they nodded agreement. Goulart turned and said to the driver, "Okay. Get us moving."

A fresh stab of fear hit David in the chest. He hopped off the trailer and looked back at Heather. "No way. This is it. I'm going back to town."

Heather was obviously frustrated by this, but as the trailer lurched forward, she jumped off with a soft curse. "Damn it, David. These guys are armed to the teeth. We should stay with them."

The trailer picked up speed, making any further discussion pointless. They watched it trundle away, the men on board kneeling along the sides or standing with the Brazilian soldiers and old man at the front wall. None of them even glanced back. They were all fixated on the road ahead.

Heather turned and punched David in the arm again.

"Ow," he said. "Stop it."

"I can't believe you jumped off. Now what?"

"We walk back to town. Or we could wait here and catch a ride with them on their way back."

The road in front of the trailer began to grow brighter; a flickering light now framed it and the men. In addition, as the rumble of the tractor faded, it was replaced with the sound of cracks and pops, as if from the breaking of thousands of tree limbs.

"What's that?" Heather asked. "Is that a fire, or...what?"

More light appeared to the left and right of the road. The cracks, pops, and snaps merged into a kind of crackling roar. The trailer had covered two hundred or so yards when gunshots rang out. David and Heather instinctively crouched down and then looked at each other with strained faces.

"What the—" said Heather. She gripped David's arm as a scream and a fusillade of shots roared from up ahead. It sounded as every man was firing as fast as he could. A long burst came from what had to be one the soldiers' rifles. The tractor swerved right and hit a tree, and the men not braced against the wall went tumbling off the trailer.

Dark shapes flashed back and forth over the trailer, and they could see men firing in all directions. More screams came, and the volume of shots slowed. Panic tinged the yells and there were fewer shots. There was a final long burst, a chattering reverberation that echoed hauntingly through the trees. Then a terrified plea for help could be heard, but no more shots came. There was only the crackling, popping roar as the light coming through the trees grew brighter. By now, it had spread wider, expanding beyond the sides of the road all along the tree line where the trailer now sat in silence.

David turned and ran, his arms pumping and his heavy stomach jiggling. Fear propelled his legs with a speed he never knew he could achieve. Despite this, Heather ran up and past him. She held her arm out in front of him while casting a glance back the way they had come.

"Slow it up, big boy," she said, barely winded. "We have a long way to go. Easy."

David slowed and looked back down the road. He was already panting from the exertion of running only a few dozen yards. The line of flickering light was moving forward at a steady pace, but not so fast they couldn't stay ahead of it by moving at a brisk pace. Not having the breath to respond, he nodded and began striding forward with determination.

They had to make it back to town, they had to. A chill went through him—*so what if we do?* What was there in town to protect them now that the men behind...had...died? *Had all those men just died?* He shuddered with the certainty that they had, every one of them, all dead.

"Oh God," he muttered. "Oh God, oh God, this can't be happening."

Heather met his eyes, her face mirroring his own confusion and fear, but didn't say anything.

"What were those things?" David asked, fighting back a sob. "It looked like they jumped over the trailer."

Heather shook her head. "I don't know. Whatever they were…I don't know, it seemed as if they had six legs."

"Do you think everyone is dead?" David shuddered. "What if those things come after us?"

Heather shrugged. "I don't know. For now, let's just focus on getting back to town."

"Is the forest on fire—is that what's making the noise and that weird light?"

"No, I don't think so. No smoke for one thing. Also…I think I saw something really big against the light. I think something is ripping up the trees."

"Demons take the trees. That's what the boy, and that woman, said. Do you think those could be demons?"

"I don't believe in demons. But…something is doing all this, so I guess demon is as good a name as any right now."

David had a million questions, but he knew Heather did not know any more than he did. Therefore, he saved his breath and concentrated on moving as fast as his exhausted legs could carry him. They half walked and half jogged up the road toward town, gaining a little on the noise and strange flickering light behind them, but not much.

No more monkeys scrambled overhead, though creatures flashed by in the forest to their left and right; shadows that moved in leaping bounds did not look quite right. Large, bear-sized shapes that David swore had four legs and two arms and carried long, serrated swords. He shook his head, refusing to accept what his eyes were telling him.

"This is impossible!" said David after another of the shadowy shapes leaped past them. "Whatever these things are, do you think they came from the mountains?"

Heather looked over her shoulder at the advancing line of light and shrugged. "Probably, but I don't know. We need to keep moving."

"What will we do when we get to town? Lieutenant Goulart was the closest thing the town had to a police force. Now...?"

Heather shook her head again and said in an annoyed tone, "For the hundredth time, damn it, I don't know. I don't know, I don't know. One thing at a time. Save your breath and keep going."

Huts began to appear along the road as they entered the outskirts of Rio Estrada. Where people had been working before, there was now no one in sight. The crackling and popping behind them masked any other sound, but David doubted there would have been anything to hear anyway.

At long last, they spotted the tall spire of the church marking the center of town. Even Heather was panting at the frantic pace, and Davie was near collapse.

The plaza was empty when they stepped onto the concrete that marked the border of the town square. They both searched the area with desperate eyes, seeking escape or shelter. The roaring cracks and advancing light was not far behind them.

"Where now?" asked David, fighting for breath. "The church?"

Heather frowned and shrugged. "I don't think so. I don't want to get trapped in there. I'm not willing to bet a church will stop them, even if those things really are demons."

"The river!" David said. "The canoes."

Heather nodded, and they hurried down the road towards the docks. They ran hard along the concrete road between the stalls and shops and then ran past the bars to where the road crested the hill. Once there, they skidded to a stop.

One look at the scene below made it obvious there was no escape there. The area seethed with violent confusion. David guessed at least two hundred people were fighting for maybe a half dozen small boats. The result was a full-scale riot on and near the docks.

Damn, everyone in the village must have headed here to escape. David felt sick and panic battered at his self-control.

"Oh my God!" said Heather. "That man shot that woman!"

The sound of a shot echoed up the hill as a dark-skinned, bare-breasted woman in a grass skirt staggered backward and toppled into the river. A few people paused, but most were oblivious to the murder and continued to fight for the few available boats. The normal cooperation of the frontier town was gone, inundated by a wave of pure terror.

After giving a terrified glance back up the hill where David and Heather stood, a man decided to brave the river. He jumped into the brown water and began swimming with fear-laced energy toward the far bank. A moment later, three other men and one woman followed. Then six or seven more leaped in after them. They did not get far.

First the lead swimmer and then the woman following began to convulse, thrash, and scream in agony. The voracious red piranha had been drawn to the splashing water. Now blood joined the thrashing, and the fish went into a frenzy. The water around the man and woman boiled red.

Two more men started to scream and thrash as more murderously aroused fish arrived. Ever larger schools of piranha rushed to the docks, drawn by the frantic splashing and copious amounts of blood. The fighting paused as people froze to watch in sick fascination. Not everyone in the water was attacked, but nearly so. A young girl standing in the shallow water beside the dock also began screaming and ran for the bank. She did not make it.

Large swaths of the river now boiled red. The sight triggered an even greater panic, and the mass of people seemed to convulse nearly in unison as the fighting resumed. More shots rang out as the fight for the few boats grew even more violent and desperate.

"Maybe this is the apocalypse," muttered David. Bile rose in his throat; he had never seen so much blood outside one of his precious games. In addition, this blood was real, too real by far. "There's no escape that way. Now what?"

With her eyes fixated, almost as if mesmerized, on the docks, Heather said, "Let's head through the jungle along the ridge, go upriver away from that mess. Maybe we can slip past, or at least get far enough up stream that we can risk crossing. It looks like every damn piranha in the Amazon is down there for the feast." A loud crash came from nearby and she jerked around, searching for the source. "Those things are getting closer."

David nodded. The sounds of the village's destruction roared from all around. Chickens and pigs ran squawking and squealing in all directions. They didn't have much time. Turning to the right, they ran off the road and into the trees.

After running a short distance, the exertion caught up to David and his side cramped up, doubling him over in pain. Heather came back, placed her arm around him and half carried, half dragged him through the foliage.

The bulk of Rio Estrada sat on a hill above the high watermark of the wet season. The undergrowth along the ridge and leading down to the river was almost park-like due to the traffic of villagers going to the water. However, there were still a lot of trees, and the light was dim. The thick trunks quickly dampened the sounds of battle at the docks. Although the hissing cracks and pops, which were characteristic of the forest's destruction, roared from all around.

Shadows fleeted through the forest to their left and right as they stumbled forward. Most of the shadows that passed them came and went too fast to determine if they were even real, much less what they might be. Some of the shadowed forms were villagers seeking escape. Sometimes the shadows rushing past were, odd, lumpy, dark shapes. These inhuman shapes could be seen running down villagers and leaping on them. Twice when this happed, an anguished scream echoed through the forest that cut off with bone-chilling abruptness.

David's legs felt like rubber and he gasped for breath. His side was a blaze of pain. The terror coursing through his veins was not enough to overcome years of physical inactivity. Heather tried to bear some of his weight and had her shoulder under his arm to help support him. They staggered drunkenly as they hurried through the half-light under the trees. David expected her to leave him any moment and clung to her like a drowning man.

The dimness seemed to brighten a bit, and David looked up in confusion. All around them, light flicked through the trees. This was very important, but in his exhausted, lumbering state, he couldn't remember why. He looked down at Heather, but her head was bent under the weight of his arm and she was focusing all her attention on the ground right in front of them, trying to avoid roots and vines.

Disaster struck from the shadows cast by the flickering light. David spotted a huge shape as it emerged from behind a large tree. Stumbling to a stop, he screamed, "Stop, damn it, stop!"

Heather stumbled as he stopped, his sudden resistance staggering her. She slipped free of David's arm, skidded on some damp leaves, and fell, rolling to the foot of a monster that came straight from any sane person's nightmare.

This creature was far larger than the bear-shaped things in the forest. It towered over them, twenty feet tall or more. It was snapping branches off a large tree with no more effort than one would a twig, even though each branch was as thick as David's ample waist. Heather was still on the ground, looking up in frozen terror and amazement.

The creature ignored them and continued working on the tree. Four thick legs supported a heavy body covered in sharp spikes. A powerful torso sat like a centaur over the front two legs. The torso was equipped with two long, powerful arms that ended in three-fingered hands, each finger tipped with a heavy claw. It had a small head compared to its body with two gigantic eyes and a short snout that ended in a hole instead of a mouth. Antenna or more spikes sprouted from all over its head.

More shadowy hulks began to appear out of the murk, all slashing or ripping at the surrounding trees. Two stepped up to the same tree as the one towering over them and attacked the base, tearing up huge clumps of soil and hunks of root.

After a moment's hesitation, David surprised himself by stepping forward to help Heather. Her head snapped around, her face contorted with fear.

She yelled, "Go! Run! Run!" She clambered to her feet with her head craned back, looking up at the creature as she staggered back from it. The movement caught the monster's attention and it looked down at her. Before she could turn, white material gushed out of the hole in the short snout, striking her in the head and chest. The enormous force of the stream threw her back into David, knocking both of them down and off the ridge.

They tumbled toward the river, slamming to a halt against a tree forty feet down the hill. David was speckled with the tough, sticky material, but Heather's head and shoulder were covered under a thick, whitish shroud. She began thrashing on the ground, clawing at her face and throat. David shook his head in an effort to clear it and then scrambled over to her side, heedless of the creatures on the ridge above them.

David attacked the material on Heather's face, grabbing the now-solidified substance and pulling with all his might. He screamed as three fingernails on his left hand tore loose, splattering blood across her blanketed face. He ignored the pain and continued wrenching at the webbing, but it was too strong.

Remembering his camping knife, he jerked it from the scabbard on his belt and began sawing, cutting away chunks of material in an effort to clear a patch over her mouth or nose. When he managed to cut away enough to see the lower part of her face, it became obvious the task was hopeless. The material had gone into her mouth and nostrils and congealed. David had seen a show once where someone had cut into a choking person's throat, but he didn't have a clue how to do it.

"Please don't leave," he said. "Please don't leave me all alone."

What could be seen of Heather's face turned blue and her struggles grew weaker. David sat back and stared, helpless as she died in front of him. With a final arching heave, she stopped moving.

David began trembling all over and his eyes misted with tears. Standing, he stumbled back, barely aware of the lumbering monsters coming down the hill until they were right on top of him. Upon reaching Heather's lifeless form, one of them picked her body up and casually impaled it on a spike protruding from another creature's back. A red stain appeared and began to spread across the white material.

David backed away, his mind blank. He knew he should run but couldn't tear his eyes off Heather's form on the side of the creature as it turned toward him. His foot snagged on a root and he fell, landing hard on his rump. The shock of the blow prodded his mind, triggering fear and panic that sent new vigor into his exhausted legs. Digging in with elbows and heels, he scrabbled backward with frantic energy for a short distance, then flipped onto his stomach and pushed himself up off the jungle floor.

Fighting to regain his feet, he staggered forward a few steps and ran headlong into a massive leg. Bouncing back, he looked up into a pair of large, emotionless eyes. He threw his arms up just before a terrific force struck him, slamming him back down.

Dazed, David found himself on the ground with waves of pain searing his left side. One of the creatures jerked him up by his feet and swung him through the air. A second later, he slammed into the side of another creature's spiked back. A searing pain lanced into his back along with a blow that knocked the breath out of his chest, leaving him gasping. The pain spread up his back as his body shifted down and he realized one of the creature's spikes had pierced his backpack and he was stuck like a bug on a pin.

The spike had a slight downward tilt and he slid a bit, easing the pain. He could feel himself inching forward. The ground looked like it was far below, but falling had to be better than where he was. He began rocking his body back and forth and the backpack began to slide a little faster and then pulled free. His motion caused him to fall face first, but only a short distance. The left side of his body from shoulders to his legs was covered in the white, sticky web stuff. As he fell, the webbing around his legs snagged on another spike. He continued to swing down until his plunge was brought to a jerking halt.

His momentum carried him under the behemoth and he barely missed being impaled on another spike protruding from the creature's massive back leg. He swung back and forth several times, spinning around and around.

Only luck had spared him. Bad luck probably, since now this nightmare could only drag on. There was no reason for hope as the creature turned its ponderous bulk and began trudging toward the strange white mountains in the distance.

David's body was a mass of pain from where he'd slammed into the creature and where the initial blast of webbing had struck his left arm and shoulder. The shock, dizzying motion, and hanging upside down conspired to make him nauseated, and he threw up. Tears leaked from his eyes as he choked on the snot and vomit in a struggle to breathe. Hanging from the creature, whose every step made him sway and caused fresh waves of pain, he watched the final moments of Rio Estrada.

By now, the area was stripped bare. The creature David was hanging from joined a long procession of lumbering giants headed toward the mountains. All of them were loaded with trees, white bundles, and people. In addition, several carried objects from the village. Through blurred eyes, David saw two carrying a tractor. Another had the town's diesel generator, and another had the spire from the church. For what purpose, David had no clue. On the other hand, none of what was happening made any sense. If not for the pain, he would believe it to be a nightmare. However, everything was far too real for such a mercy.

The Ruins of Rio Estrada

Scattered about the ravaged expanse where a thriving frontier town once existed were several piles of stone and brick, but only the docks remained intact to give testament that people once lived here. A few hundred inhabitants escaped across the river and began spreading wild tales about the arrival of strange mountains and demons carrying off trees. However, most of the two thousand two hundred and twenty-six souls who lived in the village vanished with their homes.

In place of Rio Estrada and the surrounding jungle, there was now a vast field of reddish-orange soil, ripped and torn in to large clumps as if the entire area had been turned with an enormous plow. In the heart of the Earth's mightiest rainforest, the source of one-fifth the world's oxygen, a new desert was in the making.

Chapter 9

Marcus

Marcus Antinasio pushed the Brazilian marines of Patrol Boat Group 31 as hard as he dared through the gloom under the immense trees. Yet every mile they covered made it tougher to face the next. The men walked with their heads hanging low, stumbling over roots and dripping with sweat. The hyperactive awareness exhibited after the encounter with the strange tick creatures that morning faded with each kilometer traveled.

Marcus knew that over time the heat, humidity, rough terrain, and constant stress could be as deadly as any enemy they might face. Nevertheless, he relentlessly kept them moving. His determination to accomplish their mission, to find the answers his country desperately needed, was an unwavering force.

By mid-afternoon however, even Marcus began to sag. They were going slower than they had yesterday. He suspected that as the forest wore them down, they would go even slower. Looking up through the layers of trees, Marcus tried to determine how much time they had before darkness but could not even tell where the sun was through the interlocking branches. According to his watch, they might have two more hours before total darkness.

Someone called from up ahead, the sound echoing with a strange resonance through the trees and vines, but the words were indistinct. The person doing the shouting came closer, and Marcus made out his name.

"Here, over here," he yelled.

A moment later, Private Julio Arente rushed up, showing a level of energy that was in direct contrast to every other man. His uniform did not even have the same stains or wear as the others did. Marcus supposed his small frame allowed him to weave through the fallen trees and undergrowth more efficiently.

"Sir," said Julio. "The lieutenant needs you right away."

"More casualties?" asked Marcus with concern.

Julio shook his head with his brow creased in confusion. "No…but, ah, well sir. There is a mountain, and…a desert."

"A mountain? Up ahead? Are you sure?"

"Absolutely sir. It is… Well, maybe I should have said there is a huge wall up ahead. But…sir, you should come see for yourself."

Marcus knew there were a few large hills, but certainly no mountains in this part of Brazil. Puzzled, he motioned the private to lead him. This was certainly turning into an eventful day. He hoped that whatever waited at the end of this trip would be better than the encounter that morning.

As they weaved their way through towering mahogany and rubber trees, a monstrous Brazilian nut tree blocked the view ahead. The tree was a giant of its kind with a trunk half again as wide as he was tall. The thick wooden column sliced upward through the canopy, and Marcus knew the upper branches would cast shadows over the surrounding trees. Julio led him around the wall of wood, both men looking up with some trepidation. Stories about huge nuts falling from the tree and hitting unwary travelers with killing force were commonplace.

A little way past the Brazilian nut tree, shafts of dazzling sunlight cut through the canopy's gloom like spotlights on a stage. This indicated a large clearing of some kind just ahead. Large clearings were unusual this deep in the jungle, so it was unusual for so much sunlight to pierce the normal gloom of forest. However, it was hard to believe there was a desert up ahead, much less a large mountain.

As they drew near the light, through the thinning trees, he spotted the orange soil so prevalent in the Amazon Basin stretching away from the forest. It appeared to have been churned into large clods and clumps. It reminded him of a farmer's plowed field.

Hardly a desert. As they advanced, the soil seemed to go on and on. *A very large clearing indeed.* Doubt crept into his mind. It would appear there might indeed be a desert up there. Marcus shook his head, but to what he was saying no, it was hard to say.

They crossed from the shadowy forest into a blinding shaft of late afternoon sunlight. Marcus blinked, struggling to adapt to the sudden brightness. Looking up and squinting, he froze with his breath caught in his throat. His mouth slowly dropped open. Across an expanse of churned orange earth, a grayish-white wall thrust skyward. He stepped forward to be clear of the overhanging trees and craned his head back, looking up, up, up at the monolith before him.

"Oh my God," he muttered.

Julio stood beside him, his head also tilted back, and said the only thing he could think of. "Yes, sir."

Perhaps three kilometers from the edge of the jungle, the wall rose straight and sheer for a half mile and more. It was mostly white and light gray with frequent dark red lines, like rusting iron, running through it. There were also areas splotched with dull yellows, greens and light browns. In some areas, the red streaks had reacted with the frequent rains to send rust colored, tear-shaped streaks down the face that looked very much like dried blood.

There were countless jagged ledges, deep fissures, and sharp, craggy spires along the top of the wall, looking like battlements on a huge castle. Marcus looked left and right and saw that the impossible barrier extended out of sight in both directions. High above to the far to the left, almost lost in the hazy humid air, two peaks could be seen poking above the rim of the wall.

The area around the mountain was devoid of life. Julio's comment about there being a desert suddenly made sense. A wide expanse of roiled orange soil stretched out from the edge of the forest, bare except for an occasional large, grayish boulder that appeared to have fallen from the wall. It was like nothing he had ever seen before. None of it should be in this part of the Amazon. If anything, it was as if the wall from a massive lunar crater had suddenly thrust up from the Earth.

"This is impossible," he said in a hoarse whisper. "It cannot be."

Lieutenant Viana walked over and joined them. The three men

stood in silence for several long moments, absorbing the scene before them.

Marcus said in a low tone, "Is that the source of the interference?"

Viana nodded, holding up one of their small tracking devices. The arrow on the dial pointed straight at the imposing white wall.

Marcus shook his head. How could they search such a thing? The sides were steep and scarred with deep crevasses. Travel would be almost straight up, and they did not have any rope or other equipment to undertake such a task. He believed they had prepared for anything. This notion had just been proven utterly and completely wrong.

Shaking his head to get his brain working again, he took out his phone and called up the camera. The mountain itself would be of extreme interest to General Fernando. Antinasio wondered if the joint chiefs would believe his report, even with pictures. Although it towered skyward right in front of him, he found it hard to believe himself.

Viana said, "What are we going to do, sir? Are we going to try to climb it?"

Marcus shook his head. "Not unless we have to. We are not equipped for mountain climbing." He looked at the wide strip of torn orange soil between the wall and jungle. "We will circle it for now. Perhaps we will find a way up. Or maybe we can find some Indians or loggers who have some useful information on how this...this thing, came to be."

Viana nodded. "I believe there is a village, Rio Estrada, not far from here. My family used to go there for supplies when I was a boy. It is on a small tributary that feeds into the Negro River. I am not sure of the exact location, but it should be southwest of here, maybe thirty or thirty-five kilometers. We could reach it in a couple of days. Plus, it is close enough that someone may have seen or heard something."

Marcus took off his hat and squinted in the direction of the mountain. He was leery of getting too far from the boats. They were his only means of communication and, if need be, escape. But having them move would shorten his line of communication and supply, which would be a good thing. So, the village did seem like a logical destination. He nodded. "That is an excellent idea."

Viana looked at the setting sun and gestured to the left. "That way is southwest. We can travel along the tree line. That way will have more light and we should make better time."

"All right," replied Marcus. "We can also keep the mountain in sight." He placed his hand on Viana's arm. "We must keep our eyes open and our wits about us, Jeronimo. I do not like what we have stumbled onto one little bit."

"What can this mean, sir? Mountains where there can be no mountains?"

Marcus shook his head. "I don't know. It is totally beyond me." He squared his shoulders and turned away from the towering wall. "But the general sent us here to find out, and that is what we will do. Get the men up here. Give them a little time to take this in and get over the shock. Then we move out for Rio Estrada."

Sally
The girl died. No big fuss accompanied her passing. One moment she breathed, and then she didn't.

As sad as this made Sally, no tears came. After all the crying she had done the last few days, it would be a wonder if she ever cried again.

"She's dead, Myra," she said. "I'm in a crypt."

A soft chuckle. "Maybe you're a ghost," said Myra, her voice a husky, wooden rasp.

"Am I dead, too?" Sally asked. She pondered that. Maybe she was. Her pulse was strong, though. What would a ghost feel if she tried to take her own pulse? She pursed her lips and shrugged. Who knew? Besides, it couldn't hurt this bad to be dead, could it? "Does it hurt to be dead, Myra?" There was no answer. Myra didn't always answer. Was that a good thing? Sally didn't know anymore.

She studied Myra's ruined face seeking answers. It was getting dark, and there seemed to be an awful lot of flies crawling across it. Sally hated the flies. There was nothing she could do about them except keep herself covered in insect spray. It helped some, but they still landed on her. Each time they did, she flinched, as much from fear over where they had been as the odd tickling sensation they made when crawling on her skin. She hated the flies.

"You are not dead," an answer came at last. "You need to live. You made a promise."

Sally snorted. "Promises. No one made me any promises. Why

should I care?" Then she felt guilty. Her mother had always kept her promises. After all, she hadn't promised not to die. Neither had her father. Although in a way, having children carried a promise of sorts, didn't it? And her father had died on purpose.

"Keeping a promise is more important to you than those you make it to," said Myra.

That was what Sally's mother had always said.

"Okay, okay," Sally said. "Quit badgering me."

As darkness descended on the wrecked helicopter, Sally stirred herself to do her exercises. Every few hours she practiced moving. She had been able to force a little more motion each time. However, it was getting harder and harder to get motivated to start. It hurt like hell. She knew she might be doing damage to her insides, but if she could not recover enough motion to get out of the helicopter, she was dead anyway.

"God, please give me strength," she prayed. It was a prayer she said each time she started to exercise.

"He will, Sally, He will. But you have to make your own strength as well," came Myra's voice from the darkness.

She rolled over inch by inch and pushed herself up onto her hands and knees. Her side was better. However, the impact of the crash had left her bruised and stiff to a degree she had never before experienced. This was what made moving so painful. The internal hurt was easier to bear, but scared her more.

With a moan, she straightened, grabbed a dangling seatbelt strap, and managed to pull herself to her feet. The pain was intense, but so was the elation. She let go of the seatbelt, eased her arms over her head, and touched the opposite wall of the helicopter above her next to the passenger door.

"Good girl," game the creaking rasp.

Sally nodded and grunted with pain as tried to stretch a little further. There was a way to go before she would be able to climb up to the door. At least she had managed to stand—that was a big step from where she had been two days ago. Moving slow and easy, she sat back down, panting from the exertion.

"I'm sorry I talked you into going to Rio Estrada," Sally said in a quiet, guilty voice. "If we had stayed at the camp, none of this would have happened."

There was no reply. With a sigh, Sally closed her eyes and prayed for a restful sleep. The hard floor, terrible smells, tickling flies, and horrid dreams tended to make this difficult. Night came early in the forest canopy and it settled around her, dark and deep. With a sigh, she began another long, lonely night in a tree-bound prison tomb.

David

David faded in and out of awareness during the long, agonizing journey to the mountains. The constant swaying and jerking, combined with shock and pain, both physical and mental, left him in a state of heightened anguish and dim perception. After a long, painful struggle, his mind refused to deal with reality anymore and he escaped into oblivion.

An indeterminable time later, he was roused against his will. His mind tried to cling to the safety of unconsciousness. However, a strong odor of death and decay overlain with a sweet smell intruded his safe haven of denial, demanding his attention. The sweet odor reminded David of chocolate chip cookies, but rather than help dispel the foulness, the sweet tinge magnified it. The smell was so repugnant, the desire to get away from it so powerful, it managed to force him into awareness where mere pain could not. Like a fighter given smelling-salt, he came awake with a spasm.

The spasm hurt. It also served as a reminder that his feet and left arm were bound by webbing. His right arm was free, although this seemed a meager consolation. The worst pain came from his left arm, which was plastered to his body at an odd angle. His back throbbed from where the spike punctured it, but there was no telling if the wound was still bleeding. He remembered how Heather's head had been enveloped in webbing and her frantic struggles growing weaker…and then stillness. An almost warm tingle ran through him when it occurred to him for the second time that maybe that would have been for the best. At least then, this nightmare would be over. The warm tingle was not unpleasant, not unpleasant at all.

The fog around his brain continued to fade and he noticed he was no longer hanging upside down, but rather laying on a rough surface that vibrated beneath him. There was a hum in the air. It was accompanied by squeaks and clanks that came and went from no discernable direction. Blinking his eyes open, he saw that he was in a tunnel with the walls and ceiling sliding by at a steady pace. This last fact required several moments of pondering while his mind struggled with too many strange sights and sounds. Then he realized the walls weren't moving; he was. The rough, vibrating surface underneath made him conclude he must be on a huge conveyor going through the mountain. This was unsettling, but in his confused state, he could not think why.

The walls and high, arched ceiling were made of a white material that looked like granite. There were sparkling sections of quartz and places with rust-colored veins shot through it. Pipes or rods of different diameters and lengths were everywhere, either protruding straight out or running along the wall in no apparent pattern.

Some of the rods set in the roof cast a harsh blue electric light that strained the eyes. The resulting glare produced dark shadows that made details difficult to distinguish.

Nearby were three large lumps that he realized must be people. They lay in contorted positions, partially covered in blood and whitish webbing. *Dead.* It seemed strange how little emotion the concept stirred in him.

The material of the conveyor appeared similar to the white webbing but felt like leather made from some kind of scaly hide. The surface was brownish-green overall, except for patches that were a dull white. The darker parts were from stains and the lighter from repairs would be his guess.

A variety of animals, trees, and dirty white bundles shared the belt with him. Except for the trees, almost everything in sight was wrapped to some degree in webbing. None of the animals showed any sign of life, except for one gray rat that sat a few feet away calmly gnawing at the bindings around its rear legs.

Okay, I'm on a conveyor, nodding to himself with approval, as though the realization were a great accomplishment. *I'm inside the White Mountains*; another nod. He looked at the bundles surrounding him and took a tentative sniff of the foul air.

"Oh my God," he croaked.

His head snapped back and forth and his eyes rolled in their sockets searching for a way to escape with terror-powered desperation. His breath started coming in short gasps with the realization that the conveyor he was riding would end at the smell.

"No!" he screamed and exploded into frenzied motion. He

struggled against the webbing, pulling and jerking at it with his unbound arm. Waves of pain racked his body, but they did not slow his desperate struggle. Rocking from side to side, he thrashed while screaming in fear, pain, and frustration.

The rat stopped gnawing and watched his antics with suspicion, its whiskers quivering in search of danger. David's struggles lasted nearly two minutes. Then, exhaustion and the pain from his injured arm forced him to stop. He lay still, panting like the terrified animal he was, sobbing as tears ran down his face. Awash in despair and self-pity, David cried like a lost, hopeless child.

After a few moments, the panic and fear began to ebb, replaced by a sense of fatalistic acceptance. The smell told him things he did not want to know. He looked over at the rat and found it still working at its bindings with single-minded focus.

Damn, while he wasted time and energy in despondency, the rat kept working toward gaining its freedom. This angered him, which he knew was foolish, but at least it was better than being terrified.

He kicked his bound feet at the rat. "You stupid bastard!" he yelled.

The rat flinched and studied him, its nose wrinkling as small pink eyes evaluated him. After a few seconds, it must have decided he wasn't a threat because it went back to work.

Great, dismissed by a rat. How much lower could his life get? He started to lash out again, but the anger faded. What was the point? He sighed. *What is the point of anything?* It would all be over soon anyway.

He watched the rat work with fatalistic detachment for a while. Damn it, he was not going to let a rat be the better man. *I am probably going to die, but I would at least like to get my feet free.*

He began paying more attention to how he was bound. At least his right arm was free. His left arm, which he had thrown up in a vain attempt to protect himself when the creature had sprayed him, was plastered at an odd angle right below his chin. It was messed up, that much was obvious. How bad would have to wait for later, if there was a later.

A good bit of the webbing was red with blood. It must have flowed down his back while he was hanging upside down. Nothing he could do about that right now either. His waist and torso had only a few white globs plastered here and there. His calves and feet, however, were hopelessly entangled.

He reached for his knife and found the scabbard empty. *Crap.* He remembered using it in the vain attempt to clear the webbing from Heather's face. He must have dropped it. There was another knife in his left pants pocket. A small folding one his father had given him many years ago. Reaching across his body with his free arm, he felt for it. Yes, there it was, underneath the material. His hand found that the entire area was plastered with the tough webbing binding him. He needed his knife to get to his knife.

He tugged at the tough substance for several moments, his already torn and bleeding fingernails leaving red trails across the white. No good, he would never get through the tough material. Then an idea came. Feeling foolish at the simplicity of the solution, he reached inside his pants and grasped the pocket's lining. With a few hard tugs, the thin cotton of his pant pocket pulled free and he had the small knife. The small accomplishment gave him intense satisfaction.

Opening it with his teeth, he began sawing at the bindings on his legs. The feeling of satisfaction faded as the tough material refused to yield to the small blade. The knife was pretty dull since he did not sharpen it very often, and it was not very effective at cutting through the material. He now regretted all the times he used it as a box cutter when they were setting up camp. His father had chastised him for dulling a knife on cardboard when he was only eight years old. As with many things in life, one rarely gave much credit to what parents said until it slapped one in the face.

He looked back at the rat and saw it chew through a final strand. In one fluid motion, it sat up on its hind legs and sniff enthusiastically, seeming to enjoy the reek permeating the air. Then, with an almost disdainful look at David, the rat ran off in the direction the conveyor was traveling.

David knew that if he got loose, he definitely would not head that way. The rat probably smelled something enticing and thought more of food than escape. The idea made David's stomach twist as he turned back to cutting.

The conveyor belt lurched and there was a change in the vibrations, the belt must be going over a different surface. A faint rustling noise carried over the sounds of the conveyor, catching his attention.

Something rustled some white bundled brush just ahead. Then a shadow moved along the wall heading against the flow of the conveyor. Was something coming toward him? He peered anxiously at the top of a small tree near the edge of the conveyor.

There was a movement! Then he relaxed as the rat came scampering back. Unease crept into his awareness when he considered what the rat's return might mean. Nothing he could think of was good.

The rodent ran past him, though it was moving noticeably slower than the speed of the conveyor. "Good luck, dude," David said as it scampered by. It seemed unlikely the small animal would escape whatever fate awaited David.

The conveyor belt gave another lurch, and the belt underneath bumped him around for a moment as it crested a hump. The steady vibrations resumed, though now he was going down a slight slope. This allowed him to see over the debris a little farther down the belt for perhaps two hundred feet until the branches of a large rubber tree blocked his view. Visibility was poor in the harsh, electric blue light. Now he could tell there was a faint haze in the air that glowed blue in the strange light. The smell got steadily worse and his eyes began to water.

David stopped sawing at his bindings when the rubber tree up ahead dropped from view. A muffled crunch came right after that, carried over the sounds of the conveyor. More objects began to fall out of sight. He took in a deep breath to quell his rising panic as he realized The End of the conveyor was fast approaching.

The End of everything as far as he was concerned, and for several long moments, David couldn't tear his eyes that dreadful edge. He gave up trying to cut through his bindings. So far with the dull knife he had only managed to cut a third of the way through his bindings. There was no way he could finish before this ride ended. In resignation, he folded up the small blade and put it in his other pocket. His father had given it to him after all…as if such things would matter much longer.

There were several dozen people ahead of him on the conveyor, none of whom showed any signs of life. *Those are the lucky ones.* It was evident to David humans no longer occupied the top of the food chain, not in this part of the world, not anymore.

A cluster of small trees, and then some people, and then a stream of various animals and plants, vanished. No muss, no fuss. One moment they were there and the next they weren't. The End.

As the conveyor rumbled along, he thought of Sally. *Had she survived?* He seriously doubted it. Ever since they'd watched the airplane explode and fall from the sky, he had feared Sally was gone. The fear had transitioned to near certainty when they'd reached the village and found out the helicopter had already left. Sally's chances of surviving a crash in the jungle were slim at best. He wanted her to be well, but at this point, he did not hold much hope. There seemed even less hope for his own chances. He wondered if he would see Sally and his parents when he died. That would be nice.

The tree preceding him went over The End. The three people a few feet ahead of him fell, along with numerous bundles, all followed by thumps and crunches. Now it was nearly his turn. He prayed that whatever was going to happen happened quickly. As he got to The End, he took in a deep breath, like a swimmer, and then he fell.

Chapter 10

Marcus

Traveling across the torn earth along the tree line proved to be even slower than cutting a trail through the jungle. The churned clumps of soil were wet and sticky. Marcus hated to imagine what it would be like once the rainy season started. The clay-like mud sucked down on the men's feet and clung to their boots in weighted chunks. After stumbling along for a short distance, Marcus moved them back into the jungle.

By staying a short distance inside the tree line, they had more light and avoided the mud, a compromise that allowed them to make decent time. However, the looming never-ending wall served as an unsettling distraction as they traveled. More men stumbled and fell in the first kilometer after they found it than in all those previous. Marcus considered taking them deeper into the jungle, but his burning need to learn more held him, and his men, to the edge of the trees.

Near dark, they came upon a five-hundred-meter-wide swath of torn earth cut at an abrupt angle from the path they were following. It made a wide muddy orange road through the jungle heading directly away from the mountains.

Viana approached Marcus with a worried expression on his face and said in a low voice, "This is close to where I would have turned for Rio Estrada. I was planning to angle more southwest to find the river and then follow it upstream to the village. But I have a strong feeling this trail...err, road, leads toward the village."

Marcus frowned. Until now, they had assumed whatever caused the mountain to appear, or thrust up, grow, or whatever had also been responsible for the wide strip of barren soil around it. Now they had evidence that something else was ripping up the land. The fact that it might lead to Rio Estrada was very disconcerting. "How many people live there?"

"I am not sure," replied Viana. "I would guess two thousand, maybe more. I have not been there since I was a boy. But it used to be a large town during the Rubber Boom days."

Marcus looked up at the darkening sky. "It is too late to go much further today. I want good security set up tonight, so we will stop now. Double the pickets around the camp and make sure everyone stays alert. Hopefully, we will find the village tomorrow and get some answers." He kneeled on the ground and spread out a map. He found the village and traced the river that ran beside it with his finger. "Damn, we could have taken the boats to Rio Estrada in the first place."

Viana nodded. "The directional finders were not accurate enough for us to tell."

Marcus traced a route from where the boats were anchored, back down the Amazon, up the Negro River, and then up the tributary that led to the village. "Nearly five hundred kilometers," he said, taking off his hat and scratching his head. "Well, it makes the most sense for the boats to meet us there. Send a runner at first light to Lieutenant Pereira. Also send orders for the relay posts to fall back to the boats as well. We won't need them anymore."

Viana said. "Yes, sir. It might take Pereira two or three days to get to the village."

"Yes, I know. But it would take us that long to get back to the boats anyway. This way we will have our resources concentrated and close to hand. We will set up a command center in the village." He looked up from the map and scowled at the surrounding forest. "It will be good to get out of the jungle for a while."

David

David landed with a grunt on a pile of leaves and white bundles after a surprisingly short drop. He felt cheated. It was supposed to be The End, after all. Now he was faced with an After, which sucked. Once again his hope faded that this nightmare would end in a painless flash. It was not fair. Now this crap would just keep dragging on.

There was no telling how long his unnatural calm acceptance would last. For now, at least, his emotions were beyond exhausted and he could care less about…well, anything. Belying his lack of concern, he lay back, sighed, and wondered what would come next.

The pile he landed on was very near the center of a huge pit that was covered by a large, rough-cut, domed ceiling. The room was a couple of hundred feet in diameter. The sides of the pit were smooth, but the doom appeared to have been chiseled out of the white granite of the mountain. The pit sat in the center of the chamber, took up about three-fourths of the area covered by the dome, and was surrounded by a wide walkway.

The rough walls of the huge dome had the same crazy arrangement of pipes and rods as the tunnel. Many of the rods gave off the harsh blue light these things seemed to love so much. The bluish tinge gave everything a surreal look. A haze hung over the contents of the pit, thinning to wisps higher up.

Death, and the smell of death surrounded him, making him gag. Human and animal corpses, along with uprooted trees and plants, made a gruesome mound of the dead and the dying. Fluids from the plants and animals merged into a vile concoction that covered everything. The odor made his throat water and his stomach tighten.

Muffled wails and cries came from somewhere out of sight but seemed to come from below. Poor souls who were in an even worse position than David, if that were possible.

The detachment he was maintaining was amazing—no fear at all; he just felt numb. He always considered himself less than brave, but here he was, calm as could be, discounting his nausea, in the most nightmarish situation imaginable. The analytical part of his brain knew this detachment was most likely shock. However, he felt no desire to do anything with this knowledge. He held firm to his belief that death would be a merciful release.

His dive into lethargic acceptance was interrupted by a shout from somewhere above. "Hey, you! Can you hear me? Are you alive?"

The intrusion irritated David. He looked up and saw what appeared to be a large red ape wearing camouflaged pants, a black tee shirt, and a wide canvas belt from which hung a huge pistol and a multitude of pouches.

"Great," he mumbled, his words coming out in a slur. "I mush be worsh off than I thoush. Now I'm halsusinating."

"I saw you move," said the ape. "Can you hear me?"

"Go 'way," David replied, exasperated at the intrusion. "I don' wan' spend my last breaths talkin' to a crazy dream."

"Hey buddy, snap out of it! And I mean right now. I'm trying to save your ass. In a few minutes you'll be mush if you don't get out of there!"

David forced himself to focus on the figure. Damn if it wasn't a man. A short, very wide, hairy man, but a man nonetheless, and he had a rope. Hope flooded through David with the realization he might have a chance to live. He tried to focus his attention and thrust away the lethargy that engulfed him as he rolled over to face the stranger.

"Do I have your attention now?" asked the ape-like man. "I'm going to throw you this rope. Tie it around you, and I'll try to pull you up."

David nodded, fearing to speak lest his benefactor disappear, being in fact an actual hallucination. A thin green rope landed across his back, and he fumbled with his one good arm for a few moments before securing the rope around his chest, right below his injured arm. The rope was thin, maybe a bit over a quarter of an inch thick. It seemed too thin to hold David's weight, but what the heck.

There was a hissing sound, followed by a rumbling noise from somewhere below.

The ape-man glanced down and said, "We're running out of time. I see your arm is messed up, but help as much as you can."

With his feet still bound and only one arm free, David couldn't help much. But between his feeble efforts and the incredible strength of the red-haired man, they made progress, although from David's viewpoint it was agonizingly slow.

The man's arms and chest were huge and his muscles bulged with every tug. Each time the rope pulled him across the debris, it jerked his injured arm and forced out a grunt of pain. The thin braid cut painfully into his skin, but at least it did not break. David nearly called for the man to stop. However, terror had returned with hope and the combination gave him the will to endure.

An eternal two minutes later, the man managed to drag David to the wall of the vat. Then, in a demonstration of unbelievable, raw power, especially considering how thin the rope was, he hoisted David's two hundred sixty pounds hand over hand straight up. At long last, David reached the safety of the rock ledge surrounding the vat and flopped over a low wall to land on a hard, gritty surface.

The man looked almost as much like an ape up close as he had from the pit. He stood maybe a head shorter than David but had to weigh at least as much, all of it muscle. David's fingers would not come close to touching if he tried to encircle the man's massive biceps with both hands. The man appeared to be in his early forties, but it was hard to tell. His hair was a burnished red and cut close to his scalp, actually shorter than the hair covering his arms. He had a heavy brow that made it look like he was squinting all the time in either anger or deep thought. Mostly anger David concluded.

The hissing and rumbling in the vat grew louder. Two or three seconds later, the pile in the pit, made up of the entwined mass of animals, plants, and…people, gave a violent lurch. While the red-haired man began cutting through the bindings on David's legs with a huge knife, David stared down at the pit with wide-eyed amazement and horror.

"My name is Josh O'Brian," said the man. "Welcome to the party. I don't think you'll like it here, but at least you're alive." The dark brown eyes of the heavily muscled redhead looked him up and down appraisingly. "At least for now."

David was not paying much attention to what Josh was saying. Besides shock, he was engrossed with the vat. The contents underwent increasingly violent lurches that rippled through the mass below. Fresh screams of terror, muffled yet easily heard, came with each sporadic jolt.

Josh noticed him staring and paused clearing away the webbing on David's legs, which pretty much entailed the destruction of his blue jeans.

Josh said, "Frog in a blender."

David, puzzled, glanced at him. Josh's gaze was cold as he stared into the pit.

"An old, sick joke," he said. "What is green, red, and white and goes ninety miles per hour?" He didn't wait for a reply. "A frog in a blender."

The contents of the vat continued to lurch spasmodically, accompanied by more screams and loud crunching and grinding noises. The hissing was very loud, and David could see a brownish, slightly viscous fluid creeping up the sides of the vat. As the stuff rose, the smell of chocolate chip cookies grew stronger. The screams faded away, most of them with blubbering, gasping pleas.

The chamber's horrible death smell was not masked in the least by the sweet cookie odor. Rather, it combined with the stench in a nauseating combination that brought bile to the throat. The lurching, crunching, and grinding came faster and faster. Then, in a colossal surge, the entire mass began to rotate. Slow at first, then faster and faster, a huge blender going from chop to liquefy. David now understood Josh's bizarre comment about frogs.

Unidentifiable chunks covered in ooze bubbled up from the depths of the pit. There were frequent bone-chilling crunches and pops from the madly roiling concoction. After a few minutes, the contents of the vat were mixed into a thick, dark soup. The material began to flow smoothly with an occasional lump sucked down into a small dimple in the middle, very much like his blender at home.

All those people! And he had nearly been a part of that disgusting concoction. Bile erupted from his stomach and he threw up over the wall.

Josh looked at him without sympathy. "Yeah, I know how you feel. This thing makes me sick, too. But I got kind a used to it by now."

The level of the mixture in the vat began to go down. The contents drained away revealing large, multi-bladed structures dripping with the ooze. They were spaced evenly around the vat and looked sharp and mean. Except for the edges, each of them would look at home on the stern of a ship. The vat emptied quickly leaving a small puddle at the bottom situated in the middle of four large holes that must be drains.

David looked up at Josh. "Thanks for saving me from…from that."

Josh shrugged. "Yeah, well, I was wanting some help." He looked David up and down, his expression making it plain he didn't hold much hope for that. "Maybe you'll do if we can fix you up. Where did all the blood come from?"

It took a moment for David to understand the question. The webbing around his arm and his shirt were stained red. Seeing the blood made him remember the pain from his back when he was thrown onto the creature's back. Now it started to burn. "My back. I got a spike through my pack."

Josh nodded and eased him forward. With a few swipes of his big knife, Josh cut the pack free and set it to the side, then cut away the webbing on his shoulder and back, along with most of David's shirt. "You have a puncture wound back here, but it doesn't seem to be too deep. Looks like it's almost stopped bleedin'." **He** trimmed off the webbing on his chest and arm, then placed a wad of the webbing onto the wound and bound it in place with strips of the same material. "Well, it don't look like you'll bleed to death. Let's look at that arm." He pushed and prodded David's arm and shoulder for a bit, prompting several grunts of pain. "Hmmm, looks pretty bad. I think your shoulder's dislocated. Upper arm may be broken, too. We'll have to try to pop it back in and hope the break is not too bad."

Josh had David lay back on some webbing. The makeshift bandage made an uncomfortable lump, and the material felt rough and scratchy. David squirmed, but stopped after a stern look from Josh. Josh bundled up more of the material, shoved it under his feet, threw more on top of him, and then walked over to a pile of wood and white bundles sitting against the outer wall. He mused over the pile for a moment, selected a small branch, and nodded. Using his knife, he trimmed it until he had a straight rod two feet long and maybe two inches in diameter. He picked up a smaller stick from the trimmings and some more webbing. Placing the webbing and rod next to David, he then squatted down beside him.

"This is going to hurt. But it will only get worse if we wait. I've never done this before, but at least I seen it done. Bite on this stick, and try not to fight me if you can."

Josh tied one end of the webbing around the rod and the other around David's wrist. He stretched out David's arm and then began pulling on it. David gasped as fire radiated from his shoulder and upper arm. The pain got even worse as the big man worked the injured arm around, trying to get it to pop into the socket.

David tried not to fight, but pure agony coursed through his entire upper body and he began pulling away in an attempt to escape the pain. Josh barely seemed to notice other than to tighten his grip a little. David whimpered with panting gasps, tears streaming down his face.

Josh muttered, "Sorry, kid. Like I said, I've never done this. One more time." With each motion, David could swear that the ends of his bones were grinding together.

David felt a distinct pop and the sharp pain lessened considerably, but it was replaced with a deep ache that was nearly as bad.

Nodding, Josh said, "Okay, I felt it. Now I know." He pulled David's arm across his chest and began binding it in place. "I don't know, maybe you'll be lucky. I felt it pop back, but there is a lot of swelling. You might have a broken collarbone. You may have fractured your upper arm, too. Not much we can do about it. We'll just have to wait and see how much motion you get back."

David said nothing, hardly aware of what Josh said. The pain from around his shoulder and arm was only slightly better and he sure as hell didn't feel particularly lucky. In addition to his arm, his whole body was battered and bruised and throbbed with pain.

Josh squatted beside him, brown eyes staring into David's green ones with his head cocked to one side for several long moments. The older man treated David like he was nothing more than a piece of equipment being evaluated for use or disposal.

Finally, Josh said, "I'm not a cruel man. But I am a hard man and we are in a cruel situation." He tossed his head over his shoulder toward the vat. "I done seen several hundred people, men, women, and children, go into that thing today. A lot of them was still kicking and screaming as they fell. So let me tell you right now, life here is pretty damn cheap."

A shrill metallic screeching noise made David jump. Josh half turned and looked up. The conveyor began moving again. Several white objects fell; David could hear them strike the bottom of the vat, each impact making a sound somewhere between a thump and a sickening wet splat. Josh turned back and resumed looking at David as though trying to determine if he was worth spending any more effort on. Then he shrugged, like maybe he couldn't decide.

Josh glanced up at the conveyor as more bundles and a tree tumbled off. "There ain't much point in worrying about what goes in the vat until stuff gets near the top. It's too deep to fish anything out of the bottom."

A terrified shriek that tapered into desperate, wailing cry made David flinch. The anguished sound came from above their heads, then a squirming brown-and-white bundle toppled off the belt. The bundle flashed down in a blur with the wail following it down, slightly muffled as the unfortunate victim passed behind the wall. The scream ended with another of the sickening splats.

Josh said in a flat tone, "Monkey. They sound kind of human, but after a while, you can tell the difference."

David's gut clenched in horror at the casual way Josh stated this horrific observation.

Josh snorted. "Like I was saying, life in here is cheap. It might be cheap for a long time with the gatherers around."

David managed to croak, "Gatherers?"

Josh nodded, "Yeah, that's what I call 'em. Cause they gather stuff. Anyway. You look soft to me. I don't know what the hell you were doing in the middle of the damn jungle. I don't really care. But if you're going to make it, you've got to get tough. Like I said, I ain't cruel. But I don't have time to be a damn nursemaid to the likes of you."

Josh began rifling through David's backpack. He set David's canteen within easy reach of his uninjured arm along with a few breakfast bars that had been in a side compartment. Josh grunted when he found a small plastic bottle of ibuprofen. He opened the bottle and shook out several of the little rust-colored pills.

David reached for them gratefully, but Josh held them out of reach. "Like I said, you got to be tough. I know you think you hurt now, but you don't know shit. It's like after a car wreck. Right now, your body is full of natural painkillers. Give it a few hours. Then you'll see." He stood up and said, "I gotta get back to the others." David's eyebrows went up, and Josh grunted again, "Yeah, others. I'm starting a goddamned Amazon Hilton."

David said tentatively, "You…you're going to leave me here?"

Josh nodded with a blank expression. "Yeah, I am. Like I said I ain't running a nursing home." He laid the pills on David's chest. "Besides, it's best if you lay still for now. I think you might go into shock. It would be a good idea if you just lay here with your feet elevated." He tossed more of the creature's webbing over David. "For warmth," he said without a trace of warmth in his tone.

He began picking up various objects: wood, two dead monkeys, several branches laden with fruit, and David's pack, and piled them onto a sled built out of two wooden poles with webbing strung between them. He bent and picked up the ends of the poles.

Nodding toward David's chest, he said, "Remember what I said about them pills. I know they ain't much, but they're all we got. And we don't got many of them either. Like I said, you got to be tough."

"But, but…they're mine."

Josh laughed. "Tell you what, if we get out of this alive…" The edges of his mouth twitched up in a humorless smile. "If you get out of this alive, I'll write you a check."

He turned and began dragging the sled around the lip of the vat toward a round, dark opening in the wall. The sound of the wooden poles rasping on the rough floor seemed loud at first, but was quickly drowned out by the squeaky rumble of the conveyor and the dull thumps and splats of falling Amazonian plants, trees, and animals. David's sense of hopelessness grew as the rasping sound diminished.

Hurt and alone, except for the falling victims of the gatherers, he felt very far from being tough. He fingered the little pills on his chest. Only four, barely enough for a bad headache. Tears welled up in David's eyes and he took two of the pills, put them into his mouth, and swallowed them dry. He looked up to see Josh standing at the round, dark opening, staring back at him. The big man shook his head with a look of disgust and then turned and disappeared into the tunnel.

Marcus

The Amazon dawn greeted the men of PBG 31 with another round of rain and mist as they set out. The mountains were now to their backs as they followed the new torn track through the jungle. Although behind the men and shrouded by trees and fog, the mountains' looming presence could still be felt, a tickling trace down each man's spine.

The men pressed onward and the rain tapered to a stop and the mist lifted bit by bit. Through the trees, white tendrils still crept like ghosts through the forest, limiting visibility. The sounds of men calling to one another other echoed through the quiet morning air, the only way they had to keep in touch with their fellows. If not for the plowed track, they could easily have become lost and wandered in circles through the maze of huge trees, thorny vines, and silent fog.

They traveled through the quiet, dripping jungle for several hours. Then Marcus heard a familiar voice calling his name. Drawing in a deep breath and letting it slowly, he wondered what was about to happen this time. He yelled in response to the shouts and in a few moments, Lieutenant Viana's favorite runner, Julio Arente, appeared out of the mist.

"What have you found, Julio?" asked Marcus.

"A helicopter, sir. It is in the trees about two hundred meters ahead. The lieutenant wants to know if we should stop and investigate or continue on."

Marcus raised his eyebrows in surprise. "A helicopter, here?" Really, he shouldn't be surprised with all the aircraft going down. Helicopters were not uncommon in the region. A lot of logging and mining companies used them. "I think it would be worth our while to learn more about it." He ordered the nearest troops to set up a perimeter. His command echoed through the forest as soldiers relayed the message to unseen companions. "It would be good to know why it crashed. Are there any signs of survivors?"

"No sir, but it is hard to tell."

Marcus frowned at this. A short time later, when he saw the helicopter suspended in the trees thirty feet in the air, it was easy to understand. It was difficult to even see the blue and white fuselage wedged up in the branches, much less tell anything about its contents.

Julio led him to Lieutenant Viana, who was looking up at the helicopter with a concerned expression.

"I am surprised anyone spotted this," said Marcus as he walked up. "It is very difficult to see."

"Very," replied Viana. "Corporal Marco stumbled over some wreckage." He nodded to a soldier nearby. "I doubt we would have noticed it otherwise, even with everyone searching the trees for those big tick things." He pointed up at the wreck. "I think I know this helicopter. It has the same coloring and markings as one that belongs to a drinking buddy of mine from Manaus. He is a North American, but not a bad fellow."

"What would he be doing here in the middle of the jungle?"

Viana shrugged. "He rents out his services to many organizations, even the government from time to time. It wouldn't be unusual for him to be in the region."

Marcus looked up at the helicopter, disappointed it was so inaccessible, and wondered if it would be worth the time, effort and, no doubt, the risk, to climb up to inspect it.

Sally

Sally dozed on her makeshift bedding. The makeshift pallet was made from Keith's and Myra's clothing she found in their packs at the back of the chopper. She did a lot of dozing. It helped pass the time. Her food was holding up well and she still had a good supply of water. If need be, she could move well enough now to use some of the plastic sheeting stored in the back of the chopper to gather rainwater.

The smell of her decomposing friends had lessened to the point that with the help of the alcohol-soaked rag over her nose, she hardly noticed them. But a bit of her soul slipped away every hour she spent trapped in the tree. It was getting increasingly difficult to tell the difference between reality and fantasy. Sleep helped her avoid having to decide which was which.

After the breakthrough of last night's victory when she managed to stand upright, she had been able to repeat the feat at first light. This time she even moved around the cabin a little. Small movements still hurt enough to make her wary of trying to climb down. At least that was what she told herself. After all, it would be very bad to fall out of the tree after keeping it together this long. But it lightened her heart a little to realize she was making progress.

Myra had been very proud of her. "Climb down now," she had urged her. "Get out of here." Sally found herself talking to Myra an awful lot. As the pain and shock faded, the loneliness and guilt seemed to swell. Expressing these emotions to her best friend helped. There was lot of comfort in carrying on the conversations, even though they were starting to scare her more and more.

During moments of clarity, such of those that came, she was pretty sure she was going insane. Was talking to dead friends a sign of mental stability? No, no it was not. But the discussions with her dead friend were her only escape from the horror of buzzing flies, the smell of rotting flesh, and the spectacle of feasting maggots.

"No," she responded to Myra's urgings. "I'm still too sore. Look, I can hardly lift my arm above my head."

Myra's glaring eye observed as Sally demonstrated. "You can do better," she responded. "Now you're only hiding."

Sally felt ashamed that Myra could see through her so easily. Did she fear leaving the helicopter? A little…maybe. Maybe more than a little. Where would she go? David…she needed to go find David. That sounded well and good, but she had no clue where he was, or where she was, or which way she would need to travel.

The idea of walking alone through the forest for who knew how far was pretty intimidating. Plus, leaving Myra behind would cut her final link to her old life. It would require a painful rebirth, a new beginning. A birth into an uncertain future she may not have the courage to face. The world was a very different place than it had been a few days ago. She forced her mind away from such things and tried to sleep as much as possible, although the fear often followed her into her dreams.

Now Myra called to her through the fog of sleep. The voice, as usual, was a combination of rasping metallic screeches and soft, rustling whispers. "Hey! Wake up! Sally, you need to wake up!"

Sally kept her eyes firmly shut and said in a low, husky voice, "Go away, Myra. I don't want to wake up." Other than Myra, lethargy had become her most faithful friend.

Myra's voice seemed to deepen. "Hello, anyone there?" she said in Portuguese.

Yes, her voice was definitely deeper and with no rasp at all. *How odd*, s*he knows perfectly well I am here. And why did she speak Portuguese? Myra can barely speak Portuguese.*

Myra's voice faded into murmurs. Curiosity forced Sally's eyes open. She looked at Myra, and then through her. *No, that wasn't Myra.* Excitement welled in her chest as she sat up. *No, those are real voices.* Hope, a commodity on the verge of extinction, filled her.

A sudden wave of paranoia caused her to pause. Should she call out? She must call out. But did she really know what was going on in the world? She was sure the helicopter had been shot down. But why, and by who? Her head swirled in confusion as it failed to come up with logical answers about the mysterious mountains and the strange creatures in the helicopter. On the other hand, what did it matter? Better to be a prisoner than stuck in this stinking haunted hell slowly going mad.

She yelled out in Portuguese, "Help, help me! Can you hear me?"

Silence answered her. Had she imagined the voices after all? Madness seemed an ever-stronger possibility. She called out again, "Help, please help me! I'm trapped inside."

This time someone answered, the voice muffled by the walls of the helicopter. "Who are you?"

Relief washed over her. She shouted, "I am Sally Morgan. I am with a university team from the United States studying the rainforest. Who is there?"

"We are Comando Naval Marines," the voice replied. "Don't worry, we will get you out. Do you think the helicopter is safe for someone to climb up?"

"I think so," she yelled back. "It hasn't moved or shifted much. But I can't be sure."

She heard a brief, unintelligible discussion between several men. Then the voice called out, "Someone will be up in a moment."

Sally laid back to wait. Her excitement swelled as she looked out the window. She heard leaves rustling as someone negotiated the maze of branches below. The sound was a bit like Myra's voice, but no words came.

"Well, Myra," Sally said in a low voice. It wouldn't do to have whoever was coming hear her talking to a dead woman. "I guess this is it." There was no answer. This made Sally sad. "So that's how it's going to be is it," she said with a wry smile. "Well, thank you for helping me." After a moment's reflection, she added, "I just hope the price wasn't too high."

In a short while, the face of a young, dark-haired Brazilian marine in a camouflaged uniform gazed down at her through the broken window in the passenger side loading-door.

"Hi," she said in Portuguese.

"Well, hello miss," he replied. "Are there any other survivors?"

Tears welled up in Sally's eyes; so she hadn't lost the ability to cry after all. She shook her head and said, "No."

"Are you hurt?"

Sally nodded. "Yes, my side. I hurt my ribs in the crash. But I think I can move with a little help."

"Hmmm," the young man said as he looked over the outside of the aircraft. "Well, we will find a way." He leaned back and looked at the door. "Do you think this door will open?"

"I don't know. I have not been able to try."

The young man moved around the door, transferring his weight with care as he took each step. Reaching the handle, he turned it and pulled. The hinges squawked as the door swung up. It stuck about a third of the way, but with a few tugs, he managed to get it up and clear of the opening. "Well, that wasn't so bad."

The young Brazilian lowered himself gingerly from the branch to the doorframe. After each cautious step, he hesitated a moment to check for any sign the helicopter was shifting. The smell must have hit him because he grimaced and choked a few times before shaking his head and squatting down at the edge of the opening.

The young man's eyes swept the interior of the battered helicopter with revulsion. Sally almost felt offended; these were her friends, after all. Then some sanity came back and she wondered what the hell she was thinking. Here was a live human being coming to help, and she was worried about insulting dead people.

The soldier shook his head and blinked rapidly for a moment before continuing his slow descent into the helicopter. He stopped about halfway in with one foot braced on the side of the stretcher that contained the body of the male patient they had been transporting. When his added weight did not appear to be on the verge of trigging a catastrophe, he smiled down at her. Sally noted how small and slender he was. He couldn't weigh very much anyway.

"My name is Private First Class Julio Arente. What is yours?"

"Sally," she said. "Sally Morgan. You have no idea how glad I am to see you!"

His smile widened, obviously relishing his role as rescuer. "Can you stand?"

Sally nodded and slowly pulled herself to her feet.

"Is there anything here you need?"

She nodded toward the front of the helicopter. "What about my friends? I mean, their bodies?"

He looked sad and shook his head. "We are not in a position to carry them out. They will be better off in here for now. There is less chance of scavengers. Anything else?"

She looked around the small chamber that had been her prison, and her shelter, for the last three days. She gazed at the forms of her dead friends and sighed. Wiping away her tears, she said a quick, silent farewell to each and promised to pray for them. She automatically picked up her backpack and then looked up at Julio. "This is all."

"Okay, hand it up to me." She passed the pack up, and he slung it onto his back and then extended a hand to her. "Slow and easy now. Let me know if I hurt you."

With his help, she was able to climb out of the helicopter. After a few agonizing moments, she was outside. Then they eased over to a large bough and began to descend. The young solider was small, but surprisingly strong and agile as he supported her and helped her ease down from branch to branch. With each motion, her ribs sent flashes of pain through her chest. Several times the agony was so intense they had to stop as tears streamed down her face. But after a moment, the pain faded and they continued downward.

To some extent, the slow, painful descent actually made her feel wonderful, almost giddy. The rebirth back to the world was as physically painful as she feared. At least she didn't have to do it alone. While the journey out of the tree was hard on her body, it was a blessing for her soul. Finally, gratefully, she stepped onto the jungle floor and as a near-orgasmic wave of relief swept through her.

Sally threw her arms around Julio and hugged him as hard as her battered body could stand. "Thank you, thank you, thank you."

The young man was obviously embarrassed, yet pleased. After a moment, she pulled away, and he eased her to the ground. As he stepped back, she noticed a tall, athletic Brazilian officer in the same type camouflage uniform as Julio, smiling down at her.

"Well, Julio," he said to the young private. "It looks like you have an admirer."

Julio stammered, "Uh, yes, sir. I mean, no, sir. I, uh…" He stopped, his dark complexion showing a distinct blush.

The officer laughed. "Do not expect all of your missions to involve rescuing pretty women. I assure you this is a rare occurrence."

Now it was Sally's turn to blush. After being in a helicopter crash, battered, bruised, and then stuck in hell for three days, she doubted her humanity, much less her looks. Silly, but for some strange reason, the comment, delivered in such a natural and sincere manner, made her heart a bit lighter anyway.

Being around people, living people, and out of the helicopter at long last made her drunk with elation. The response she felt to the officer's comment gave reason to hope that her soul had not been lost in the grim confines of the helicopter, or at least, not all of it.

Julio regained his composure and said with a slight flourish, "Sally Morgan, may I present to you Major Marcus Antinasio, commander of Patrol Boat Group 31."

Marcus bent over and shook her hand.

She said, "Major, I am very glad to meet you. Thank you all coming to my rescue."

Major Antinasio nodded. "The pleasure is ours. You say you are with a university team from North America? Your Portuguese is very good."

"Yes, we are in the area under a Brazilian grant studying deforestation. As for my Portuguese, my mother was from Portugal."

The major smiled; his teeth were bright white framed against his brown skin with two-day beard. "Ah yes, I thought I detected an Old World accent. I see you are injured. Let my medic take a look at you."

Sally was sitting propped against the larger of the two trees holding the chopper. Big, solid mahogany trees she noted. She had suspected as much from the leaves she could see through the windows. There was an opening in the trees here, maybe twenty feet around. At the edge of this pseudo-clearing stood four soldiers, one of whom wore a green patch with a dark Red Cross embroidered on it. All of them were watching her talk to their commander with open curiosity.

Marcus called out, "Corporal Barros, please see if you can help Miss Morgan." With a slight wave, he led Julio and the three other soldiers around a large Jaboto tree to give them some privacy.

The medic wasn't much older than Julio, but he was a bit bigger, at least half a head taller than Julio, though shorter than Major Antinasio. He looked at her shyly as he approached.

"Miss Morgan?" said the medic. "Hello, I am Corporal Jef Barros. Looks like you have been through a rough time."

Sally nodded. "I suppose you could say that. It is nice to meet you, Jef."

"For me as well." His eyes darted away from hers. "Um. I need you to remove your shirt."

"Okay," she said. As she shrugged gingerly out of her brown bush shirt, she noticed how it smelled. She hadn't been flexible enough to change in the confined space of the chopper. The shirt was soiled with all manner of disturbing fluids, and it felt really good to take it off.

The young medic almost seemed relieved to see her wearing a sports bra under the shirt. Sally imagined he didn't examine women very often. The Brazilian culture was somewhat patriarchal. While woman served in many roles in its military, they were not known for extensive gender integration.

Jeff nodded in approval at the bandages she had applied to her ribs and then removed them. He spent a few minutes patting and lightly probing her injured side, causing her to wince several times. "Uh, have you, uh…passed any blood?"

"No. Not that I have noticed."

He nodded. "Can you cough?"

She scowled but forced a cough, although the effort made her wince.

"Hurts? I guess that is to be expected. It is good that you can stand to do it though." Jef took out some gauze and tape and rewrapped her ribs, having her lift her bra enough to get under it without exposing much. The young man was tentative in his manner, like he was embarrassed to touch her. He looked relieved as he finished taping the wrap in place.

He pulled out three foil packets of aspirin and handed them to her. "I have stronger medicine if you really need it, but it would pretty much knock you out. Let me know if you start to experience worse pain." Meeting her eyes at last, he said, "It would be best if we could get an X-ray, of course. But since you do not have any sign of internal bleeding, I think you will be okay. Can you walk? If not, we can rig up a litter for you."

Sally stood and walked around in a small circle with care. Her ribs burned, but it was bearable. Climbing had been pretty tough, but she should be okay to walk. "I...I think I can. I would like to give it a go anyway."

"Fine," said the corporal. "We can rig something up latter in need be."

"Thank you. Uh, would you please ask the major to give me a minute? I would like to put on some fresh clothes."

"Yes, certainly." With a nod, he walked around the jatoba tree.

With a cautious glance at the tree, Sally stripped off everything. From her pack, she pulled out fresh underwear, shorts, and a green bush shirt. She loved bush shirts because of all the pockets, they were a researcher's best friend. The shorts would not be her first choice for hiking in the jungle, but she had not packed any long pants for her 'vacation' to Rio Estrada, so they would have to do. The clean clothes felt wonderful. No doubt, she still stank to high heaven, but at least she had on clean underwear.

"Major, I'm dressed," she called out.

Major Antinasio walked around the tree accompanied by Julio and another officer. "This is Lieutenant Jeronimo Viana."

"Hello, Miss Morgan," the officer said. His face looked a bit strained. "Um, by any chance was Keith Anderson your pilot?"

"Uh, yes, yes he was. Did you know him?"

Lieutenant Viana nodded with sad eyes. "Yes. We had a common favorite bar in Manaus. He was a good man."

"Yes, he was that," she said. "I wish I had known him better."

Marcus said, "We are investigating many strange occurrences in this area. We would like to ask you a few questions. First of all, what happened to the helicopter?"

Sally told them of the horrible impacts that shattered the aircraft's windows as something tore through the cabin. Then how Keith had jerked, and jerked, and jerked, and then the crash. "I am sure we were shot down. Do you have any idea who would do such a thing? Is that why you are here?"

Marcus nodded and said, "Yes, that is basically why we are here. Many aircraft have been shot down in the last few days. But no, we do not know who did it or why. Is there anything else?"

"Well, you might think I am hallucinating or something. But...well, we saw some white mountains, huge mountains. We flew into Rio Estrada one day, no mountains. When we left the next day, there they were." She searched their eyes, trying to see if they believed her. To her relief, they both nodded.

"Yes, we have seen them," Marcus said. "Rather, we saw a huge wall at least a thousand meters tall and kilometers long. There were some peaks visible, so it is easy to believe there are mountains on top of the wall." He shook his head. "None of it is on any of our maps. Lieutenant Viana used to come here as a boy, and he is positive he would have known of such mountains. So, we know they are new. But now you tell me all that appeared from one day to the next?" He did not sound harshly skeptical, but it was evident he was having a hard time believing her. "We thought it might be a volcano."

Sally frowned and shrugged. "I would think an eruption big enough to create what I saw would be pretty devastating. A volcano would kick up huge clouds of ash and smoke."

Marcus nodded in agreement. "Yes, that is a good point."

Sally continued, "There was some kind of strange earthquake that caused a lot of damage to Rio Estrada. But still..." She shrugged. "Have you heard anything about the researchers I was with? They are in a camp about seventy-five kilometers from here."

Marcus shook his head. "We weren't told of them when we were ordered here. Once we get to the village, I will see about sending someone to check on them. Is there anything else you can tell us?"

She hesitated. "Yes," she said after a moment. "But it is nearly as crazy as the mountains." She told them about the strange spider-like creature prying open the window and entering the helicopter.

Lieutenant Viana interrupted her. "Was it about this size with many, many legs?" He held his hands about a foot and a half apart.

She nodded in surprise.

He continued, "Yes, we have seen them. They killed one of my men and wounded another. You were lucky."

Major Antinasio said to Viana. "How much further would you estimate it is to the village?"

"Not far. Between ten and fifteen kilometers."

Marcus considered this for a moment. "We still have a way to go then." He looked at Sally and said, "Do you think you are okay to walk? If not we can—"

A shout caused him to pause. A soldier hurried over to Julio, Jef, and another soldier standing by the Jaboto tree. After a flurry of excited voices, Julio pointed in their direction. The marine looked about for a moment, fixated on the officers, and hurried over to them.

Running up, the man struggled to catch his breath as he said to Major Antinasio, "Sir! Lt. Campos sent me to find you. A large group of creatures left the wall and are heading this way!"

The major was obviously puzzled. "Creatures? What kind of creatures?"

The private shook his head. "We could not tell, sir. They are moving fast, though. If they keep up the same pace when I was sent to find you, they should be here in about fifteen minutes!"

Chapter 11

Marcus

Unknown creatures from the mountain? A cold surge of fear ran up Marcus's back and gripped his heart. Taking in a deep breath, he pushed the fear into a small knot at the center of his stomach, squared his shoulders, and forced his expression into one of confident determination. He didn't have the time or luxury to be afraid. Yet inside, his gut churned at the memory of poor Juan sprawled dead in the mud. He prayed this was not the beginning of another such occurrence, or a worse one.

"Corporal Barros, you, Carlosa, and Pieter stay with Miss Morgan," he commanded to the soldiers near the Jaboto tree. Turning to Lieutenant Viana, he said, "Jeronimo, detail some men to watch our rear. I don't want any surprises. Miss Morgan, if you will excuse me." He turned to the private who had delivered the message. "Okay, Valdir, take me to your lieutenant."

The private nodded and hurried off with Marcus right behind.

He found Lieutenant Dante Campos standing inside the tree line, looking through binoculars across the barren strip of land. The young officer was shifting from foot to foot as if he could not decide to stay or run.

"Where are they, Dante?" asked Marcus as he hurried up.

Campos turned. His relief at seeing his commander was obvious. He handed over the binoculars and pointed. "There, sir, about three kilometers out."

Marcus raised the binoculars and stifled a gasp. Shuddering, he forced himself to draw in a long, slow breath. *Stay calm*, he told himself. *Please God, help me stay calm.*

Bounding down the wide strip of churned orange soil with the towering white wall behind them came a mass of impossible creatures. Oversized back legs propelled them with ground-eating rhythmic jumps...leap, bound, leap, seemingly unaffected by the clinging mud. They were dark in coloring and traveled in a tight group, making it difficult to pick out details. The head and body were covered in spikes or antennae. With nothing to compare to, it was hard to determine their size, but he would guess about the size of a small bear, only with longer legs.

Six legs? They have six legs! Rather they had six limbs, four legs, and two arms. *What is the size of a bear with six limbs?* This could not be happening, however, like the huge wall and mountains in the distance, he could not deny what he was seeing.

Marcus lowered the binoculars and looked at Lieutenant Campos. Fear verging on panic contorted the young officer's face.

"Demons," said Campos in a hoarse voice.

Lieutenant Gale stood nearby, his face pale, crossing himself repeatedly as he stared out at the approaching creatures.

Marcus turned and surveyed his men. Most of them huddled around those with binoculars, taking turns staring through them in open-mouthed astonishment, or talking in apprehensive, fear-laced tones. A few hid behind trees. One man was on his knees with his hands clasped and raised toward the sky, a rosary between his fingers. Nowhere did he see anyone ready to confront what was coming.

Anger swelled in his chest. "Marines!" he barked, causing most of the men around him to jump. "Form a line! Along the trees. Now!" He turned to his two junior officers. "Gentlemen! You are supposed set the example here, so get to it. Form your men up on either side of me. Move!"

The forceful commands and resulting activity had a calming effect. A series of clatters and clicks came from both sides of Marcus as men took cover behind trees and checked their weapons. In a few moments, a wall of rifles pointed out at the approaching creatures.

Marcus knew they were all scared. He was himself. However, his men at least looked like soldiers once more. He shouted, his voice carrying up and down the line. "That is better, marines. Whatever these are should fear us, not us them!" He turned to Campos and Gale. "Go up and down the line and tell your men not to fire unless I give the order. We have no idea what these things are about. I don't want to provoke them if we can help it."

The two men nodded and headed off in opposite directions.

Marcus stood gazing at the rapidly approaching creatures. *Can they be demons? My God, am I about to go to war with real demons?*

For that was what they looked like to him as well. They seemed unreal. As the dark shapes drew closer, the knot of fear in his stomach grew. He had to keep himself under control, if he lost it things would get very bad. It occurred to him that his hands were clinched into tight fists, making his forearms hurt. With effort, he forced his fear down and his fists to relax. *These are only strange animals, nothing more,* he kept telling himself. It was very important he focused on this line of thinking. They were only animals, strange animals, but animals.

The creatures continued traveling along the open strip of churned earth until they were about five hundred meters from the Brazilians. Then they came to a sudden halt and spread out into a ragged line consisting of small, tightly packed groups. This made it difficult to tell their numbers, but somewhere around fifty or sixty. Stopping right in front of the Brazilian position did not bode well.

Campos and Gale finished organizing their men and rejoined him at the center of the line. The two younger officers watched Marcus carefully, as did the men close enough to see along the line. Marcus nodded to acknowledge their return and, casually as he could, lifted the binoculars to his eyes and resumed studying the strange beings facing his command.

It was hard to define, but their coloring and general shape reminded him of the tick-like creatures they'd encountered earlier. It was if one lived in a world of reptiles and came upon a bear and squirrel. Even if you knew nothing of mammals, they would seem related if compared to a lizard. Though they are very different in size, a bear's and a squirrel's fur, paws, and general shape are similar enough to spot a relationship.

The tick-things and the creatures in front of them were akin like that. Like the tick-things, the larger creatures had heads small in proportion to their bodies, topped with spikes and antennae of various lengths and dominated by oversized eyes. They had scales that looked vaguely like a caiman only less flexible with wicked spikes protruding from many, though not all, of them. The six limbs were fewer in number than the smaller creatures, but the resemblance was still there. Were these things adults and the smaller ones children?

With the things being closer and not moving, he was able to firm up his size estimate. Yes, the body was about the size of a small bear. The back two legs were especially large and powerful, like a frog's. The middle limbs were a little shorter, with flat paws and short claws. The head and front arms were lower than the midsection, giving the creatures the menacing look of a scorpion, only without the segmented spiked tail.

The front arms were especially disturbing. They were obviously made for fighting and killing. The appendages were strangely jointed, heavily muscled, and oddly proportioned. One was short and powerful, with an oversized forearm ending in a large, three-fingered hand with short claws. The other was longer and slimmer, but rather than a hand or paw, it was tipped with a meter-long serrated talon that looked the blade of a sword.

When not moving, the creatures sat low to the ground and appeared tense as though poised to spring. Their antennae, arms, and legs quivered like harnessed hounds that had caught the scent of their quarry. Marcus had to keep swallowing to prevent his mouth from going bone dry.

Lieutenant Viana jogged around a tree and joined them. "I have men deployed to cover our rear. Per your instructions, Jef, Carlosa, and Pieter are with Miss Morgan."

Marcus gave a curt nod in reply while continuing to stare through the binoculars.

With a frown, Viana followed the line of the binoculars back down the churned strip and gasped, "What in the name of God are those?"

Marcus shook his head. "That is something we need to find out. I do not believe it too wild a guess to think they are connected to the interference." Taking out his camera, he set it to maximum zoom and took several pictures.

He expected the creatures to surge forward and attack. However, they just sat on the orange soil, quivering, with their oversized eyes gleaming in the tropical sun, impossible to read. The marines stared back at them, tense and ready.

After what felt like an eternity, but was closer to ten minutes, Lieutenant Viana said, "So, what do we do now, major? Should we send someone out to try and talk to them?"

The other three officers turned and looked at him as if he had lost his mind.

Lieutenant Campos said, "Are you crazy? Those things do not seem like they are much for talking! Look at them—they're demons!"

"How do we know?" retorted Lieutenant Viana. "Maybe they think we look scary. We know nothing about these things or where they came from. Maybe they mean us no harm."

Marcus drew a deep breath, held it, and then let it out slowly while trying to think. He had been in the military for ten years, a third of his life. His father had been a soldier, so he had grown up in a military family, had gone to the Brazilian Military Academy, and studied countless military situations. None of that meant a damn thing right now. Never had he felt so unsure of what to do.

Nevertheless, that did not matter. Drawing himself up with a mental kick, he squared his shoulders. He was in charge, damn it! *Quit feeling sorry for yourself.* One thing he did know was that one had to make decisions when one was in charge. Right or wrong, you had to make the call and live with the results.

"No, Jeronimo," he said. "We will not try to talk to them. Our mission is to find the source of the interference and gather information. *And* get that information back to General Fernando. We are not here to establish communications, or fight a battle if we can avoid it."

Viana looked annoyed, but nodded.

Marcus held up the memory card from his camera. "We know the source of the interference and we have some very valuable information. It is obvious we need more men and equipment to truly get to the bottom of what's happening here. As for now, we need to get this back to the general."

There was a yell for Lieutenant Viana from the rear.

He said, "Excuse me, sir."

Marcus nodded and the lieutenant trotted back into the forest. He continued with a slight wave toward the line of creatures, "1st and 3rd Platoons will keep our friends under surveillance. Lieutenant Campos, you and 2nd Platoon will continue on to Rio Estrada and meet the boats. You will make sure this gets to General Fernando personally." He handed over the memory stick.

Lieutenant Viana called out, "Major, you need to come see this!"

Marcus frowned at the interruption, but turned and jogged back to Viana. The lieutenant was with Julio and both were staring up at a large kapok tree.

"Tell him what you saw Julio," said Viana.

"Yes sir! Major, back at the helicopter I noticed something moving through the branches. I only saw it for a second and thought it might be a monkey. But I have been keeping a lookout." He pointed up at the kapok tree. "Look up where those three large branches meet, there at the edge of the shadows. It is one of those tick-things that attacked Ernesto and Juan."

Marcus squinted up into the tree. It took him a few moments, but then he spotted a dark shape crouched in the gloom amid the indicated tree limbs. Two oversized eyes gleamed from the shadows.

It was watching them. Marcus could tell it in his bones. "Shoot it."

Julio nodded and in one smooth motion brought his rifle to his shoulder and fired. The creature lurched and fell from the tree.

Marcus would later wonder what triggered the following events. Was it the noise of the shot? Or did the small creature emit some kind of silent cry? Possibly the smaller beings were working with the larger ones in some orchestrated plan. Regardless of the exact cause, immediately following the shot, a panicked shout came from Lieutenant Campos.

As Marcus turned and sprinted back to the tree line, he heard a sound like a score of axes thudding into the trees come from ahead. Men started screaming. Someone, Campos probably, yelled, "Fire!" Assault rifles began chattering, at first sporadically and then in a sustained thunderous roar.

When Marcus reached the edge of the clearing, the mass of menacing creatures were bounding forward across the torn earth. Already they were little more than two hundred meters away and closing on the tree line with amazing speed. Glancing down, he saw Lieutenant Gale lay on the jungle loam, obviously dead with a bloody hole torn in his chest.

Smoke filled the air as men fired their rifles all up and down the line, but it did not slow the wild charge. After what seemed a long time, one of the creatures crashed into the mud. A moment later, another went down. For the most part, however, the fusillade of rifle fire seemed to have little effect.

They really are demons. The monsters hurdled forward, their appearance becoming odder as they closed. The creatures looked wrong, like the parts didn't fit together right. Drawing his pistol, he chambered a round and made sure the safety was off. The weapon seemed pathetic after seeing the beasts shrug off the combined fire of ninety assault rifles, but it was all he had. When he looked up, the leading creatures were less than thirty meters away. Glancing to the left and right, he saw the frightened faces of his men as they fired frantically, trying in vain to stop the charge.

He sighted the pistol on a demon headed directly for him, but a split second before he pulled the trigger, it surprised him by leaping up and over his head. All up and down the line, the others did the same. Soaring over the heads of the men, they slashed down with their long, serrated talons.

A soldier to Marcus's right was hit in the chest and thrown back into a tree trunk. The man slid down with a soft exhale of death. Most of the soldiers had taken shelter behind tree trunks or amidst massive roots and spared similar fates. However, any cover the trees provided vanished once the demons landed among them. The entire line broke into a huge melee, each man fighting for his life.

Marcus twisted around to follow the creature that leapt over him, aimed, and began firing. The bullets chipped the hard scales but did not penetrate. The demon turned and raised the limb with the heavy forearm and pointed it at him. In the center of the three claws was a short, fleshy tube with a huge opening.

Marcus's eyebrows shot up and he dove behind a tree. *Thok! Thok! Thok!* The tree vibrated from three hard impacts. Chancing a quick glance around the trunk, he saw the creature take another mighty leap and disappear into the trees. Leaning back against the rough bark, he paused to draw in several deep breaths. His entire being screamed at him to dig into the soft dirt under the tree and hide. However, with a final deep inhalation, he stepped into the surrounding chaos to help his men fight the terrifying onslaught.

Sally

Sally and the Brazilian marines with her all jumped as several haunting screams echoed through the forest, followed immediately by the roar of assault rifles. The young soldiers moved hesitantly across the small clearing in the direction of the firing, fingering their rifles as if to draw courage from the hard metal, unsure what to do.

Sally tensed but remained sitting, leaning against the mahogany tree and nursing her throbbing side. It was plain the soldiers felt torn between their orders to guard her, their obligation to help their friends, and the desire to turn and run.

She opened her mouth to tell them to go help when a nightmare crashed through the lower tree branches. It thudded to the ground ten feet away, between her and the soldiers. Her words turned into a gurgle of fear at the sight of the menacing gray-and-black creature.

The creature looked so bizarre, so beyond her framework of expectations for an animal, that it took a moment for her to realize the thing had landed on its back, evidently snagging a branch or vine on the way down. Its six limbs waved in the air in an effort to right itself, reminding Sally of a huge misshapen insect. The jagged projections on its scaled back dug into the jungle floor and caught on vines, hampering its effort to roll over.

Sally tried to scream, but only a squeak came out as terror clamped down on her vocal cords. The earsplitting echoes of gunfire from the tree line drowned out the creature's landing and Jef, Carlosa, and Pieter continued staring through the foliage, unaware of the danger behind them. Sally sat frozen as the creature got a grip on a tree root with a three-fingered, clawed hand and began to pull itself over.

She found her voice just before the misshapen body thudded heavily onto its legs, but her scream of warning came too late. The creature raised the three-clawed hand and pointed it at Jef and the soldiers even as they turned. The first hollow *thok* sound made her jump. It was followed by four more of the strange retorts in quick succession.

To her left, Jef was hit and knocked back into the jatoba tree, where he slumped to the ground. Pieter followed with an awkward back flip and came down on his stomach. Carlosa nearly got his rifle up before spinning violently and staggering sideways. With a shrill scream, he sank to his knees.

The fear Sally felt in the helicopter was nothing compared to the sheer terror that now coursed through her. This went beyond fear of death. The monster in front of her was straight from her deepest subconscious hell. Childhood fears of giant spiders assailed her mind. She kicked her legs blindly, half trying to stand, half trying to ward off the nightmare as the thing started to turn, to come for her.

Before it completed the turn, Carlosa sat up, his face confused. Sally could see the fear form in his eyes as he focused on the terrible creature a short distance away. The movement must have caught the thing's attention because it turned away from Sally and began advancing in his direction.

The respite allowed Sally to get to her feet and back away. Her whole body shivered uncontrollably and she became aware of warmth going down her leg. She staggered backward into another tree and stopped. Horror numbed her mind, freezing her in place as she shook her head in denial at the scene unfolding before her.

The creature scrabbled toward the soldier, moving a little sideways as it advanced, somewhat like an oversized crab. It was better suited for leaping than crawling through the forest. Carlosa tried to stand and made it part way to his feet before falling sideways, grabbing at the bloody wound on his thigh. After falling, he began crawling frantically, dragging his injured leg behind.

The creature hesitated, as if not sure how to react to the frenzied motions of its quarry. Almost as if the notion of running away was beyond its comprehension. The private scrambled behind a kapok tree and peeked out at the monster, like a child playing tag with the Devil.

Sally's fearful panting began to slow. The human body could only sustain such hyper-emotions for so long. Her initial surge of blinding fear ebbed and she realized she needed to do something.

Run. Run now. Run far.

Instead, she continued to watch the one-sided cat-and-mouse game unfolding before her. The kapok tree was huge with twisted, intricate roots. The creature resumed moving and closed on the private's shelter. It lashed around the trunk with its long, serrated claw as it circled to the right to reach him. Carlosa cried out in terror as he dodged and crawled over the long, exposed roots, trying to keep the tree between himself and the creature.

Something happened inside Sally. A will to fight, to protect, that she had never called on before, never even had known existed, rose in her soul. Carlosa seemed so young, so scared, and in such pain that Sally found her mind and heart focusing on him, overriding her own desperate fear.

A grim, fatalistic resolve stole over her as the eternal power of motherhood filled her heart with a steely resolve, giving her the kind of strength that prompted a teacher to step between her students and a killer's gun, or a firefighter to run into a burning building on the verge of collapse.

"You will not have him," she said, iron in her voice. "You will not!"

With determined desperation, Sally looked around and spotted the rifle dropped by Corporal Barros. Forcing herself into motion, she hurried toward the weapon. Mama bear was going to war.

Carlosa screamed in pain and Sally flinched as she snatched up the rifle. She whirled and saw that the creature had stabbed the youth with its sword-like talon, sticking it entirely through his already injured leg. Carlosa thrashed and pounded on the claw, screaming and crying as the thing dragged him closer.

The Brazilian assault rifle felt strange in her hands, but not completely alien. In happier times long ago, her father had taught her to shoot. They'd made a hobby of it, going to various target and skeet shooting competitions where she'd more than held her own.

However, the military weapon was unlike the rifles and shotguns that she was used to. The peep and blade sight, trigger, and magazine were familiar. But the weapon had extra levers, buttons, and knobs that were strange to her. *There...the safety.* It was stiff, and she fumbled with it for a moment before slamming it all the way down. She braced the folding stock against her shoulder and grasped the weapon tightly. Drawing in a deep breath, she aimed at the creature's back, released the breath as Father had taught her, and squeezed the trigger.

Fire and thunder assaulted her senses. Sally had accidently placed the weapon on full auto. The recoil of the strange weapon caused her damaged ribs to flare with pain while the rifle bucked like a living thing in her hands. With a chattering roar, a stream of bullets stitched up the creature's scaly back, but most went into the jungle. The purplish-black scales cracked and splintered where the shots struck, but none seemed to penetrate. However, the blast got the thing's attention and it flipped Carlosa off its claw and began turning to face her.

"Oh my God, oh my God, oh my God," she said over and over in a hoarse whisper as she fumbled with the rifle.

Like it had in the helicopter right before they were shot down, everything slowed to a crawl. The creature's weapon appeared to move through jelly, and the shell casings from her wild burst hung in the air, or slowly glistened and tumbled across the ground in the dim light under the trees.

Fear again caused her throat to constrict, but she held her ground. There was no running in her soul now, only determination. The safety had clicked twice when she'd flipped it, so it had to be a selector as well as the safety. She switched it back a notch.

In addition to getting the creature's attention, she noticed that her initial burst had cracked a section of scales, from which oozed a thick, purple fluid. *Okay, that's where I need to aim.*

The three-fingered limb housing what had to be the creature's weapon was almost trained on her. Moving faster than she ever had in her life, she slammed the rifle up to her shoulder. It slapped against her cheek as she sighted on the cracked section of scales. Her whole world focused on that one spot even as she awaited the blow from the creature's weapon. As she had in competitions in the past, she took in another breath, released it, and squeezed the trigger.

CRACK. A purple haze misted the air around where she was aiming. Not waiting to see if the round had any effect, she kept shooting. Aim, breath, squeeze, *CRACK.* Aim, breath, squeeze, *CRACK.* She fired over and over until, with a click, the breach locked open, indicating the last bullet had fired.

As though released from a trance, she blinked and took a step back. She knew she had done what she could and it was time to run. As her muscled tensed, she saw it wouldn't be necessary. The creature was motionless and its weapon arm was lying on the ground. Where her concentrated fire had struck, there was now a splintered mess gushing dark purplish fluid.

Relief more than elation flooded over her as she hurried over to Carlosa. It was hard to move very fast because her side blazed in pain with every step, making her wince and stumble like a drunk. But Carlosa was even worse off, squirming in agony with blood flowing freely from the large tear in his thigh. She kneeled beside him and grasped the wound with her hands, trying to stem the flow. He groaned and looked up with fear and a deep sadness in his eyes. Blood was everywhere contrasting vividly with the surrounding green.

"I'll hold it," she said. "Quick, get your belt off."

Carlosa nodded and fumbled with his belt, his motions getting clumsier as she watched. The blood flow had slowed under the pressure, but she did not dare let go. He pulled the belt free, wobbling as he did so. Then he passed out, falling back in the jungle loam with a soft thud and dropping the belt to the ground.

Sally was forced to let go to grab the belt. Now things were moving much too fast. With clumsy hands, she wrapped it around his leg. A tourniquet was only to be used as a last resort, but if this wasn't a last resort, nothing was. Fastening the buckle, she looked around for something to twist it tight. Nothing of any use presented itself, so she used the barrel of the rifle, sliding it under the belt and then twisting it around and around.

The belt cut into the Carlosa's leg and the blood slowed to a trickle. It was the best she could do right now. At least the boy was still breathing. She wedged the rifle between the young soldier and the ground and sat down beside him, trembling under an onslaught of emotions.

Terror, anger, elation, and sorrow all jumbled together, swirling through her head. *God*, she prayed, *please give me strength*. Myra had told her He would, but she had to make her own as well. She placed her shaking hands under her armpits and hugged herself tightly, rocking back and forth.

A series of shots nearby penetrated her emotional storm, pulling her back to the here and now. What should she do? It came to her that there might be more of those things near. She stopped rocking and focused on the surrounding forest. It was impossible to tell where the sounds of gunfire came from. Were they winning or losing? She had no way to tell.

The rifle was bound up in the boy's belt. *Not good, not good at all. Wait, what about the ones carried by the other soldiers?* For that matter, what about Jef and Pieter? Guilt over forgetting them, even for a moment, washed over her. Wincing with every step, she stood and hurried over to Jef.

The young medic was leaning against the tree. His face was peaceful, and his expression still had a boyish shyness to it. He was staring off into the great beyond with a half smile on his face. His chest was a blood-soaked mess. The creature's weapon had torn a large hole right through the middle of his sternum. Knowing it was useless, she checked for a pulse. There was no surprise when she didn't find one.

"I'm sorry, Jef. Thank you for helping me," she said. Pulling the medical satchel off his shoulder, she hurried over to Pieter.

The other boy, Pieter, was covered in blood and she knew there was no point in checking for a pulse. His throat had been torn half away. His rifle was lying beside him, and she snatched it up and went back to Carlosa.

Should she use the medical bag to try to tend his wound, maybe sew it up? After a moment, she decided against it. The bleeding had slowed to a trickle and while she was a good biologist, she was not up to doing jungle surgery, especially if it involved repairing a torn artery. She hoped the Brazilians had another medic who could help. For now, it would be better to keep an eye out for another of those things.

Sally clutched the rifle to her chest and huddled against the kapok tree. She stared at the bodies of Jef and Pieter. Until the helicopter crash, she had only seen two dead bodies in her entire life. One had been her mother at the funeral. The other had been her father after he'd hung himself in the garage. Now the victims of violent death constantly surrounded her. She shuddered again, shook her head at how crazy her life had become, and focused on the surrounding jungle.

Julio Arente
Private Julio Arente strove to be a model for his ideal of bravery. As a child, he always imagined himself to be the leading man in a movie who laughed in the face of danger. Climbing the tree where Sally Morgan had been trapped was a good example of the kind of duty for which he typically volunteered.

Today, reality dealt a hard blow to his heroic self-image. Right now he was scared and confused. He had been instructed to watch the rear. But that order had little meaning now, didn't it? Huddled next to a tree with his heart pounding, he tried to see everywhere at once. The sounds of gunfire and tormented screams echoed through the trees from what seemed a hundred directions. There was no telling who was shooting or what was going on. He felt terrified but believed he should go help his friends. However, fear held him in place, and it shamed him.

Honor and a strong sense of what was right, instilled in him by his mother and father, could not be pushed aside so easily. His friends were out there, brothers he could not let down. Taking a deep breath, he forced himself to stand, wiped his eyes, and fatalistically squared his shoulders. On weak and trembling legs, he stepped away from the dubious shelter of the tree. Most of his old friends from civilian life would consider him a fool. But at Julio's core was a faith that a soldier's true strength was loyalty to the team. Ultimately, he did not go forward to be the hero of his childhood dreams, but to help his comrades.

After his first shaky steps, surprised to be alive, his breathing steadied and he gripped his rifle with more assurance. One cautious step followed another, and his confidence built. Julio looked around, appraising his situation as a calm settled over him. *I can do this.*

Walking with more assurance, he began weaving through the trees at a steady pace. He noticed the sounds of fighting had slowed from a constant roar to a series of intense, sporadic flurries of shots and screams. The noise echoed among the trees, confusing direction. A loud burst from his left made him jump. The shots were close enough to reverberate in his chest. A few heartbeats later, more shots came. About a half dozen or so were fired quickly, but in a controlled, deliberate manner. His senses felt raw and hyper-tuned to every sound and movement. With as much stealth as shaking legs would allow, he moved forward slowly, expecting to encounter God knew what at any moment.

Something warned him—he did not know exactly what, a small noise perhaps, or a fleeting shadow that alerted his hyper-tuned senses. Something triggered his reflexes, and he dove down and to the side. As he did, a dark shape sailed by, and blinding pain lanced up his back.

The thing that missed slicing him open flew past and slammed into a tree. Julio, his back ablaze with pain, spun to see an impossible and alien shape bounce hard off the bark and flop onto its back, multiple limbs flailing as it struggled to right itself.

He stared in horrified fascination for a fraction of a second before swinging up his rifle and stitching a line of bullets across the exposed belly. Purplish, sweet-smelling fluid spurted in all directions as the bullets impacted. The legs convulsed outward, then curled slowly toward the body and the black-and-gray carcass went still.

Elation and revulsion almost made him giddy as he stared at the thing on the jungle floor. Whatever this alien looking thing was, he had beat it. It was terrifying to think that there were most likely more of them out there, but at least now he knew what he faced.

More screams and gunfire echoed through the forest, causing him to jump, though they were a little farther away than the previous shots. The close ones had come from his left. Moving cautiously in that direction, he tried to ignore the wound on his back. There was no telling how bad it might be, and he could not take the time to find out. The pain served as a vivid reminder to be alert for an attack from any direction at any moment.

Moving quicker now, he advanced by going from tree to tree, trying to make himself a difficult target. Entering a small clearing under the overlapping canopy, he froze. The body of Corporal Barros was slumped under a tree not far away. The man was obviously dead, his head hanging down with blood dripping down his chest and soaking his pants.

Pieter lay face down in the mud nearby, unmoving with half his throat torn out.

Spotting the menacing form of another creature like the one that attacked him, his heart leaped high in his throat, and he swung the rifle in its direction. Then he noticed the scales were badly cracked and oozing a lot of purplish fluid. It showed no sign of movement and appeared hurt, or better yet, dead. Bringing the rifle up to his shoulder, he snugged it place, looked down the barrel, and crept toward the still shape.

If it isn't dead, it soon will be. He almost shot it just to be sure. However, the shooting had nearly stopped, and he feared the noise might attract unwanted attention. As he approached the form, it remained motionless, and he spotted a large puddle of purple gore around it. Relaxing slightly, but still wary, he nudged the body with his rifle a few times. When he got no reaction, he let out the breath he didn't even know he was holding.

"Julio?" a voice called out, causing him to jump. He turned and peered into the shadows to locate who had spoken. Sally Morgan, a wry smile on her face, stepped out from behind a tree. "I am very glad to see you. Do you know what is happening?"

Julio shook his head as he moved forward to join her. The gunfire had subsided. Was that good or bad? He considered going to the tree line but decided he should stay with Miss Morgan. Joining her behind the tree, the two waited with rifles ready, watching over Carlosa and keeping wary eyes on the surrounding jungle.

Marcus

Marcus stood dazed and bleeding in the midst of carnage. *Is it over? Did they win?* Even if they had won, what did that mean? He didn't even know what they were fighting for.

It was obvious Patrol Boat Group 31 had been badly hurt. But how bad? The bulk of the fighting took place within twenty meters of the tree line. There were at least twenty camouflaged forms lying dead or badly wounded nearby. Three dead creatures were also in sight, not a good ratio. It boded poorly for his men. At least two dozen demons were leaping through the orange mud toward the mountains. He had no clue why they had attacked, or why they'd stopped, but felt grateful they were gone.

Becoming aware of pain and a sticky wetness, he glanced down to find a nasty gash across his chest. There was a dim memory of a creature slashing at him with a long, serrated claw while he and two other marines had blasted away at it, though he had not felt the cut at the time. Transfixed, he watched blood seep out of the wound for a moment before blinking his eyes and looking up. It hurt like hell, but it could wait.

He needed to…well, to do something. His mind seemed unable to latch onto a course of action. Nothing made sense right now.

The area was silent in the aftermath of the battle. Only the wind stirred except for a few distant animals' cries echoing through the forest. Everyone still standing was staring at the demons heading away from the area. Then one man stumbled into motion to help a nearby comrade, and two others moved to do the same.

This acted like a catalyst that released more men from their after-battle trances, and they too began moving, going to those in need of assistance. Marcus nodded in satisfaction, though he still could not focus on what to do next. He knew he must do something, to take command, but his brain refused to work. *Shock.* That seemed right. *I'm in shock.* No time for that, we have to…what? We have to do something.

There was a rifle in his hands. The realization surprised him. A dim memory surfaced of picking it up sometime during the fight. After staring at it for a moment, he went through a basic safety and function check, finding comfort in doing something simple, something useful, no matter how small.

The process of reloading the weapon and engaging the safety helped steady him. The fog in his brain began to lift, and he glanced up to make sure the creatures were still moving away. They were, and he breathed a silent prayer of thanks. Things that needed doing began to pop into his head. Set up some lookouts, take care of the wounded, and get the hell out of here.

Must set an example. The men need an anchor. Drawing in a deep breath, he straightened his back and squared his shoulders. Holding his head up, he went to try to put his battered command back together again.

Chapter 12

Marcus

Marcus slowly stood and nodded to the marine helping him wrap yet another lifeless body in a sleeping bag. The other man nodded back, his face sad and grim. Marcus looked down the long line of shrouded forms. *Fifty-seven. Oh my God, fifty-seven.* He knew the number would haunt him for a long time to come.

Looking at his watch brought a frown to his already haggard features. Two hours since the attack had ended. *Too long, too damn long.* They needed to be on their way. The creatures could return and finish the job at any moment. It was a wonder they had not done so already. There was too much to do, too many wounded to tend to and way too many dead to account for.

Viana came up, moving with slow, deliberate steps. His face reflected pain and determination as he forced himself to move despite a mangled arm and broken ribs. During the height of the fighting, one of the creatures had latched onto his left forearm, crushing it and then flinging the large man against a tree like a child's doll.

"Two unaccounted for, sir," he said. Each breath seemed to cause him pain, though he insisted he felt fit to travel.

"We can spare no more time looking for them, Jeronimo. We must be away from here."

Viana looked through the trees at the looming wall beyond. "Do you think the war demons took them?" he said in a fear-laced tone.

Marcus half shrugged and shook his head, then turned toward the mountain. "Is that what we are to call them, war demons?"

"Well, sir, that's what the men are calling them. And the name certainly fits."

"Yes, I suppose it does. I do not like it, though. It gives them an aura of the supernatural, of something we cannot fight." He turned and pointed at the carcass of one of the dead creatures nearby. "And they may be tough, but we can kill them."

"Do you want me to tell them to stop?"

"No," said Marcus with a sigh. "As you said, the name fits. It is the label I find myself thinking as well. And if we try to stop them from using it, it would only make them think we are trying to hide something."

Viana chuckled, but there was no mirth in it. "What do we have to hide?"

Marcus shrugged. "True enough." He gestured to the long row of shrouded bodies, his heart so heavy it was a wonder he could still carry it. "We have paid a terrible price and have only discovered more questions."

"Sometimes knowing what to ask is part of the answer," said Viana.

"Maybe, but do we even know what to ask yet? Whatever is happening here keeps getting stranger and bigger. I fear for our country. Maybe for the whole world for that matter."

Viana gave a grim nod, and the two men turned as one to look at the towering white wall for several long moments.

Marcus shook himself and said, "How long before we can get away from here?"

Viana gestured toward eight litters being prepared for the seven men too weak to walk, and one of the dead demons. "We are nearly ready, sir. Maybe ten or fifteen minutes. But it will be slow going."

"I fear that is a bit of an understatement, Marcus said, his voice grave. Almost every one of the thirty-four marines who'd survived the battle had been wounded. Many, like Viana, could barely move on their own, much less help carry the more severely wounded. They would have to make frequent rest stops. If not for the overwhelming threat of staying, he would not risk moving at all.

He spotted Sally Morgan replacing the bandage on one of the injured men.

Viana followed his gaze, a slight smile managing to fight its way onto his face. "There is a true warrior spirit."

The corners of Marcus's mouth also twitched up slightly. "I heard she killed one of the demons single-handed."

Viana nodded, "Yes, sir. Stood her ground and kept firing single, aimed shots until she punched through the scales. She also refuses to give up that rifle," he said, pointing at the weapon slung across her back. "The men are calling her 'Demon Slayer'."

Marcus surprised himself with a soft chuckle. "Let her keep it. Brazil will not miss it and she certainly earned it." He noticed his battered men walked a little taller, looked more determined when she was around. He needed any source of strength and inspiration he could find. God knew he could not provide enough on his own. Suddenly he felt very grateful they had found Miss Sally Morgan. "What time do you think Lieutenant Pereira will reach Rio Estrada? Sometime tomorrow?"

"Yes, sir, if the runner we dispatched this morning got through okay."

"Pray that he did."

"He would no doubt dispatch at least part of the group immediately. So…five hundred kilometers at, say, thirty to thirty-five kilometers per hour." It took a moment to do the math. "Something less than sixteen hours." He looked at his watch and shrugged. "I would think that someone would be there in the morning, almost certain before noon."

Marcus nodded. "My thoughts as well." He looked at the lieutenant and drew in a deep breath. "Jeronimo, General Fernando must know what happened here, about the wall, the mountains, and about the creatures we fought. Pick two healthy men and get them headed for Rio Estrada immediately. I want them to go all night if they can. If they push, they can meet the boats as soon as they arrive."

Viana turned and looked at the wounded men on their makeshift litters. "Sir, we are so shorthanded, that will slow us down even more. What if those things come back?"

Marcus let out a slow breath. What choice did he have? "I know. But at this point, the information is worth more than any of us."

Viana rubbed his face and said, "I'll go, sir. I'm not so good for pulling the wounded anyway." He held up his mangled arm. "But my legs are good enough."

Marcus looked him over for a moment and then nodded. "All right, Jeronimo. Still, I xwant you to take one other man. And make sure he is totally healthy," he said with a faint smile. He handed Viana two memory cards, one of them stained with Lieutenant Campos's blood. "As long as you are going, I want you to take the boat back to Manaus and report personally to General Fernando; he will probably be there by now." The young officer's face began to cloud in protest, but Marcus held up his hand. "Go with the boat. I can't go, and you are the best person to give details to the general. I bet he will want you to go to Brasilia and report to the Joint Chiefs in person. Besides, I don't want you hanging around here with one arm flopping around like a wounded chicken."

Viana nodded, but he did not look happy about it.

Marcus smiled. "This might be the last time I will see you for some time. You have done an excellent job. I will miss you."

The young lieutenant nodded with a thin smile. "It has been an adventure, Major; I would not have missed it. As soon as the general finishes with me, and they get my arm fixed, I will be back. I have a feeling that whatever we are facing, it will not be over quickly."

David

Quiet voices carried over the squeaking of the conveyor. David opened his eyes and saw two women, or actually, one woman and one girl. They stood not far away, watching objects drop into the cauldron. The girl held a coil of rope made from the creature's webbing. The woman held a long wooden pole with a loop of the same material at the end of it.

The woman had dark skin with shoulder-length hair that was straight and coarse. She was short, maybe five feet tall, of medium build and rather pretty in a rugged sort of way. David would guess she was in her mid-thirties. She wore a white sports bra that stood out against her dark skin and blue jeans cut off at the knees.

The girl was slender and half a head taller than her older companion, with lighter skin, though darker than David's. Her glossy dark hair was pulled back in a ponytail that flowed past her shoulders. She wore a blue cotton polo shirt that swallowed her slim frame and came down to her thighs, which were bare. The shirt looked familiar, and it dawned on him that it was one from his backpack. After a second look, he decided she could have been a little older than his first impression, perhaps fourteen or fifteen.

The girl noticed him looking at them and nudged her companion. They walked over and knelt beside him.

"You are David Morgan, yes?" asked the woman in English.

David's eyebrows went up and he nodded.

The woman said, "I saw you at the police station when you and your friend were talking to Lieutenant Goulart. People there told me who you were."

"So you were in the plaza?"

She nodded. "Yes, we both were. My name is Paula Jobim. This is Alessandra da Silva."

The girl gave a small smile and nodded. The smile did not linger long. She looked into his eyes, as though searching his face for answers.

Also speaking English, she said, "Did you see anyone escape? My mother is tall and slender, with skin and hair like mine. Did you see her?"

David recognized her and said, "Oh, you and your mother were with the boy in the plaza, weren't you?"

Alessandra nodded. "Yes, we took him to the church. Only…only the demons came and tore it down around us." The girl's face contorted with pain. "We…we ran, but I lost her. I…I don't know what happened to her."

Paula put her arm around the girl.

David shook his head and said, "I did see some boats get away. But I have no idea who was on them."

Paula pulled the girl closer and asked, "Do you have any idea what is happening?"

David shook his head again.

Alessandra, tears streaming down her face, said, "We are in Hell. We have been captured by demons and are in Hell. They will come for us any second. I know they will!"

Paula began stroking her hair. David wanted to comfort her also, but could think of nothing to say. They sat in silence, watching the cauldron go through its grizzly cycle. A fly landed on David's face, and he swatted at it with a mumbled curse. He hadn't noticed them earlier, but it made sense that they would arrive; the smells of the chamber must be like heaven to the little bastards.

Paula said, "Are you up to moving? Josh said we should you bring you back to camp if you were still alive."

David frowned but nodded. He was grateful Josh had saved him, but the man was an asshole. Paula had to help him stand, which proved more difficult than he would have imagined. His whole body ached, and he remembered what Josh said earlier about the pain getting worse. This just made him more irritated at the older man. Standing up made his head spin, and he stood on wobbling legs for a moment.

Alessandra said, "Are you okay?"

He nodded. "I hurt like hell, but I really want to get away from this damn vat."

"We'll take you to the cave," said Paula.

They stood on each side and helped support him as they walked around the pit to the tunnel entrance on the far side. David moved like an old man, bent over with short, shuffling steps. The opening David assumed to be round from the other side of the chamber was shaped more like an arch. It reminded him of a cartoon representation of a mouse-hole. *How appropriate.* It was wide enough for Paula to walk beside David as she helped stabilize him. Alessandra dropped behind as they traveled about fifty feet to the far end.

The tunnel had smooth sides and had been cut in a straight line through the mountain. A dozen or so rods protruded from the ceiling with half of them emitting the harsh blue light.

The tunnel led to a domed chamber thirty feet across and about the same distance in height. In addition to the tunnel they were in, half a dozen openings of various sizes and shapes were spaced around the room. The chamber was rough cut and had pipes and rods set into the stone like the vat chamber. Several of the rods cast electric blue light. Deep shadows contrasted with the dazzling glare as the light reflected off the whitish stone and sparkling patches of quartz. Paula led him to the left to the smallest opening, a jagged crack in the wall.

This tunnel was narrower and much rougher than the previous one. It appeared to be a natural cave rather than a cut tunnel. The glowing blue rods lit this space as well, a distinctly unnatural feature. Why had they been placed there? Did the creatures that had abducted them come here often? This last thought was especially upsetting. *Please don't let them come here.*

The path they followed wound around boulders and through sections that were only wide enough for one person to pass. David noticed the air smelled much better. However, the sickly-sweet smell of chocolate chip cookies still permeated the air. After about a hundred yards, the passage opened into an even larger cave that also appeared to have been formed naturally.

The cave was dim. Even though the glowing bars of blue light were here as well, there were not as many and they were spaced far apart. Again, David wondered why anyone, or anything, would bother. How often did whoever installed them come here? Both Alessandra and Paula seemed at ease, so he decided not to worry about it.

The cave was filled with rocks and boulders of all sizes, from pebbles the size of a marble to some bigger than a house. Stalactites hung from the ceiling, and stalagmites rose from the floor, some so big the three of them could not span them with linked arms and others not much bigger than his little finger. In some places, these had merged into columns of stone joining the floor and ceiling.

Blue light sparkled off quartz in the distance where openings in the rock permitted an unobstructed view deeper into the cave. Water splashed somewhere in the distance, which was heartening. The air was dry and cool, at least compared to the rainforest. It was impossible to determine how big the cave might be, but from what he could see and hear, it felt huge.

The women led him along a path through the boulders and stalagmites for a hundred paces or so. The smell of smoke wafted through the air and as they rounded a final pillar of rock, a faint yellow glow appeared. In an open space among the boulders and stalagmites, a small fire burned, which was the origin of the yellow glow. It was a welcome respite from the harsh blue glare.

"Home at last," he said, only half-jokingly. This was so much better than being in the room with the noisy, foul-smelling vat.

As he approached the fire, he noticed a small figure on the ground next to it. He squinted and then recognized the young boy from the village who had run into the plaza screaming of demons. The boy lay on his back, unmoving, with one leg heavily bandaged with webbing. More webbing material lay around him, which Alessandra went over and began arranging on top of the still form.

"The poor boy. His leg is badly infected," said Paula sadly. "He is running a fearful fever. I am not sure he will make it."

David eased down to the ground across the fire from the boy and leaned against a large boulder. In a rough circle around the fire were several neat piles. One pile was of firewood; another was of webbing material that had been braided into rope. Another, smaller pile included David's pack, a rolled-up bundle of shiny material that appeared to be a poncho, and a small satchel that had a military look to it. There was also a pile of fruits, nuts, and vegetables common to the forest. Finally, there was a large battered yellow cooler full of water with no lid on it. He wondered how the ice chest had wound up in the pit. Beside the fire were several forked sticks and wooden stakes that appeared to be used for cooking.

After covering the boy, Alessandra tried to coax him to drink from a canteen cup. She did not have much success. The small bottle of ibuprofen lay nearby, making him lick his lips. His whole body throbbed with pain, but David resisted asking for some. Seeing how the women were fussing over the sick child made him doubt they would be forthcoming with any.

With a grunt, David got onto his knees and scooted over to his pack, picked it up, and returned to the boulder. The first thing he noticed about the pack was a large hole. The sight of it made his back itch. Leaning back against the stone didn't hurt at least. Alessandra gave up trying to get the boy to drink and watched as Paula set the forked sticks up on either side of the fire.

"Um, excuse me. Alessandra?" he said.

She looked at him, saw the pack in his lap, and blushed. "Oh," she said, fingering the shirt. "I…I didn't think you would mind. My clothes were ruined when Josh cut off the webbing."

Paula frowned at him as if he were going to demand the girl give back the shirt back or something.

"Oh no," he said. "You can keep the shirt. I was just hoping you could look at my back."

Looking relieved, she nodded and came over. She pulled away the web bandage and removed the wad Josh had used to cover the wound. David was very conscious of both her cool touch and his big white belly hanging over his belt.

"It is still bleeding a little, but I don't think it is infected." She stood, went to the pile with webbing, brought back a fresh wad, and tied it over the wound. "There, I think it will be okay."

David thanked her, and she went back over to the boy and sat down. There were three shirts in the pack besides the one Alessandra now wore. Pulling out a khaki-colored safari bush shirt, he put his right arm through the sleeve and draped the left one over his shoulder, leaving the shirt unbuttoned. It felt good because it provided some warmth against the coolness of the cave and covered his oversized stomach.

"Paula, I have an extra shirt here if you are cold."

The older woman nodded gratefully and accepted a green polo shirt. It swallowed her as the blue one swallowed Alessandra. "Thank you. It can get a bit chilly in here."

Paula went deeper into the cave and came back with a two-foot-long sharpened stick with several hunks of bloody meat on it. She placed it on the forked sticks and a few minutes later, the smell of cooking food filled the air. The smoke wafted up and away however, indicating there must be a steady airflow through the cave.

The sights and smells of the vat were still fresh in David's mind and the smell of the meat made him nauseated. The questionable appearance of the meat did not help. Nor did the chocolate chip cookie smell that seemed to always hang in the air. With a shudder, he turned his attention back to his pack.

He pulled out his tablet and found a hole punched through the left corner. This made his gut lurch. Thinking back, he dimly remembered one of the creatures picking him up and tossing him onto the spiked back of another creature. The spike had hurt, but it should have killed him. Instead he had just slipped off. Now he knew why. The tablet must have taken the brunt of that first blow and probably saved his life.

It made him sad to see it mangled and broken. Sally had given it to him for his sixteenth birthday. It was almost obsolete, but it had been his constant companion for two years, not to mention a sentimental link to his sister. Now it was dead and most likely Sally was too. It was doubtful the tablet would have provided the comfort and escape it once had, but now there was no chance to try. With a sigh, he placed it to one side along with a hand-cranked charger Paul had given him.

Other than the tablet, his pack held a pair of shorts, the blue jeans he had worn down the river, now dirty, and extra socks and underwear. His bathroom kit was still there, minus the ibuprofen, along with some breakfast bars, bug repellant, and a small camping kit that included a metal plate and bowl clamped around a knife and fork. Items that might be handy if he were here very long, but nothing that had any meaning to him right now. He tossed the pack next to the meager pile containing the poncho.

He picked up the pad of webbing Alessandra had removed from his back and examined it. It was not really a web, more like a mesh, and felt like a plastic pot scrubber. The material was no longer tacky, but was coarse to the touch. It did not absorb like cloth; his blood flaked off it easily. It was very strong, too. It was odd how it had stuck to his clothing. Evidently, its properties changed as it dried. With a shrug, he tossed it into the fire. It shriveled and melted, then burned with an oily black smoke. Paula frowned at him but didn't say anything.

Josh came striding into the area wearing shorts, black combat boots, and a pistol belt that had a mammoth handgun hanging from it, along with two canteens and various pouches. His massive chest, covered in red hair, glistened with sweat despite the cool air of the cave. He stopped and stared at David for a moment before grunting and sitting down.

Paula lifted the spit off the fire and used a leaf to pull a piece of meat off it. She handed the leaf to Josh and said, "Any luck?"

Josh took a bite of the meat and shook his head. "Every damn passage is blocked. I got one more to check, but I don't see why it would be any different. It looks like the only way out is the way we came in."

"The conveyor?" said David with alarm.

Josh stopped eating and looked at David over the piece of meat. "That is one of the stupidest goddamn questions I have ever heard. Of course the conveyor—ain't that how we got in?"

David looked away blushing as Josh shook his head and resumed eating.

Paula glanced at Josh and then said hesitantly, "David? Would you like something to eat?"

To his surprise, now that the meat was fully cooked, David found himself very hungry. He nodded, and she brought him another leaf with some of the cooked meat and a breadfruit. Josh watched without comment but frowned at David's ample midsection.

Paula gave a leaf with food to Alessandra, who began trying to coax food into the boy, then took a leaf for herself and sat down. They ate in silence for a time. Then Paula asked, "How were you captured, David?"

He told them about his sister flying to Rio Estrada and coming down the river to look for her. Then about going to the forest with Lieutenant Goulart and described what happened to the men on the trailer. When he talked about Heather and how she died, his throat closed up and he had to stop for a moment.

After he finished, he said, "What about you?"

Paula told about being captured just outside her hut. A neighbor's screams had warned her and her husband, but they had been netted when they went to investigate. "I saw my man get impaled through the chest on a spike," she said, looking down with tears in her eyes. She drew in a deep breath and looked up, eyes glistening. "At least my son and daughter are in Manaus, thank God."

Alessandra told about hiding in the church with the boy and her mother. The day in the plaza had been a shopping day for her entire family. Her sister and two brothers had hidden in the church as well along with dozens of other villagers, all seeking refuge in vain. The church had trembled and shook and then began to collapse around them. She and the boy barely escaped the roof caving in on them, only to be netted together right outside.

When a creature threw them onto another's spiky back, one had snagged the webbing holding them together, and another had punched into the boy's leg. Blood and gore were everywhere and that was probably why his leg had gotten infected.

She also told of seeing her sister and two brothers captured. Her voice became very quiet as she finished in a near whisper, saying they had gone ahead of her into the vat. After Josh had pulled her out, she could hear her younger brother screaming at the end. Her voice broke as she finished and she began to sob softly.

They sat in silence, respecting the girl's loss. For that matter, they all had losses to reflect upon and mourn. The silence stretched to an uncomfortable level before David looked back and forth between Alessandra and Paula and said, "Your English is really good. Are both of you from Rio Estrada?"

Paula nodded. "We were both born there. My husband is from Atlanta, Georgia, though. His family owns the mill and he came here to manage it over twenty years ago. I have been to the U.S. several times and decided I needed to learn the language." She nodded toward the girl. "Alessandra's father is from Manaus and worked as an engineer for the mill. We sponsored a program for English in the school, and she was one of the star pupils."

The girl looked down, blushed, and said, "I had hoped to be a translator working in a big city one day. Now...who knows?" Again, the group sat in silence. Then Alessandra looked at Josh. "Did you see any sign of them, the gatherers?"

He shook his head, a puzzled expression on his face. "Nothing. Not that I'm complaining mind you. But it's strange. Like they don't care we're here."

"Maybe they just don't know," said David.

Josh shrugged. "Maybe. But we need to find a way out of here before they do."

Remembering how Josh had humiliated him a minute ago, David started to point out that was pretty damn obvious too. Wisdom overruled and he decided against it. What would it accomplish? The big goon would probably beat him to a pulp. He sighed and shook his head as tears filled his eyes, feeling more lonely and worthless than ever.

Crap, crap, crap, why me? It would have been just as well for it to have all ended at the vat. In a haze of self-pity, he joined the others in staring at the fire, wondering what the future had in store for them. This time the silence stretched on and on.

Sally

The jungle was less dark than the last time Sally opened her eyes. Had she slept? If so, it couldn't have been for long. Soft moans and the sounds of a poncho being shaken and folded let her know it must be time to wake up. *Thank you, God for getting us through the long night.* A little prayer never hurt, but moving did. Sally winced with pain and forced herself to her feet. The poncho scavenged from a dead man spread over the hard ground had been her bed for the night. It had not been a comfortable one. Even with capacious amounts of insect repellant, she had numerous bites. She tried unsuccessfully to blink away the grit that seemed stuck to her eyeballs.

While the dark gray of the forest turned into a lighter gray, Sally pondered how her life had come to this. Getting down from the tree had been a wonderful moment. It had proved to be a terrifyingly short-lived moment, however. Now she was a survivor of a battle against unimaginable creatures in the shadow of an impossible mountain. If anything, she was now more tired, in more pain, and even more terrified than she had been in the helicopter. Her ribs pounded, her legs cramped, and her back ached. As more and more of the men began to stir, she sat on the poncho in numb disbelief at her situation, dreading when she would have to get up and start moving.

From the haggard looks of the men, she was not the only one struggling to get started. The men moved carefully, trying to be quiet, fearful of attracting unwanted attention. The battered group had moved every bit as slow as Major Antinasio had feared, making a scant five kilometers before grinding to an exhausted halt. Everyone was highly aware how close they were to the wall and mountains.

There was now enough light to see Major Antinasio as he moved about his men, having a quick word with each of them. After each brief exchange, whomever he spoke to often had a slight smile, or at least a less worried expression. He seemed to radiate confidence and assurance, and it warmed her to see him draw near.

"How are you today, Sally?" he asked. "I trust these magnificent accommodations were to your liking."

Sally surprised herself with a crooked smile. "The room service could be better, but the beds are wonderful."

He smiled, nodded, and moved on. She gazed at his departing back, amazed at how such a small thing could raise one's spirits. It wasn't so much the corny joke, but rather that he made it all. She recognized him as that special kind of leader; one that men would follow into Hell itself. This, in fact, was pretty much what they had already done. Sally hoped he would also be able to lead them out again.

Julio walked up and nodded toward the major. "He is a great man," he said as if reading Sally's thoughts.

"He is, isn't he?" she said. She turned to the young private. "But then, so are you, my hero."

Julio blushed. "Please, Sally, do not call me that."

She actually managed to laugh. "All right. I'm sorry." The laugh was short, as was the levity, absorbed by the misery around them. "Well, I guess we should get Carlosa."

Julio nodded, looking over at the man Sally had saved. He lay unmoving on the makeshift sledge they had been pulling him on. One of his legs was a bloody mess with a belt still pulled tight around his thigh in a tourniquet. All the medics had died in the battle and no one had been able to stop Carlosa's bleeding. Sally feared the boy had a severed artery.

"Do you think he will make it?" Julio said in a whisper.

Sally shook her head. "He won't if we don't get him some help soon. I think the leg is already a loss."

The sledge was a simple affair. Two long branches stripped of leaves and twigs fastened together at one end with green straps from a discarded backpack. More straps suspended a one-man tent between the branches and supported Carlosa.

With a resigned grunt, Sally lifted one of the branches and slipped a strap over her shoulder. Julio did the same right beside her. It was an awkward arrangement that made her ribs seem like they were grating together with every step. Others were hurt worse than she in the battered group pulling the sledges, so she set her jaw and resolved to keep going without complaint. She was determined to help until her strength failed completely.

The tattered troops set out, fighting for every step as they pulled the sledges between the mammoth trees, over jutting roots, and through patches of tough vines covered with thorns. Their pace through the forest maze would make a turtle look like an Olympic runner. Their clothes were ripped, torn, and soaked, from perspiration as much as rain. Sally had numerous painful scratches on her legs. The shorts she had chosen for the trip to the village were pitifully inadequate for the jungle.

Flies buzzed in ever-greater numbers. Sally and Julio had to stop frequently to fan them away from Carlosa. The smell of dead meat coming from his leg acted like a beacon for the insects.

It started raining hard around mid-morning. The pounding water cascaded down through the layers of trees in such a torrent that visibility dropped to nothing. This brought the group to a reluctant halt. They just did not have the strength to fight both the jungle and the weather.

Even Major Antinasio sat silent and grim, leaning against a tree with a poncho draped around his head and shoulders. The group kept moving in large part because of his constant urging, drawing strength and energy from him with every step. Now it appeared even his considerable reserve had reached an end.

Not sure why, only that she felt the need for the company, Sally went over to him. He smiled despite his obvious fatigue as she sat down beside him.

"How are you this fine morning?" he said in a hoarse voice. He offered her part of his poncho.

She nodded with a tight smile and held one corner over her head. It helped—not much, but at least the water wasn't pounding on her head. Sally looked down and grimaced when she saw the blood soaking his uniform. "I'd better check that for you," she said, frowning up at him. "If you aren't careful, we'll wind up carrying you."

He gave a small snort but didn't protest as she pulled the torn shirt away from his chest and removed the tape holding a blood-soaked bandage over the wound. Despite her efforts not to hurt him, Marcus flinched several times but remained silent.

"You are a remarkable woman," he said, catching her by surprise. "Many women, most men, too, for that matter, would be a blubbering mess if they had been through what you have."

She looked up at him, pushing rain-soaked brown hair from her eyes. "Actually, Major, I am a blubbering mess, on the inside. But I guess I got most of the hysteria out of my system while trapped in the helicopter. I very nearly lost it during the attack. In fact, I am amazed I can function at all."

"I think you have done better than merely continue to function. You killed one of the creatures single-handed and have done more than your share helping the wounded. That is why I say you are remarkable."

Sally felt her spirits rise. Once again, he managed to lift her above the tension and weariness of their predicament. "You have quite a way with words, Major," she said. "I can see now why your men are willing to follow you, even into..." she gestured around them with a brief wave, "this."

He studied her face a moment and asked, "What about you? My medic told me your ribs were probably cracked in the crash, yet I have not heard a complaint out of you. How are they feeling?"

While she worked on his chest, she grimaced at the ragged slash. It looked red and angry, though the bleeding seemed to have almost stopped. It must hurt like hell, but he never complained either. How could she do any less? She dabbed the wound with antiseptic from Corporal Barros's bag and covered it with a fresh bandage. "Not too bad. They hurt, but I'll live. It is nothing compared to the injuries of some of your men." She finished taping up his chest. "That should hold it," she said with a smile.

"Thank you," he replied. He looked up as the rain abruptly slackened, as it was prone to do in the heart of the Amazon. A hint of sunlight painted the upper branches as steamy tendrils began seeping from the ground. "It looks like our break is over," he said, struggling to his feet. Sally also stood, and he looked down into her face. "I am truly glad we found you. You have been more help than you realize."

Sally smiled at him, trying to think of something nice to say. Instead, she nodded and turned to go find Julio so they could resume the grim and laborious task of pulling Carlosa through the jungle.

David

Despite some disturbing dreams, David slept far better that night than he expected, aided by exhaustion, the gentle patter of cascading water from deep in the cave and the soft sand floor.

The dreams were bad enough. The worst involved Heather's shocked expression as she was inundated with the sticky webbing. Such images roused him several times, causing him to mutter and roll over but not fully wake.

Josh's loud, insistent voice, however, was another matter. "All right everyone. Up and at 'em. Time to get moving."

The sudden intrusion on his sleep caused David to jerk erect, expecting a gatherer or some other threat. Seeing nothing, he leaned back. Josh must have been talking to the women. Paula and Alessandra looked confused as well but climbed to their feet. The little boy stirred, but did not rise.

David asked, "What's going on?"

Josh glared at him. "I said up, fat boy. We're going to do a little P.T."

"P.T.? What's that?"

Josh snorted. "Physical Training. Something you obviously don't get enough of. Civvies call it exercise."

"I...I don't understand."

Josh took two long strides over to David and kicked him in the leg. "You don't have to understand. Just get off your ass."

David swallowed hard. Looking up at an angry Josh was unnerving. He rolled over and struggled to his feet.

Josh nodded. "That's better, now come on."

They went through the cave and down the tunnel to the vat room. A droning sound echoed through the chamber, indicating the vat was in the final stages of churning its contents into a soupy mixture prior to draining. The smell was as bad as David remembered, and he nearly gagged.

As they entered the chamber, Josh pointed at the wide ledge surrounding the pit. "We'll keep it simple for now. Start running."

"In here?" whined David. "We can hardly breathe."

Josh frowned at him. "Is bitching and moaning all you can do? So it stinks a little. You'll get used to it."

Alessandra and Paula glanced at each other. Paula shrugged and they set off at a slow jog.

Josh watched them a moment and grunted in satisfaction. He turned to David. "Well, get moving."

David gestured to his arm. "I can't run like this."

Josh's eyes flared with anger. "If you bitch one more time…" His voice trailed off, but his eyes completed the threat. David wilted back, his face going white. After a moment, Josh's expression returned to his normal scowl. He said, "As for running, I beg to differ, fat boy. I don't see a damn thing wrong with your legs." He leaned forward, his face inches from David's. "I tell you what. Start walking, go as fast as you can, but get moving."

Despite being at least six inches taller, David felt very small as he recoiled from the older man's glare. Fearful to speak, he started walking. He had not gone far when he heard a clump-clumping coming up from behind, followed by a stinging slap across his rump.

"Ow, shit!" he cried.

Josh clumped on by carrying a long, thin stick. "I'm going to swat ya each time I pass," he said, looking over his shoulder with a savage grin. "We'll see how long it takes you to start running."

David began walking faster, watching Josh's steady progress around the cauldron. Passing Paula and Alessandra, he gave each of them a light rap with the stick. They frowned and then smiled, obviously not hit as hard as David. When he saw how quickly Josh was catching up, he broke into an awkward jog.

The vat emptied, and the conveyor squalled to a start. A progression of large trees and white bundles began tumbling off the end. The noise was loud enough to cover the sounds of Josh's approach until he was right on top of David. Clump, clump, clump came Josh's boots from behind. David found it difficult to run with one arm bound across his chest. Moreover, the jostling hurt, but so did his butt for that matter. He managed to pick up his pace a bit more. He made it a dozen more steps before Josh caught him.

Whap! The stick struck again. Josh did not bother to look back this time.

"Umph," grunted David. He did not want to give the goon the satisfaction of crying out. Despite panting in an almost doglike fashion, he bumped up his pace a little more. In a few minutes, his head started to spin and he had to concentrate on placing one foot in front of the other.

Josh caught up to him again. *Whap!* The blow came, but not as hard this time. David completed six circuits of the cauldron. Finally, as he came huffing and grunting back to the tunnel, he found the others waiting for him.

Paula and Alessandra looked out of breath, but nowhere near as bad as he was. Josh was sweating, but not breathing hard at all. When David came up, Josh said, "All right, fat boy. We're going to check on the boy and then do a few calisthenics. You—" he pointed the stick at David, "—keep going. Walking is all right, but you'd better not let me come back and find you sitting. Got it?"

David nodded, panting, and started to walk. Josh and the women turned and disappeared into the tunnel. David stopped and glared at the opening. *Damn, what is it with this guy?* He almost sat down, but with a long look at the tunnel mouth, turned and kept walking.

David felt like he had been walking around the cauldron forever before Paula and Alessandra emerged from the tunnel, carrying their rope and grappling hook arrangement. Alessandra had freed her hair from the confines of the ponytail and it flowed free about her shoulders and upper back. She had transformed the voluminous blue shirt into a short dress by tying a strip of webbing around her waist. The outcome of these simple changes was startling; her figure looked much more womanly and her face more mature. He bumped her age up from girl to young woman.

Seeing them with their "fishing gear," as Paula called it, made him decide P.T. must be over. He walked over to where they stood looking into the pit.

"How's your butt?" asked Alessandra with a small smile.

David managed an embarrassed grin. "A little sore, but I'll live." He frowned. "Josh is such an asshole."

Paula bristled. "That asshole saved your life. Saved all of us."

"Well, yeah. But what's the point of this P.T.?"

She poked him in the stomach. "Why worry about it? It's not like you don't need it."

David blushed; this wasn't at all how he wanted this conversation to go. "Well, I guess I just don't see the point. This doesn't seem like a good time to start worrying about our health."

"You still think they will come for us?" asked Alessandra, her eyes darting around the cave.

He shrugged. "I am amazed each hour they do not."

"And that is why we need to be able to run," said Paula forcefully. "When Josh finds a way out, we need to be ready to take it. There is your reason for P.T."

David stared off into the vat. As much as he hated to admit it, that did make some sense. He had been so angry he had not considered it in that light. Did Josh actually have some kind of plan? If so, why didn't the son of a bitch simply say so?

Alessandra, her smile gone, said, "I don't think there is an escape. I still believe we are in Hell." She crossed herself.

David nodded. Though not overtly religious, he felt much the same way, if for different reasons. Sally was gone; his heart knew it. They were trapped in a mountain by things that could not exist. Nothing made sense. What was the point of fighting anymore?

Paula shook her head. "All those people died, and yet we live. I think there must be a reason for it. And you two are ready to…" she snorted, "just give up. Why don't you jump and get it over with?" she finished, pointing into the vat.

David looked down and considered it for a moment. With one blinding flash of pain, there would be freedom from this nightmare. Damn, he didn't have the courage to do it, and he did not have the strength to go on. Self-loathing filled him. "I'd better go check on the boy," he said, the only excuse he could think of to escape her accusing glare.

"Pedro," said Paula. "And we already did so."

"Huh?"

"His name is Pedro, since you have been too full of yourself to even ask." Her expression was scornful, and even Alessandra was looking at him like he was an asshole.

David's face flushed and he nodded, turned, and hurried into the tunnel. He had felt a strong impulse to actually jump. A tinkling, electric burn clutched his heart and sent jolts up and down his back. It felt icky, but good too. Is this how his father had felt? This brought 'The Memory' forward from his now rather black and cold existence. But as it played across his mind's eye, it didn't seem to hurt as bad. Tears still found their way down his cheeks as he shambled up the tunnel.

That afternoon, Josh had them do another round of P.T. This time he lapped David four times, giving him a painful swat each time he passed and saying, "Move it, fat boy."

David wasn't sure if the pain or the shame hurt the most. It took him back to high school during dreaded gym class. He had been even heavier then than he was now and suffered merciless teasing. However, at least back then, no one had kept hitting him with a stick.

Alessandra seemed a little sympathetic, but Paula laughed with each occurrence. David began to hate her almost as much as Josh.

Misery turned to despair and at one point, he nearly worked up the courage to throw himself into the vat. He felt more and more that Alessandra was right. This was Hell, and Josh the Devil. However, something, fear of death, or a stronger will to live than he knew he had, kept him shuffling around the vat and clear of the edge.

Later that night, The Memory came again. David didn't cry at all. Was that a good thing? Or a bad thing? That would take some pondering. His heart had less pain, but now it often felt very cold.

Sally

The wore slowly on and Sally's arms and shoulders ached more and more from dragging the sled. Her ribs sent spasms of pain through her with every step. Cramps coursed through her back and legs more and more often. With every step, she was surprised to find the will to take another.

At least she hadn't fallen down. This was becoming a common occurrence among the men struggling to transport the wounded away from the looming mountains. Everyone in the battered group expected the demons to return and finish them off at any moment. There was no fight left in them, only the desire for flight. Fear of the demon's return and constant encouragement from Major Antinasio was the only thing that kept them staggering onward.

After many painful hours, in the late afternoon, the private who accompanied Lieutenant Viana to meet the boats returned with a Brazilian officer and twenty men. They were a beautiful sight to Sally with their clean, untorn uniforms and faces free of haggard exhaustion. The men around Sally gave a muted cheer that was more a collective sigh of relief as they halted and began setting down their wearisome burdens.

Major Antinasio stepped forward, beaming. "Nelino, my God, am I glad to see you."

The officer leading the rescue party was short and somewhat stocky. He smiled and nodded, although his eyes showed concern as they swept over the tattered group. "I am glad we found you, sir. It looks like you could use some help."

Antinasio nodded and his smile faded. "Indeed we can. It has been pretty rough."

The new arrivals moved forward. Two wearing Red Cross patches like Jef's went immediately to the men on stretchers.

Sally and Julio eased Carlosa's litter down gratefully. Julio spotted a friend among the new arrivals and went to greet him. Sally checked Carlosa's pulse and found it beating slow and steady, but frowned at the fever the young man was running. She prayed they could get him to some help soon. The major noticed her and motioned her to join them.

"Sally Morgan, I would like to introduce you to Senior Lieutenant Nelino Pereira, my second in command."

"It is very, very good to meet you, Lieutenant."

Pereira shook her hand. "And you Miss Morgan. Lieutenant Viana told me about you. He said they call you Demon Slayer."

Sally frowned. "I have heard a few of the men say that. But I have discouraged it."

Pereira gave a small laugh. "Well, you should have told that to Lieutenant Viana. You might have a hard time shaking it now."

Sally shrugged with a slight grimace. "Well, I've been called worse. Lieutenant, how far is it to Rio Estrada? I hate the idea of spending another night in the jungle."

The officer looked uncomfortable, but said, "We are about ten or eleven kilometers from the boats. If you were fresh, maybe three hours, but considering everyone's condition, it will probably take at least eight."

Antinasio looked apologetic. "Sorry, Miss Morgan. It looks as if we have to spend one more night in the forest."

Twelve soldiers led by a sergeant gathered the four men in worst shape, including Carlosa, and immediately left at a brisk pace. Lieutenant Pereira had ordered them to travel after dark if necessary to get them back to the boats as soon as possible. Sally watched Carlosa's stretcher go by, thankful to see him getting help, but also grateful not to have to pull him anymore. She reached out and patted his shoulder, but the unconscious marine did not stir.

As the men passed by, Lieutenant Pereira continued to look uncomfortable. "Uh, sir, there is something you need to know."

Antinasio looked at him, his eyebrows raised. "Yes?"

"Well, sir, Rio Estrada, it is gone."

"Gone?"

"Yes, sir, this track leads straight to it. But the entire village is missing—people, huts, animals, everything."

"Oh my God," said Sally.

Pereira shook his head. "According to the few people who got away, it wasn't an act of God. They all describe demons." He gave a brief overview of what he knew about the destruction of the village.

Sally watched Major Antinasio as for the second time since she met him, fear played across his features. It lasted but a moment before grim determination took its place. "Thank you, Lieutenant. It sounds as if we still have many challenges before us. Well, we have time to get a few more kilometers between us and those damn mountains before dark. Then we will get some rest. Hopefully, we can make it to the boats in the morning."

Chapter 13

Sally

For the second night since the attack, Sally refused to sleep in a tent, even though it would have provided blissful relief from the insects and a steady light rain. The idea of being in a flimsy nylon prison with demons large and small populating the jungle terrified her. Even if she didn't believe in demons, the things from the mountains were close enough as to make no difference. A restless night on the damp ground was better; at least she could get up and run if need be. Or fight if it came to that. She was not the only one who felt this way. Three-quarters of the marines slept outside with just the layered canopy of the trees for shelter. In addition, she slept with the rifle she had picked up during the battle close to hand.

Sometime during the night, as she slumped back against a large mahogany tree, Myra came to her. A single staring eye came drifting toward her through the maze of huge tree trunks, like a mutated Cheshire cat from a twisted Wonderland. Then the ruined face and battered bloody body of her dead friend solidified before her. This time Sally found no comfort at all at the sight of her friend's mangled visage. In fact, it was disgusting and disturbing.

"Hey girl," said Myra in a moist, drippy voice.

Sally felt confused, disconcerted, at her friend's appearance. It felt…wrong somehow. Her days in the helicopter already seemed to belong to a different person from a different life. "Myra, you shouldn't be here. You're dead."

Myra laughed with the sound of wet, rustling leaves. "That's for sure. You didn't seem to mind that little fact a couple of days ago. And yet, here I am." Behind her, other figures wavered in the mist.

Keith's bloody form solidified and peered at her. She could see the accusation in his blank dead eyes. "Why did you leave us in the helicopter?"

Sally shook her head. Before she could reply, Jef and Pieter loomed out of the darkness.

"You saved him," they said in burbling unison. "Why didn't you save us?"

"I tried to save you. I really tried."

They shook their heads, and again in unison they said, "You never made a sound. You could have warned us; you could have saved us."

Tears began to stream down Sally's face. Her life was nothing but terror, guilt, and tears.

Two more figures wavered into existence, at once near and far away. They had no faces, only the accusing eyes, but Sally still recognized them. The man and young girl in the helicopter they were taking to Manaus. They said nothing, just stared with those…those accusing eyes. *Why, why, why?* There was nothing she could have done. Why were they here? The ghosts didn't scare her, although their battered bodies and faces left her with a deep sadness.

All six began shaking their heads timed to a beat only they could hear, as though to a metronome of sadness. Sally shuddered—what did they want with her?

"It's not my fault. What could I do?" she mumbled. Her heart hurt worse than her ribs as tears continued to flow down her face.

Myra's mouth opened to an incredible extent, wide enough to engulf Sally's head, and her one eye gleamed as a shriek of death and desolation erupted from her ravaged throat.

Sally started awake, grasping the rifle like a life preserver. The screams continued, and she looked around in panic before realizing they came from the jungle. The sounds faded, followed by a roar of triumph. Taking in a deep breath, she forced her fingers to ease their white-knuckled grip on the rifle and wiped the tears from her face.

The screams were from a monkey, the roar a jaguar. Sounds she had heard before, a common enough drama in the heart of the Amazon. She shuddered, now having more sympathy for the monkey than ever before. Now she too knew what it felt like to be hunted.

She leaned back, considering her experience with Myra. *God, am I going crazy? Or are there truly ghosts loose in the jungle?* She did not like the answer to either question, though the idea of going insane really scared her the most.

In the grand scheme of things, if demons were afoot, why not spirits? Sally was a disciple of science and had always discounted the idea of ghosts, but the world was not the same place it had been a mere week ago. *Stress*, she told herself. *It must be the stress.* She stared up into the shifting layers of darkness above her. After a time, exhaustion forced her to sleep again.

Despite the restless night, Sally woke to the gray, shadowy dawn in better spirits. It was a relief to know they had made it through another night. Today they should get out of the jungle. In addition, all she had to carry was her backpack and newly acquired rifle, heaven after the last two days of hard labor pulling the sledge.

However, even with lighter loads, the jungle still presented challenges for the bone-weary group. They moved a little bit faster than the day before, but not much. Many in the battered group were weak from blood loss. It rained for a little while, cutting visibility, though not enough to force them to a stop as it had yesterday.

The last stretch of the journey was the worst. The jungle ended, and they had to cross a wide expanse of torn, muddy earth. The cloying soil sucked at their exhausted legs with every step. However, with the added strength of the reinforcements, they pushed on and came upon the ravaged site of Rio Estrada a bit before noon. They passed a small observation platform at what would have been the edge of town. Walking became easier as the ground became packed down and the mud less sticky. Three Brazilian marines operating optical equipment trained on the mountains waved and called out encouragement as they passed by.

Exhaustion, emotional and physical, muddled Sally's awareness, and she did not even realize they had reached the town until she spotted a pile of bricks. She drew up with a gasp. Her already heavy heart weighed even heavier in her chest as she looked around and spotted the floating docks at the bottom of the hill. She turned slowly, struggling to comprehend, knowing what she was seeing but unable able to accept it.

Over there would have been the church, there the office of Naval de Brasilia, there the hotel, and all around should have been the thatched huts and ramshackle houses that had made up the thriving frontier village. Even the small fountain at the center of the plaza was smashed beyond recognition. There was nothing left but the docks, the paved road, lots of red soil, and numerous piles of stones.

Julio came up beside her. "Are you okay?"

She shrugged and let out a deep sigh. Her eyes were tortured with remembrance. "Not really," she replied. "I have been here several times. I was here just a few days ago." Such a short time ago and an entire village had been here having lunch in the rainy plaza. The millworker who saved the small child, the mayor, the nurse, and so many others had all been there. "Does anyone know what happened to the people?"

"One of the guys with Lieutenant Pereira said they were taken by demons."

"Yes, I heard that. But taken where?"

Julio looked back at the imposing bone-colored mountains, clearly visible through the parting clouds. Even here, he had to tilt his head back to see the tallest misty summit. "I guess they were taken there," he said in a low voice.

Sally followed his gaze.

Julio drew in a deep breath and said, "It doesn't look good, does it?"

"No, Julio, it doesn't look good at all," Sally said a quick prayer for the townspeople and then another prayer that no new faces would join her haunted dreams. Her dreams were crowded enough already. With a slow shake of her head, she began walking down the hill toward the river.

Two patrol boats floated next to the docks, looking fast and sleek. Men stood at guns mounted on their decks. Soldiers also watched from two log bunkers at the top of the ramp leading down to the docks, the snouts of large machine guns poking out of the structures. It made Sally happy to see the defenses. She would feel even better if there were a battleship sitting in the river.

Julio nudged her and pointed across the river. "Wow, would you look at that?"

Sally looked up and saw two patrol boats cruising across the water. However, this was not had what caught Julio's attention. The river was wide here, even in the dry season, over a half mile from bank to bank. On the far side was a riot of color. Boats and tents, obviously civilian, dotted the water and land.

Julio looked at Major Antinasio. "I bet he isn't going to like this. I wonder what they all want?"

Sally said, "Survivors from the town maybe? Possibly some sightseers? But where could they all come from?"

Julio shrugged. "There are a lot of small villages along the main river. More than most people realize."

The gathering on the far shore reminded Sally of a carnival. It seemed especially strange compared to the ruins of Rio Estrada, disrespectful somehow. There was a curious contrast between the light-brown water, dark-brown mud flat, the green jungle, and the riot of color assembled on the far bank.

The mud flat was quite large, stretching almost two hundred yards in places between the water and the edge of the jungle due to the shallow slope of the land. Four walkways made of wide wooden planks snaked across the mud to the shore proper. Where the land rose above the mud, the jungle had been chopped back for forty yards or more, and numerous tents were arranged helter-skelter in the resulting clearing. Two log buildings were visible with three more under construction. At least two dozen small and medium-sized boats sat at the water's edge.

A short distance off the bank, jutting out into the deeper water, were two small floating docks constructed of wood and large plastic barrels. A walkway made of more barrels and wood connected the new docks to the mud flat. Moored to the docks were two *regatãos*, a type of traveling general store that patrolled the rivers and tributaries of the Amazon.

The *regatãos* were by far the largest boats in sight. The vessels looked especially bizarre with their multi-colored merchandise crammed into and onto every available space. For some reason, they made Sally think of floating Turkish bazaars, though she had never been to Turkey.

In direct contrast to the chaotic civilian gathering, a dozen olive-green tents sat off to the left, separated from the colorful gathering by a strip of trees. They were arranged in two neat rows. Four log bunkers sat around the tents, though she could not tell at this distance what, if any, weapons they might contain. A wide wooden causeway led across the mud in front of the tents across the mud flat to another floating dock, where a patrol boat was moored.

Sally and the survivors of the battle walked down the hill and onto the docks. Once there, she stood to one side as the boat crews greeted their returning comrades with enthusiasm. A flurry of activity erupted as those with wounds needing treatment, more than half the men, were loaded onto one of the boats for the trip to Manaus. As the men settled on board, Major Antinasio noticed her and came over.

"You should go on this boat, Miss Morgan," he said, sounding very formal. "It can have you in Manaus by tonight."

Sally shook her head. "No thanks. Not until I find my brother. And the rest of the team for that matter."

He frowned. "But you really need to have your ribs X-rayed."

She gave a dry chuckle. "They still hurt, sure. But if the last three days did not kill me, I guess I'll survive. Thank you for the offer, but no. I'll stay for now."

He was clearly unhappy about this but did not push the matter. "Very well. I suppose we can spare a boat to help you find your people." He waved Lieutenant Pereira over. "Nelino, Miss Morgan is part of a research group from the United States. They are camped up river from here. Please arrange a boat to take her to them as soon as practical."

Lieutenant Pereira pursed his lips and turned to look across the river. "That may be tough, at least for one of our boats. The river gets pretty shallow upriver from here. But I believe someone from your group is already here."

Marcus looked across the river, his displeasure evident. "I am disappointed you let them set up camp there, Lieutenant. They are not safe."

Pereira shrugged. "Well, sir. They were already here when we arrived." He rubbed his chin. "Though not so many as there are now. They just seem to keep coming in."

Sally cleared her throat. "If there are some of my people there, that would be a good place to start. Maybe David is there."

Marcus nodded. "All right." He nodded to a boat pulling up to the dock. "We can take you over easy enough, and possibly find someone to take you up river if you need. Lieutenant, please go with her."

Pereira nodded.

Marcus took Sally's hand and looked into her eyes. "Good luck, Miss Morgan. It was very good to meet you. Too bad the circumstances were not better."

"And you, Major. Thank you so much for everything."

He smiled, his white teeth very bright against the dark stubble of his beard. "Thanks to you as well. You pulled more than your share. As I told you yesterday, you are a remarkable woman."

Sally managed one last blush, squeezed his hand, and then accompanied Lieutenant Pereira to the idling patrol boat.

She stood at the front of the boat as it cruised across the river. A group of about forty people stood on the civilian side, peering at the activity on the old docks. As the boat drew near, she scanned the faces of the crowd, looking for David. He was nowhere to be seen, but she did spot

Dr. Robert Allen, Professor Jane Powers, and Paul Sanders. Seeing them made her heart soar—everyone from the camp must be all right.

She had been worried for nothing. David was probably huddled in a tent with one of his precious games. Her friends on shore saw her and began waving like they were a little on the crazy side. He began hurrying toward the makeshift dock in front of the military encampment.

Once the boat was tied off, Sally hurried across the rough planking that joined the floating dock to shore. She threw her arms around Doctor Allen, giving the short, stout doctor a fierce hug while fighting back tears of relief.

Pulling back, she said, "Oh Robert, you have no idea how good it is to see you."

His smile showed every tooth and his eyes twinkled. "I don't know about that—we feel pretty damn good at seeing you. We thought for sure you had…" He looked over at the boat. "Uh, where are Myra and Keith?"

Sally's smile faded as she shook her head.

Dr. Allen flinched and looked down at the ground. Paul seemed to fold in on himself, and Professor Powers put her arm around his shoulders. He and Myra had been good friends.

"Uh, Sally…" Dr. Allen began. His voice sounded odd as it trailed off and he looked at the ground. Paul and Professor Powers suddenly couldn't meet her eyes.

Apprehension flooded over her. "David?" she asked. "Where's David?"

Dr. Allen shook his head slowly. "We don't know, Sally. He's…he's missing. He came here…with Paul, Heather, and Darrin." He nodded toward the barren scar that had once been a thriving village. "He came looking for you."

"Looking for me?" she asked in a soft squeak. Then with more force, she said, "When? What happened?"

Paul, as unemotional a man as there ever was, was weeping, his face drawn and haggard. It was obvious he had been crying even before hearing about Myra and Keith. He said, "David, Heather, Darrin, and I came down the river in the canoes. We—"

"Wait," said Sally. She turned to Dr. Allen. "You let David go in the canoes? Why in God's name did you do that?"

The older man now looked to be on the verge of tears as well, a marked transition coming over him from the joy at seeing her a few seconds ago to the misery of delivering bad news. "He insisted, Sally. And Paul said he would take care of him."

Paul seemed to slump even further. "Oh God, Sally. I thought... I didn't know... I thought he would be safe there."

Sally said, "Where are Heather and Darrin?"

Paul said, "Darrin went to Manaus. Heather? Heather was with David in Rio Estrada when..." He glanced across the river; pain seeming to radiate from his eyes. He continued, almost too quiet to hear, "We hired a boat, and I went back to the camp. I...I talked David into staying, in the village, in case you came back." Tears ran freely down his cheeks. "Oh God, Sally, I am so sorry. I thought... I didn't know."

Dr. Allen said, "The people we talked to told of mass confusion at the docks. There was fighting for the boats, shots were fired, and some people were killed. Then things got even worse, especially as the creatures closed in. A few remember seeing David and Heather head out of the village with an officer from the Naval de Brasilia and some local men right before things went to hell. None of the survivors remember seeing them after that."

"So...so no one saw them get taken?"

Dr. Allen shook his head. "No, so we don't know for sure. It's possible they made it out on a boat or escaped into the jungle."

Sally studied the older man's face. "But you don't think so, do you?" She noted his hesitation and saw the answer in his eyes. Turning her back on him, she gazed across the river at the mounds of rock and brick that were now the gravestones of Rio Estrada. Her shoulders drooped as her spirit faded.

When she and the soldiers entered the remains of Rio Estrada, Sally didn't think she could feel any worse. She believed she had been carrying as much guilt, sorrow, and fear as she could bear. Now, on this side of the river, this proved to be very, very wrong. Completely new levels of misery wrapped her soul at the idea of her little brother braving the perils of the Amazon to look for her.

In addition to the overwhelming guilt, there was also a new fear. There was little doubt that when the ghosts came calling in the night, as she knew with all her heart they would, David's face would be at the forefront. A situation she feared she just wasn't strong enough to endure. Sally sank to her knees on the rough wooden planks at the edge of the river as though a great weight had fallen on her. Tears flowed down her cheeks in an endless stream.

"Oh God, I am so sorry, David. I am so very sorry."

David

Vibrations could be felt, albeit faintly, through the floor of the cave. Loud noises would also echo through the surrounding rock. By now, David could tell where the vat was in its cycle while sitting or lying by the fire in the cave, especially when he tried to sleep.

The conveyor created small vibrations, but none of the sounds of its operation reached the cave unless an especially large tree fell unimpeded to the very bottom. Then a distant gong-like peal could be heard. It was easiest to tell when the vat first began to churn as the initial vibrations and sounds were at their strongest, sending a dull thrum through the tunnels. As the vat spun up to top speed and the mixture smoothed out, there was almost no vibration at all. Nor was there any when it drained.

Other than the cycles of the vat, the cave remained steady and unchanging. The widely spaced light rods shed the same electric blue light over boulders and rock spires, casting sharp shadows that never wavered. Water splashed on rocks further back in the cave with the sound echoing off stone in a constant cadence. The faint smell of decay and chocolate chip cookies came incessantly from the vat room. The constant sameness gave time very little meaning. The only way to know whether it was day or night was to look at a watch.

Josh kept them on a schedule, however, at least in regards to P.T. and chores. P.T. was twice daily at eight o'clock in the morning and three o'clock in the afternoon. David never even considered not being there. Nor would he skip out on his assigned chores that included fishing duty, hauling water in the battered yellow ice chest, and dragging wood from the vat room to the cave for the fire.

All of these were a struggle with only one arm, but Josh insisted he find a way to get it done. Therefore, he dragged the ice chest by one handle, fished out the smallest bundles he could snag from the pit, and carried as much firewood as possible with one arm from the vat room. This last chore required multiple trips, and David hated every moment of it.

At night, or what Josh had dictated was night, David could only sleep in spurts. When he did sleep, his dreams were full of demons, or the fiery death of his sister, or of Heather's slow suffocation. When he was awake, he worried over what insanity Josh would come up with next. Fantasies of suicide, the ultimate escape, still held an appeal for him. It felt good sometime to think about being dead. The concept twisted his emotions and made him both warm and scared at the same time.

It was his fear of pain more than anything else that held him from actually doing it. A little bit the fear of death maybe, but not really. How much worse could it be? His dad had done it after all. *If my father could escape that way, then why not me?*

The thing was…how bad would it hurt? That was what stopped him. Thinking about ending his life brought a twisted weird feeling to his stomach that was not entirely unpleasant, and better than the knot of anxiety residing there the rest of the time. In a way, it helped him understand his father's suicide, at least a little. *But only a little.* David was alone, trapped among people who not only didn't care if lived or died but made it clear he was more of a burden than he was worth. His father had no such excuse. Still, The Memory did not hurt anymore, and that was a very good thing.

Terror of Josh and impending doom at the hands of the gathers aside, life in the cave was not hard. The air was cool and dry, especially compared to the jungle. Josh said that either the gatherers kept the tunnels cool or their cave was at least a mile high or more. With the sudden appearance of the towering mountains, this made the most sense. They were often glad of the fire.

Due to its very sameness, it was even possible to ignore the obnoxious odors, if one put one's mind to it. The floor of the cave was made of light gray rock with pockets of sand that would make for decent sleeping if not for the fear. Their fishing efforts yielded bundled animals and plants from the vat that provided food, though David had eaten things he never would have imagined a week ago.

For the first two days, water was their biggest concern, as they had been afraid to drink from the stream flowing through the back of the cave. Josh was very concerned about the kind of microbes or chemicals that might be in the water. Drinking untreated water in the Amazon was usually a sure way to a slow, agonizing death.

They argued about it, or rather Paula and Josh argued. Alessandra was as reluctant to confront Josh as David. Paula was not inhibited in the least, sometimes meeting the big man glare for glare, but generally, she supported every decision he made.

On their second day in the cave, after a P.T. session that left everyone craving water, Paula stamped her foot and said, "To hell with it. It's not like we have a lot to lose." She marched back to the waterfall with the others trailing behind her. When she reached the waterfall where the stream entered the cave, she used her hands to scoop up a drink.

Josh watched her with a disapproving frown. After a few moments, he shrugged and took a tentative sip. The others followed suit. As Paula had said, what did they really have to lose? Thankfully, no ill came from it. Two days later, they all felt fine, at least in regards to thirst. Josh surmised the water must come from rain collected in some kind of basin higher up the mountain and flowed down through crevasses in the rock.

The waterfall emitted from a small opening about thirty feet up a sheer wall and gushed down in a strong, steady stream. It hit a series of rock ledges about ten feet higher than the cave floor and flowed from there in a cascade. The water was clear with blue sparkles from the light strip nearby, except where it was frothed into white foam.

The waterfall and cascades were David's favorite place to escape between chores and P.T. The sound washed over him and helped blot out a small portion of the fear and anxiety.

Paula was getting to be as bad at Josh with her criticism. Alessandra rarely had much to say to him; she lived in Paula's orbit. And Josh…well, Josh was Josh. He terrified David with every glance. David felt like he was on borrowed time, just waiting for the big goon to decide he wasn't worth keeping around. Moreover, while suicide still had an appeal, dying was a scary prospect, in no small part because of his fear of the pain involved.

David returned from one of his pilgrimages to the falls to find Paula cooking some kind of meat, probably monkey, and Alessandra sitting next to Pedro. Paula had taken on the cooking duties pretty much single-handedly; the only nice thing David could attribute to her.

The meat smelled wonderful, making David's mouth water. The older woman glared at him as he settled down on the opposite side of the fire. Alessandra kept trying to get the boy to drink some broth. Pedro looked sicker than ever, and David wondered how much longer he would live. The boy's skin was stretched tight over his thin frame, and it was easy to count his ribs. Most of the broth Alessandra gave him ran down his face onto his chest.

Josh clomped into camp and sat down next to Paula. With everyone seated, it was if there was a line through the camp, with David on one side and them on the other. The group had assembled, and David was as alone as ever.

"Any luck?" Paula asked.

Josh shook his head. "Naw. I traced where the water goes," he said, pointing over his shoulder. "The cave gets really low when you get back a way, and the water goes down crevasse too narrow to get through. I crawled as far as I could but no use. Every tunnel ends in a dead end as far as I can tell. I really don't get it."

"Why not?" asked Paula.

"Well, that chamber with all them tunnels was built, it ain't natural like this cave. It had to have been put there for a reason. All the tunnels are filled with rubble though. Somethin' must have made them collapse, and the gathers abandoned this section for some reason."

Alessandra perked up a little. "Well, that's good, isn't it? I mean, maybe they won't bother us."

Josh shrugged. "Well, that big blender is still in use. I would think somebody would have to work on it every once in a while, so we shouldn't relax too much. There might be another way in here we haven't found yet."

Paula nodded. She glanced at Alessandra and then frowned at David before saying, "Alessandra believes we are in hell and there is no way out."

Josh looked at her, a modicum of concern crossing his brutal features. "Does she now?"

Paula gestured across the fire with her chin and said, "I think fat boy over there thinks the same way."

Josh turned his gaze on David, any hint of concern vanishing, replaced with scorn. "Tell me, boy. Do you think we are in hell, scooped up by the Devil's minions?"

David shrugged. "I could see this being hell."

Josh snorted. "So you think this is the end of days or something like that?"

"The apocalypse? I don't know, maybe." He looked up and met Josh's gaze, then looked away. "What do you think all this is?"

Josh picked up a chunk of meat and leaned back against a boulder. He tore off a large bite with his teeth. After a moment's consideration, he picked up another chunk and tossed it to David. David caught it, fumbling with the hot, greasy mass with one hand. He felt a stab of anger as Josh laughed at his impromptu juggling, but felt grateful for the meat just the same.

Josh said, "Well, this don't feel like hell to me." He glanced at Paula and then back at David. "I done been to hell, and this ain't it." He lifted up the meat. "We have food, water, a fire, and nothing's bothering us. No, this ain't hell, not even close."

Alessandra leaned forward. "But the mountains, where did they come from, and how? And…the…the demons. They must be demons."

Josh glared at Alessandra. She flinched back as though fearing he would strike her. His voice sounded harsh and threatening as he said, "Don't ever call them demons again." He leaned back and said in a normal voice, "I don't like that. Makes 'em sound special or something. Call 'em gatherers. That's what they do, so that's what they are. Okay?"

She nodded nervously with obvious reluctance.

Josh frowned and then relaxed, deciding to accept her acquiescence at face value. He tore off another piece of meat and leaned back against one of the large boulders surrounding the fire.

"Besides. Why the hell…" He smiled and gave a little snort at his unintended pun. "Why the hell would God or the Devil or whatever want to start the apocalypse way out here in the middle of the Amazon? And why haul in all those trees and animals? Are they sinners? Does that make any sense to you, boy?"

David considered this for a moment. "No, not really."

"As for the mountain?" Josh shrugged. "That one's beyond me. Rose up from the ground would be my guess."

Alessandra looked thoughtful. "So, why are the…gatherers doing this?"

"My guess? Food. Whatever they are, wherever they came from, food. And we are just another variety of cattle to them. Why else do would they blend up everything? Making soup is what I think."

Alessandra nodded with a lack of enthusiasm and leaned back, clearly wanting to believe him but not really able to. Not that being considered food was very appealing. But it was obvious she considered it to be a bit better than having been cast into eternal damnation. Everyone continued eating in silence, lost in his or her own thoughts, except for the small boy who just moaned softly in his feverish sleep.

Chapter 14

David

The next morning, David woke to a quiet giggle from Alessandra. It was brief but sounded musical and light. It made him...something. Less dead inside, maybe. It reminded him of the sound the water made at the cascade. Not the same sound, but it caused similar feelings. A hint of happiness, which was in short supply in his soul. The sound of life, and hope. It would be nice to know what had been so funny, but he didn't dare ask. For all of sixty seconds, he felt a bit lighter in his heart, and then Josh roared for everyone to get moving for P.T.

David got up as fast as his hurt shoulder would allow and hurried down the tunnel, determined not to be whacked with the stick today. Or at least, not whacked as often. Reaching the vat room first, he waited for Josh and the others so he could start out right behind the big goon and stay there for as long as possible. Josh emerged from the tunnel with a strange look on his face. This puzzled David until Paula and Alessandra stepped out behind him, wearing just bras and underpants.

Until now, Alessandra had worn David's blue polo shirt. The shirt swallowed her and came halfway down her thighs. When Josh had cut Paula free of the webbing after pulling her from the pit, her shirt had also been badly torn. David had actually given her his green polo shirt to help combat the cold of the cave. In hindsight, he wished he had kept it. For the last few days, he would have been happy to see her freeze to death. Until now, both women had worn these shirts all the time.

They looked very different this morning, and David felt his face flush. He had seen his sister in her underwear a time or three, but that had always just seemed gross. This was very different. Alessandra, who he could no longer think of as a little girl, wore a pink bra of thin material that left little to the imagination in the cool cave. Her underpants were blue, boy cut, and quite sheer. Paula wore black briefs that clung tightly to her rump. While David had seen plenty of pictures of women wearing less—after all, they were hard to avoid on the internet—this was his first time to see such scantily clad (not his sister) female forms in real life. Again, very different, and...really interesting.

Paula put her hands on her hips and glared at both men. "Shut your mouths and get your eyes on the walkway." David swallowed hard and looked away. "We don't have enough clothes to keep washing the sweat out of them every day. I knew you two sick North Americans would start ogling us like a couple of perverts. Get over it; this is Brazil, the Amazon."

The two women may be more accustomed to nudity in their culture, but Alessandra still looked demure as they started running. David could not help but look, though he tried not to.

His estimation of Alessandra's age underwent another revision upward, heck; she might even be older than he was. She had well-formed though small breasts and full hips compared to her waist. Her lithe, muscular frame moved with an easy grace as she jogged.

Paula, though heavier, still had a nice figure, and the muscles in her legs and buttocks flexed with female definition.

David considered taking off his bush shirt. It was getting pretty rank. But the idea of having his belly bounce around in front of Josh and the women deterred him. Better to stink. At least he had extra underwear he could wash and change into.

He had seen Paula eyeing one of his spares the day before and wondered if she might try to commandeer them. They would be huge on either woman, but Josh had a small sewing kit in his stuff. He considered giving them to her as a peace offering but decided to heck with her. Let her keep washing her own every day. A wet butt was the least she deserved.

David enjoyed watching Alessandra and Paula run though. It was mesmerizing though it made him feel strange inside. This was the first time he had been in such close proximity to any woman wearing so little clothing. Looking kind of shamed him. But each time he tore his eyes away from their flexing leg and butt muscles, his gaze was drawn back, first with a glance, and then with a stare. It was almost as if a spell had been cast on him.

The fluid movements as they ran were nothing like pictures from the internet. He finally relaxed and let himself look; at least they helped keep his mind off trudging around the cauldron. Regretfully they soon pulled ahead of him, and he was left staring at the ground as he plodded along.

Whap!

David yelped as a stinging pain lanced up his thigh. Josh hit him with a damn stick.

"Move it, fat boy," Josh said, clomping past.

Anger boiled in David. He heard Paula laughing from somewhere behind, joined this time by a faint giggle from Alessandra. He set his mouth in a grim line and concentrated on Josh's back, his breath coming in ragged gasps as he struggled to keep up.

As he passed underneath the conveyor, it squawked to a start. The sound was familiar by now, but he looked up with annoyance at the irritating noise. A large tree appeared and tumbled off the end. It made a resounding clang when it struck the bottom of the vat. It had looked familiar, but he couldn't place it, a species from one of his sister's studies probably. He knew way more about trees than he cared to since Sally had frequently shamed him into helping her with science stuff.

This brought up a bittersweet memory about her efforts to promote his "personal development." He sighed. In would seem he should have listened to her more.

Josh was halfway around, chugging along with seeming limitless energy. The women caught up to him and as they passed, Paula said, "Watch out, fat boy, he's gaining on you."

They giggled and put on a spurt of speed, pulling ahead. David's face flushed and all the joy at watching them run vanished.

The cauldron filled quickly. There were a lot of large trees, and it did not take long. He noticed another tree like the previous one tumble off the conveyor. Its bright green double leaves, small white flowers, and odd, long pod-like fruit tugged at his memory.

He stopped running and pointed. "A *hymenaea courbaril*!" he yelled. He started jumping up and down. "A jatoba' tree! A jatoba' tree!"

Josh ran up to him and stopped, so surprised he forgot to smack David with the stick. "What the hell are you jabbering about?" he said, mystified.

David turned and grasped his arm. "It's a jatoba' tree. We need it; we need the bark."

Josh looked at him like he had lost his mind.

David gave an exasperated grunt and said, "For the boy. It might help."

Josh frowned, but then turned and sprinted over to the tunnel opening where the hooked stick and rope lay. He grabbed them, ran back to the rim, and yelled, "Which one?"

"There, the big one with the bright green leaves."

Josh hesitated and then looked over at David as if suspecting a trick. "Are you crazy? That thing is huge; I can't pull that up."

"We just need some of the bark."

Paula came up and looked down. The cauldron was two-thirds full, the tree in question sticking straight up two dozen feet below them. "The bark can help Pedro?" she asked.

David shrugged. "Well, I think so. It was a tree my sister was studying. She was really excited about it and said it has strong natural antibiotics. It's also effective against fungal infections. If anything can help him, that's it."

Paula looked at Josh questioningly.

He shook his head and said, "That thing must be a hundred feet tall." He held up the rope and makeshift hook with a helpless shrug.

Paula grabbed the rope and began tying it under her arms. "Give me your knife."

Josh hesitated.

She looked up at him. "You're too big. We couldn't pull you back up. You have to stay here. Now give me your knife—the vat is almost full."

Josh nodded and handed her his survival knife.

David pulled off his khaki bush shirt and handed it to her. "Here, put this on. That rope will cut you to pieces."

After hesitating a second, she nodded, took the shirt, and pushed the rope back down. After slipping the bush shirt around her, she pulled the rope back up and stepped to the edge of the vat.

Looking at Josh, she said with a faint quiver in her voice, "Don't drop me."

Josh nodded.

She clambered over the low wall. Josh wrapped the slender green rope around his arms and braced himself. Paula slipped off the ledge and hung with her feet dangling over the large tree. As Josh lowered her, she swung about, bumping into the side of the cauldron. She clung to the rope with one hand and the knife with the other. The knuckles of both hands were white.

As she came to the upper reaches of the tree, the conveyor creaked to a halt, and a loud hissing noise filled the chamber. The change in sounds startled her and she glanced up, her face strained, her expression scared but determined, and then back down as Josh lowered her into the tangle of branches.

She came upon a medium sized branch and waved.

"Hold it," said David.

Paula reached out and grabbed the branch to steady herself, and then clutched a smaller limb, about two inches thick. She looked up through the leaves with a quizzical expression, and David nodded. Shifting position, she swung the knife as hard as she could. The limb parted easily to the sharp blade, catching her off guard and sending her into a spin. She fumbled with the precious knife a moment and then clutched it to her body. She looked up and nodded.

"Go," said David and Alessandra in unison. "Pull her up!"

The viscous brown fluid in the vat stopped rising a few feet below Paula. Startup was imminent. Josh started heaving upward just as the contents of the vat lurched. A branch slammed into Paula, knocking her into the wall. She dropped the limb.

Josh kept pulling, but Paula looked up and shook her head with a scowl.

"Stop," said Alessandra. "She wants you to stop."

Josh looked confused but paused. The vat's contents lurched again, and another branch hit Paula hard. She cried out and latched onto the branch. From the depths of the cauldron came a grinding noise. They had mere seconds before it spun up.

Paula let go of the large branch and grabbed a smaller one. She swung the knife again and an instant later was twirling amid the leaves with the small limb.

Alessandra and David both shouted, "Pull!"

Josh began pulling the rope up hand over hand, the flexing of his large shoulders the only sign of strain as he lifted her weight. She cleared the tree by ten feet when, with another loud grinding noise, the mass below leaped into motion with a roar, sending leaves, splinters, and pieces of bark flying up to pelt Paula. She closed her eyes and gripped the knife and the limb with grim determination. A moment later, she climbed over the low wall, breathing hard.

She looked down at the churning contents of the vat and then turned and handed the jatoba' tree limb to David. "This had damn well better work," she said, sucking in air with heaving gulps.

David nodded, and then hurried back to the cave. *Crap! I don't really even know how to use this stuff.* Of course, the options were kind of limited. He knew the bark and the resin of the tree contained antibiotics. About the only way he could think of using it would be to boil the bark in water and get the boy to drink it. Maybe make a compress of the leaves and apply it to the wound as well. No doubt a long shot, but what the hell.

Preparing the solution was easy. Getting the boy to drink was not. David sat for over an hour, holding his thin, frail, fever-racked body and slowly dribbling the fluid from his canteen cup into Pedro's mouth while coaxing him to swallow. The boy's leg was swollen from infection, and pus ran in disgusting quantities from the wound.

When the cup was empty, he gently laid the boy back on a bed of webbing. He dribbled cool water over his head and patted his shoulder. As he was staring at the boy, a slight noise came from behind, and he turned to find Paula looking at him. She gave him a small smile, handed him his shirt, and headed toward the cascading water deeper in the cave.

The day dragged by. Paula and Alessandra went fishing for food at the pit while Josh went off exploring. David stayed with Pedro. He prepared and administered more of the jatoba' tree potion, coaxing it down the boy's throat. The boy looked weaker and frailer than ever, his breathing now ragged and shallow.

"Poor little guy," David said in a soft whisper.

Later that evening, at least evening according to David's watch, they sat in their usual places, Josh and Paula now sitting closer together, Alessandra and the boy nearby. David sat alone on the far side of the fire, leaning back against his favorite boulder. No one talked. They spent a lot of time watching the boy's chest slowly rise and fall.

Sally

The early light of day was a relief to Sally. The ghosts didn't tend to visit once the sun came up. The early morning was the only time she managed an hour or so of much-needed sleep before the rising temperature forced her back to full consciousness.

Today was no different, and before long, the still air in the tent grew uncomfortably hot. The noise of people moving around the camp dispelled any further hope of sleep and, though still exhausted, she got up, dressed in olive green shorts and a white button-up shirt, and left the tent. Helping herself to a cup of coffee from a pot kept warm over a small gas stove, she sat down at the small camp table across from Dr. Allen. He looked at her with concern, noting her red-rimmed eyes and distant haunted stare.

"Are you okay, Sally?"

The question confused her; she really didn't know how to answer. After a moment, she forced a smile and said, "Fine, the ribs are coming along good."

He frowned. "That's not what I meant. You have been through a hell of a lot. Are you sure you don't want to take Major Antinasio up on that ride to Manaus?"

Sally shook her head. "No, I would rather stay here. If…if I left, I would have nothing to do. There's no one…" She choked on the words, struggling to breathe, and then managed to stammer, "There's no one to even talk to away from here." Blinking back tears, she met his eyes. "I think that would be a bad thing right now. I need to stay busy, maybe finish my research if I can."

He studied her over the rim of his cup and then put it down. "Sally," he said in a soft, reassuring voice. "David and Heather…what happened to them wasn't your fault."

The tears she had been fighting back blinded her as they flowed free. "Oh God, Robert, yes it was." She put her face in her hands. "Myra too. She didn't even want to go that day, not until I talked her into it. I…I was so selfish. I didn't need to go to town; I should have stayed in the camp." Her eyes shone with tears, and pain carved deep lines into her face when she looked back up. "And…David. I can't believe he went down the river. He never does anything. I have to…had to…" she sobbed, "kick his tail to get him out of the house. And he went down the river in a canoe…to look for me? I…I never thought…"

"Sally, you couldn't know." He stood, came around the table, and kneeled down beside her. Tears made her cheeks glisten as her chin quivered, then her whole body began to shake as she threw her arms around Dr. Allen, clutching to him like a drowning woman. She sobbed loudly as the grief and guilt tore at the fabric of her soul. She clung to him for a long time.

As the cycle of grief played out, the pain ebbed. It did not go away as much as numbness set in. With a soft gulp, she pulled away, feeling ashamed. "Oh crap, look at me," she said, wiping her face.

"Ahem." They both looked up to see Marcus Antinasio, wearing a camouflage uniform, standing nearby. Sally pulled back and turned the other way, dabbing at her eyes with a napkin. Dr. Allen stood and nodded to the Brazilian.

Marcus looked uncomfortable. "Uh, Miss Morgan, I am very sorry to hear about your brother. I assure you, we will keep looking for him. There is still hope."

Sally's eyes threatened to overflow again as she smiled weakly and nodded.

Marcus paused with a look of concern on his face at Sally's obvious distress and began to shift his weight from foot to foot. After a moment, he cleared his throat again and said, "Miss Morgan, I wanted to talk to you. Well, to Dr. Allen actually, if you would be so good as to translate for me. But if this is a bad time...?"

Sally shook her head and dabbed at her eyes again as she relayed this to Dr. Allen. She turned back to Marcus and said, "Please, Major, call me Sally."

He looked even more uncomfortable but nodded. "Very well, Sally." He pointed to the insignia on his collar. "Actually I am a colonel now," he said with a small smile. "General Fernando promoted me yesterday. The youngest colonel in the Brazilian armed forces. But please, call me Marcus. If you would be so kind, tell the doctor I have a job for him, if he will take it."

Sally nodded and translated Marcus's words for Dr. Allen.

"What is it, colonel?" he replied through Sally.

"I have heard that you already arranged for your team to relocate here."

Allen nodded. "The rest of the team should be here this afternoon. It has been slow going. The airboat can't carry very much. But we should be finished today."

"Very good. Did you know we brought one of those things, a demon, out of the jungle? There is also one of the small tick-like creatures here as well."

Dr. Allen shook his head. "No, I hadn't heard." He looked excited, already anticipating what Marcus might want.

Marcus said, "Manaus is in shambles. When the planes fell out of the sky, one hit the university campus and burned down most of the lab complex. It would take a week or more to get the carcasses to a decent facility further downriver. Sally told me your expedition is well equipped for a wide variety of research. We would like for you and your people to dissect the creature and prepare an analysis for us. We need to know what we face."

Dr. Allen smiled and nodded with enthusiasm. "Certainly, certainly. It would be an honor. Not to mention a scientist's dream to have the chance to study an unknown species."

"Good, I will have my men bring it here. And Doctor, time is of the essence. If possible, we will need your first report the day after tomorrow. I know it is not much time, but give us the best data you can."

"Certainly, Colonel. We will work around the clock if necessary."

"Excellent. I imagine your services will be of great value. We need people with your team's background. We have much to learn about the mountains and the inhabitants. I hope you will consider staying for the time being."

Dr. Allen said, "Of course. Although I can't speak for the entire team without asking them. But I would think most of them would leap at the chance to help."

Marcus nodded, stated his thanks, and walked away.

Dr. Allen turned and said with enthusiasm, "Well, Sally, you said you wanted to stay busy. It looks like you got your wish. Come on, I'll need your help with the locals to get a site ready for the team."

Sally nodded and stood up, a faint but smoldering fire in her eyes. If there was anyone, or thing, to blame for the ghosts who now haunted her dreams, other than herself, it was the monsters from those damnable mountains. While she felt responsible for David, Myra, Keith, and even Jef and Pieter's demise, the creatures from the mountains were the actual murderers. She squared her shoulders.

Sally was no warrior, despite how Marcus's men felt about the incident in the forest, but she was one hell of a scientist. It may not be a huge deal in the grand scheme of things, but if there was something she could contribute in the fight against the mountains' inhabitants, this was it.

Marcus and the Brazilian military had thrown a much-needed lifeline for her soul.

David

The morning's P.T. went a little better for David. Josh only lapped him two times and did not seem to hit as hard when he passed. David spent more time watching Paula and Alessandra's backsides as they ran, focusing on keeping up with them. It shamed him a little, but the natural endorphins he got from watching them helped him ignore the gasping pain.

After running, Josh made them do fifty sit-ups. David finished last, hampered by his arm as much as his big belly. The others were long gone when he trudged down the tunnel to the cave. As he neared the camp, he heard both Paula and Alessandra laughing. It was an alien sound in the camp and it took him a moment to realize what it was. When he reached the fire, they were sitting next to Pedro, who was looking around in obvious confusion.

Paula smiled up at him, "His fever broke. The medicine you made worked."

David nodded and sank down wearily in his usual spot. A moment later, Paula brought him some fruit. She handed it to him, smiled, nodded, and went back to the boy.

David watched the women and the boy as he ate. Pedro was sipping broth from a cup and with Paula's help managed to get most of it down. Alessandra looked up and gave David a quick smile. Then Paula's head came up and she nodded at him, a crooked half smile on her lips. Then she resumed watching Pedro and her smile widened.

The smiles from Alessandra and Paula made him feel…accepted. That was a very good feeling. Better than any video game victory he had ever achieved.

What was he going to do with his life? Choose death like his father? No, he did not want to die. He had come to believe that getting caught up in thoughts of suicide was the epitome of self-pity. He had had enough of that.

So, what did he stand for? A video game? That seemed silly now, after everything he had been through since the trip down river and everything since. It was a question he had never even considered asking before. A question he would have to ponder with great care. Something was different inside him, something that had been missing for a long, long time.

Warmth spread through his chest and it occurred to him that for the first time in a long while, maybe as far back as his mother's death, certainly since his father's, he felt good about himself.

Josh

The scene around the campfire brought a contemplative gleam to Josh's eyes and then a frown. The Morgan kid had actually shown a spark of initiative. That was good. It was a start anyway.

It probably didn't really matter, though. It was unlikely anyone besides himself would get out of here alive. He was now sure the only way out of the vat room, and the cave complex, was back up the conveyor. Just climbing up and across the dome to reach it would be very tough. Probably it would be impossible for Morgan and nearly so for the women and the boy. If it came to it, would he leave them? Wouldn't it be more merciful to kill them?

The boy, too? God, please don't force me to choose, not again...

Being a hard man was not natural, or easy, for Josh. Experience...hard, cold, cruel experience had taught him the need. *But the boy, the damn boy...* Even hard men cracked when hit in the right spot. A soft touch to shatter an iron shield.

The boy brought back memories of another boy, another time, and another hard choice. Leaving that boy and his mother with the villagers had seemed the right thing to do. They surely would have died during his team's desperate flight from the ISIL militia. It had been better to leave them with their own people.

Right? Right? No, it hadn't.

Betrayed by their own, the boy and his mother's screams were baggage he still carried in his nightmares. Before he'd left them, the mother had actually asked him, begged him, to kill her and the boy. She knew. He hadn't done it, couldn't do it. He hadn't been hard enough.

Pedro smiled up at him, the trusting gaze of a child. Josh smiled back, but his heart was heavy. Maybe...just maybe he could save a couple of them. But those he couldn't? Well...this time he would be hard enough. He would not leave anyone to the mercies of the gatherers. Even though the price would be high and more painful baggage would be added to his soul.

End of Book 1

Thanks for reading *Amazon Harvest*. Sorry it ends with so much stuff unresolved, but it is a big story. I hope that you enjoyed it so far. The second book in the series, *Demon Harvest,* is due out in the Spring of 2017. Due to reader questions, this book might grow considerably in word count. If so, it may be released in two parts. You can read an excerpt from Chapter 1 on my website. **http://johnwilsonberry.com**

In *Demon Harvest,* Sally and David are living in nightmarish worlds. David is trapped in the heart of the White Mountain and faces new fears with each blue dawn. Sally believes David is dead and struggles with grief and shock over the ordeal in the rainforest, even as stories of her bravery spread. The harvest of the Amazon has begun, and Brazil and the world scramble to understand and stop the strange creatures threatening the rainforest.

Made in the USA
Middletown, DE
21 December 2016